The

Roca Group

A Tale of
Financial Espionage

J. Jaye Gold

♦

Peradam Press
North San Juan, California

Peradam Press
P O Box 6
North San Juan, California 95960
peradam@earthlink.net

A division of The Center for Cultural & Naturalist Studies

Book design and cover by Cecelia & Johanna
Proofread by Renee

Library of Congress Cataloging-in-Publication Data

Gold, J. Jaye, date
    The Roca Group : a tale of financial espionage / J. Jaye Gold
    p.   cm.
    ISBN 978-1-885420-01-5

1. Fiction.   2. Cuba.   3. International finance.   4. Espionage.
I. Title.   II. J. Jaye Gold

Library of Congress Control Number: 2016952648

Printed in the United States of America by CreateSpace
9 8 7 6 5 4 3 2 1

Prologue

The actions of Captain George Roca were less selfless than they appeared. He was an officer in one of the first U.S. Army divisions to enter Tokyo at the end of WWII. He was personally tasked by General Douglas MacArthur to find and return, to both the Chinese government and its private citizens, valuable assets either stolen or lost in the chaos of war. Yes, the captain felt some justifiable indignation for the outrageous behavior of the Japanese conquerors, but there was also personal guilt enmeshed in his crusade. It was common knowledge that the inspiration for this undertaking came from MacArthur himself. It was to be a program for establishing the good will of the American government in a post-war environment. But common knowledge in this case, as it often is, was incorrect.

Weeks before the establishment of what would become the ROCA brigade, the captain was leading a company of 100 soldiers through the outskirts of war-torn Tokyo. When one of his lieutenants uncovered an underground storage facility filled with Chinese artifacts, it was obvious that these hundreds of scrolls, paintings, and furnishings had been confiscated in China and brought back to Japan. None of the liberators present had enough knowledge of oriental art to be able to assess the value of the objects found, but they began the process of carefully cataloguing their discovery. As it turned out, the objects, though beautiful, were of little financial value, but clearly the Chinese families that had lost these heirlooms would appreciate their return. A skeleton crew of three soldiers under the command of Captain Roca was left to complete the inventory and pursue the return of the items to their rightful owners when and if possible.

It was during the process of sorting through some large chests in order to inventory their contents that it became clear why so much trouble had been taken to store and hide so many relatively worthless items. The artifacts were only there to conceal fourteen large rosewood chests that were packed to the brim with gold and what appeared to be precious jewels. Captain Roca, a second generation U.S. immigrant, possessor of a master's degree in finance, was certainly not a man of means. He decided, with the assent of his three compatriots, that there was clearly enough wealth in the discovery for the four of them to claim a clandestine reward, while turning the bulk of the find over to the proper authorities. After finding a way to turn the gold into cash, Roca's share of the proceeds came to $350,000, an enormous sum in 1945. After being celebrated for the discovery, Captain Roca, newly promoted to major, suggested to General MacArthur that he command an expanded task force dedicated to the discovery and return of lost and stolen items of value throughout Japan.

It was not in Major Roca's mind to enrich himself further, but being a man of some conscience, he felt that he owed it to his benefactors, the Chinese, to make some reparations. General MacArthur approved the project, and for the next six months Major Roca judiciously pursued his task. He named his team the ROCA Brigade – Repatriation Of Confiscated Assets, and retained the name for future ventures after his decommission from the military the following year.

Upon returning to civilian life, Major Roca spent the rest of his days and many of his nights parlaying his newfound wealth into realizing a unique plan he developed. His project was made possible by the numerous high level international government and private sector contacts he had made in the process of returning items of value. His Roca Group became the organization of choice when a wealthy individual, a company, and eventually even a government wished to involve itself in a financial undertaking that required discretion, and often secrecy. The international scope of the Roca Group grew through the years to the point that it had been contracted by many of the most significant power brokers, multinational corporations, and national governments on the planet.

In 1996, some fifty years after the inception of the Roca Group, there were very few of its employees who knew anything other than the name of its founder. The acronym that defined it and the source of its original financing were forgotten. Repatriation Of Confiscated Assets was no longer the function of the Roca Group.

Chapter 1

Havana, Cuba - September, 1996

They could be looking for either of us. They wouldn't try to stop us, but we certainly might pick up a tail. I had to be careful getting to the airport, so I couldn't give him specifics of where to meet me. I had to trust that he would be creative about it. As it turned out, he was watching all the arriving taxis. When mine pulled up, he must have spotted me even before I closed the door of the taxi. He came up behind me and whisked me off through a side door that led to the lower level of the airport. A few minutes later we were in a private lounge near baggage claim.

"Nobody will see us here señorita," he said confidently. "We can wait in this room until it is necessary to board our flight."

"I think you're overlooking something," I said, concerned that his experience while being confined in a cell at Departamento Seguridad del Estado headquarters had thrown off his judgment. "We're not booked on any flight. We don't have tickets!"

"Señorita, if you're worried that my ordeal has left me less than sound, I can alleviate your concerns by telling you that within five or ten minutes the director of airport security will meet us right here. He will go upstairs to the ticket counter and make all our arrangements. I think we can consider him trustworthy, since he is my son," he said, with a smile meant to remind me that although when I first met him he was playing the part of an aide, he was after all a major in the DSE.

I couldn't help shyly smiling back at him. Embarrassment was not an emotion that I was used to, especially when I was what you might call *on the job*. But he had the eyes. He was not what you would call a handsome man, no, not even good looking, but he had what someone once called the "eyes of age." Not old age, but enough age that he had seen it all . . . or almost all. And if you could show him something he hadn't seen, he would be open to looking at it through those "eyes of age." Some character actors in movies can appear to have those eyes for the parts they play, but Enrique Magelinos really had them. I liked looking at him face-to-face, even though it always made me feel a little inexperienced, a little too young.

Just as Enrique had predicted, his son arrived and was soon on his way upstairs to the ticket counter with the money I supplied. Within 15 minutes we were ticketed to Santiago de Cuba. Our flight was scheduled to leave in about two hours. With the one-hour flying time from Havana, we would be in Santiago by mid-afternoon.

The day's events had left me more incapacitated by nervousness than I was used to. I knew I had to relax or I wouldn't be of help to anyone. I was sitting a seat away from Enrique with my feet up on my small suitcase in preparation for a chilling out, or at least a cooling down. That idea lasted about a minute. Instead of cooling down, the water abruptly came close to a rolling boil.

"It's time to blow the fuckin' Degüello, Enrique," I exploded. "I came down to rescue someone I love and it turns out he wasn't in trouble at all. Now, after one week of my blundering, his life is in danger. We have to get our act together Enrique. I mean I have to get *my* act together. You're doing fine."

"Señorita. I am familiar with the term *Degüello* but I have never heard it used in that combination of words. I also am not used to hearing a woman use that type of language. In fact, I have never heard a woman say that word before, and I am not referring to *Degüello*. At first I was shocked, but I have to admit I find your boldness refreshing."

I didn't know what to say, so I smiled and looked down at my hands folded in my lap.

Enrique continued. "So how do you know this Degüello bugle call? I myself learned about it in school. Cuban rebels used it when they charged the Spanish infantry."

"I heard it in a movie," I answered. "When the Mexican general ordered his troops to attack the Alamo in Texas, he had the bugler blow the Degüello. It meant, 'Give no quarter, take no prisoners.' I have to get in that mode now Enrique. No more fu . . . I mean diddling around."

"Señorita, you must calm down and think practically here. Explosions of emotion may be useful in combating inertia, but once you get going, rational thinking and deliberate acting are best."

"Enrique, I did some really careless things in the past few weeks, and I am truly embarrassed about them – one in particular. I have some serious repairing to do," I lamented, hoping that he wouldn't ask me for more details than he already had.

"We all make mistakes," Enrique said generously. "Sometimes even at crucial times. But we must move on. Thinking about our past blunders after we acknowledge them and learn the lessons they can teach us serves nothing but our self-indulgence. In this case, your recriminations won't help your friend, so perhaps you can leave them aside and we will blow the fuckin' Degüello together."

I was looking away at that moment, so I couldn't tell if Enrique blushed when he said that. When I looked back over at him he was smiling.

"Maybe you could rest your head back and close your eyes for a while. These are new chairs. They are the only new additions to our airport. You could take advantage of them," Enrique suggested.

Resisting following Enrique's recommendation would have been stubbornness for its own sake, so I put my head back and closed my eyes as he suggested. I needed some perspective, but I knew that dozing off wasn't what would get me there. Maybe going back to the beginning and getting clear on how I got to this point was what I needed. Well, not from the very beginning, but maybe from first getting to Cuba last week. No, further back. Maybe Miami, or even back at the fire.

Sure, that's it, start with the fire. Maybe then I could proceed without making blunders like the ones that put his life in danger. If I had my computer, I would try to write it all down. If nothing else, it would make a great story.

Chapter 2

New Mexico – One Month Earlier

Forest fires are tough on the local coyotes – relocating isn't very easy for them to manage. Real estate values take a beating also, not to mention people getting displaced and maybe even injured. Some say that fire is good for the forest. But none of those were my concerns as my Bronco limped out of the Sangre De Christo Mountains last Friday. You'd think with all the training I'd had, I wouldn't be one of those people who waits till the last minute and can't believe that it's really happening to them. But it wasn't till I couldn't see my 4x4 through the smoke from the porch of my cabin that I knew it was time to get out. By then there was only time enough to fill my tote bag with music CDs, my Nikon, some evidence of assorted memories with which I wasn't yet prepared to part, and as much underwear as would fit without breaking the zipper.

When I was a kid, I collected salt and pepper shakers. Not exactly regulation for a nine-year-old girl, but that's what I was into. One day a catalogue came in the mail, and without consulting either of my parents, I filled out the coupon on the back page and sent it in. Over the next year or so, numerous packages came in the mail for me. They contained ceramics in the images of animals, cars, famous people, tools, and whatever shapes lent themselves to having holes on top for either black or white powder to come out. I had only one left. It was an orphan but then so was I, so I took it along.

My attachment to this cabin was based on its willingness to grant me solitude. That made the esthetics of its shape, size, and decor less important than its location. It might be described as cute by a realtor. It had one large main room with plenty of exposed real wood, not paneling, a perfectly-sized kitchen, and a separate bedroom with a bed frame made out of logs. It also had a fireplace. Before I said goodbye to the cabin, I noted how attentive I had always been in putting on the fire screen when I went to bed or left the cabin to itself.

The Bronco and I both had a touch of smoke inhalation, so the ride down the mountain was almost as jerky as I was for postponing my departure to the last minute. The wind was blowing north, and I was riding south toward Taos, New Mexico. Once we cleared the hot spots and the smoke, it was actually a peaceful and pensive drive. It only took me a few minutes to review what was left behind. I concluded that aside from my anonymity, nothing irreplaceable was frying. Halfway down the hill I began to think more about the fate of the other solitaries on the mountain I did than about myself.

The Sangre de Christo Mountains range from northern New Mexico into southern Colorado where they merge with their big sister and lose their personal identity, being called Rockies from then on. The cabin was (it may not be any more) at 8,500 foot elevation and very close to the border. If I ever had to get a real driver's license, I wouldn't know in which direction to apply. Six months as a hermit was just beginning to whet my appetite for solitude. My previous activities had supplied enough tumult and excitement to last a reasonable person at least one lifetime and probably drool over onto the next.

As I approached town, my mind tasted tea and toast with jelly, and I groped unsuccessfully in my U.S. Olympic Team tote bag for my wallet. Most people would be alarmed at the absence of such a basic, but life experience had convoluted my value system. I was actually more relieved to have a canvas sack, a memento of Seoul, Korea, than whatever papers and plastic might be awaiting a roasting after the couch cushion that concealed them got its. Those greenish papers imprinted with presidents' pictures that I was brought up to value so highly had become less meaningful to me than they were to most of my fellow Americans. After all, I had disposed of, in one way or another, suitcases full of them. And the others – the plastic ones, may have sported my photo, but under it was an autograph that my mother, even if she were still alive, wouldn't have recognized.

The café was light on customers but heavy on fire conversation. One sniff of me was enough to magnetize those present to a potential bearer of the latest news. It was one of those places that we romanticize in our minds – a place that has something called home cooking. I've always wondered what the difference is between Denny's scrambled eggs and the variety served at mom and pop's average American diner. Since they outlawed smoking in California restaurants, and most of them upgraded the brand of grease they use from lard to soy oil, the aromas that used to distinguish "greasy spoon" from "non" have all but disappeared. One thing I have noticed is the proliferation of the practice of being asked, *What would you like to drink?* instead of having to accept or reject coffee the moment before it is about to be poured into the cup. This might indicate that the stigma of being a tea drinker has percolated away. Anyway, bathrooms are always a maybe yes maybe no deal, and that's essentially why I was here, aside from the toast and tea, that is.

I got my toast and tea and left with several offers that people everywhere are generous to give when the world is burning. I noticed that I didn't put my satchel down while I sat at the counter. I managed the tea and toast one-handed, my left arm feeling a curious reassurance as it rested on the bulk of the bag hanging from my shoulder. As I walked to the Bronco I smiled inwardly, and probably outwardly a little too, at the total accumulated material possessions of a 28-year-old woman with a 145 IQ. I had one ten-year-old truck with peeling paint, an assortment of music (none of which was more recent than the birth date of the truck), a camera more suitable for taking pictures of documents than scenery, and a tote bag. The bag symbolized the beginning of this long strange trip from which, I thought up to now, I was being given a respite.

The front seat of the Bronco was as good a place as any, and the parking lot of the café was the same. I never really picked the Bronco. It picked me. That's more easily pictured with an actual bronco, but steel, or should I say aluminum, or should I say plastic, these days can sometimes have a way of pleading its case. Anyhow, I needed a car that wouldn't resist crossing a small bumpy stream bed and some mud and ruts in the winter. The day after I first saw the cabin, I drove by a *for sale* sign in the front window of a dirt-colored truck whose tires looked like they belonged on a semi – and that was that.

It was time to figure a next step. I swung my booted legs up onto the seat notifying my body that we were going to be there for a while. I dumped the contents of the tote bag on the back seat and set it up in front of me with the words *U.S. Olympic Team* staring at me. Yes, Seoul was where it started – or maybe with that first *cómo está usted* at Monroe High School. Wherever it started, most recently I had been living in anonymity in northern New Mexico/southern Colorado as a guest of Career Management Associates, a fictitious corporation that fronted for the Roca Group, my former employer. My arrangement was compensation for agreeing not to disclose certain details of their operation. Those details would have led to the biggest scandal that they ever had to look at in their deceitfully clouded mirror.

It was hard to believe that my one-and-a-half gainer in pike position was the kind of quality that the diving experts were looking for. Sure, my ass was cute and my hair was dark, long, and stayed strait in defiance of the humidity. But I didn't make any of it available to the coaches, so it wasn't that. In college I was fastest at the breast-stroke, but my boobs were too big for a swimmer, so I reluctantly switched to diving. It was a change that followed my aborted inspiration to have a surgical reduction. When the guys on the team heard about my plan, they signed a petition and made a place for me on the diving team. But the Olympics? That was ridiculous. Sure, I was an alternate, but what if I had to perform? When it came down to it, I was so excited to be part of the regalia that I never suspected that both my family connections in Cuba, and my ability to pass for a Latino and speak fluent Spanish had anything to do with it.

Yes, I was recruited, and I never even had to jump in the water – not feet first, not from three meters, not from ten meters, not at all. As far as they were concerned, I was a 20-year-old New York piece-of-ass who could think at the speed of sound and could speak the language of Cuba. They had big plans for me.

In the 1950s my dad was a partner in a nightclub/casino in Havana. He hung out with people close to Batista but was really on nobody's side but his own. Castro changed the whole profile of things down there, and my dad moved on to Atlantic City. I was born in 1968, so all I remembered were the stories of his friendship with Earnest Hemingway and the barrels of money that the bureaucrats stole from the parking meters. The way I heard it, on the New Year's Eve that Batista left Cuba, my dad barely got out of there – probably with a tote bag like mine. His was probably full of dollars. What I didn't know at the time was that Harris Barton, my father, had spent ten years on the payroll of the U.S. government in some undercover capacity. Whoever got me into the Olympics must have thought that espionage was hereditary.

It was going to be dark soon. Regurgitating my past might lead to a clue as to how to embrace the future, but there was no way it was going to happen soon enough to get me a place to stay for the night. Summer in Taos is big on tourists, and that usually goes along with an understandable decline in hospitality among the locals. I didn't know anyone anyway except the checker-outers at Safeway and that was just for a "hello." I was either destined for the high school gym, which was set up as an evacuation center for fire victims, or finding a place to park. Probably I would end up curling up in back of my truck behind Denny's.

I gravitated toward the latter. I had no practical reason, but my acquired aversion to questions made me reluctant to embrace potentially social situations. If it weren't for that, I would have headed to the school gym. I was after all human. After six months of solitude, the possibility of some low-commitment human contact wasn't out of the attractive range for me. Not to speak of having been manless for an equal length of time – not my usual modus operandi, historically at least. When it came down to it, I opted to head out to the fields south of town. An average woman would probably avoid parking in such a remote location for purposes of truck sleeping, and wisely so. Of course, if she had spent the last eight years in my mind walking around in my body, risk would be tracked on a whole different scale.

When it's restful, sleep is one of the great gifts of life, or equalizers should I say. Mine was scrunched but deep. It was only disturbed by a coyote or two, and intermittent flashes of moonlight that hit my lidded eyes at an angle that couldn't be ignored. Since a watch was not on my list of rescued items, I didn't know how late in the morning I slept. It didn't seem to matter much, so I scrambled over the tailgate onto the ground. After taking care of a few necessities. I settled into the passenger seat to review my options.

There was my family, now consisting of only a brother and a sister, both having been sufficiently alienated by way of my past activities. Then there was Eric Lynne, codename Postman. He was my first contact with the Roca Group and probably as close as I came to real friendship with anyone there. In our eight years of association, we had covered most if not all the bases that a woman and a man can occupy. My list waned after that. My life had become so absorbed with intrigue that my only other thoughts were of college friends. Those, I hadn't seen or heard from since before I went directly from Seoul to the Roca Group's training facility on the Hudson River in Westchester County, N.Y.

I didn't know what to ask for from either of my siblings, so calling them was out. The Postman was not reachable by any conventional means and what could he do for me anyway? The Roca Group had given me the cabin and enough money to last me for a few years in exchange for me keeping out of sight. I had also agreed not to give any interviews and above all not to reveal to anyone the volume of notes I had taken describing numerous clandestine operations of which I was an integral part. These notes were my insurance, my only insurance, and nobody but I knew where they were. I still had plenty of money, and as bizarre a concept as it is, in our culture money equals security. So I slid over into the driver's seat and headed south to Santa Fe where there was a safe deposit box in which my security was stashed.

The sky was summer clear and cloudless, and the road was almost as uninhabited as the prairie. I had just enough gas to limp in on empty but that's all I needed. I didn't have an exact count of how much to expect in the box. I knew it was close to the $50,000 that Manny had originally put in there. Manny was the Roca Group's guy who had negotiated my arrangement. He couldn't be trusted, but money is money, and I had the notebook to back me up. He was the last contact that I had with the life of a conspirator that I had led. When we left that bank six months before and he put the key to the box in my hand, I was confident that a phase of my life had ended. Knowing that the double dealings of the Roca Group knew no ends, I came back later that day to check on the box and the money was there. I had visited a couple of times since, but only made minimal withdrawals. A recluse in a cabin on the mountain doesn't need much.

The bank had so many customers that it looked like a retail store, but I wasn't inconvenienced because my business was downstairs. I submitted to the procedure. I produced my key, which fortunately was on my car key ring or else it would have been immolated. I signed my fictitious name, which in my ex-line of work comes automatically, and walked behind the man through the rows of silver boxes to B495. He originally wanted me to go first. But knowing the possible motivation behind that preference, along with being trained to keep as much out in front of me and as little behind as possible, I managed to finesse the reversal. I took the box into a cubicle, closed the door, and perched atop the small desk as I opened it.

Chapter 3

The box was not as full as I had left it, nor was it empty. It contained one $100 bill. I kept my composure and turned the bill over and looked at the phone number written neatly between Ben's face and the serial number. It was an 800 number – how generous. I returned the box with the intention of asking questions about the signature card and others who might have had access to B495. Sometimes you know the answers to your questions before you ask them, and the only purpose in the asking is what I call self-calming. I was retired, but at one time I had been a pro. Sure a pro has needs, but self-calming isn't one of them. A pro needs to know *when* and *where* and *how much* and sometimes *who*. I knew some of those answers already, and the 800 number would probably let me in on the rest.

The lobby of the bank had a courtesy phone and its location even afforded some privacy, but I knew I wasn't ready. In a situation like this I had to know what was going to happen before it happened so I would have the right responses. I had to go through my training list of paranoid fantasies, none of which were too far-fetched that some variety of them hadn't already happened to me. I had a brief struggle with the urge to bolt to the phone and shout, *What the fuck is going on here – don't you assholes know that I have that notebook?*

Back in the Bronco, I listed the possibilities, not letting the concept of *ridiculous* or *impossible* inhibit my review. I knew that I had covered everything when I caught myself grasping a little too far, imagining the Roca Group had started the largest and most destructive forest fire to have ever occurred in New Mexico just to get me into this position. I was ready for the phone call. My list of possibilities looked like this:

(1) The Roca Group wanted me back inside and was looking for an opening.

(2) Manny seized on the fire as an opportunity and took the money to block my retreat.

(3) I was wanted for a job inside Cuba that only I could do.

(4) Something so big was going down that in comparison they didn't give a shit about my notes.

(5) They were going to give me an either/or threat, or offer me a huge chunk of money.

(6) Was the Postman involved?

(7) Was I still in love with him?

Over the past few months, I had begun to think that I knew myself pretty well. But I wouldn't have guessed that when I got to the bottom of my list, these last two questions would be the ones that got to me.

I was on my way to make the call from the phone in the bank lobby when my instincts took hold. I veered off course and began looking for a pay phone, a more secure phone. Shit, I was still a fuckin' spy. I still had the instincts of a spy. I thought I was becoming human again but I was wrong. I was still a spy. I was more rocked by that realization than by the lack of all that money. Money could come and go. What was in your instincts – that's what you lived with. I thought I was finished with it. Not only because they were finished with me, but because I was finished with them. I wasn't so sure now. Maybe it wasn't only Eric that I missed.

The number rang a dozen times and I hung up. *Unusual? Not unusual? Not sure. Try again later. Someone watching the phone booth? Possible? Not Likely. Not sure. Drive away. Check for a tail. Go to another neighborhood and call again.* I did.

The phone rang twice and a woman's voice answered, "Career Management, please hold."

Another unfamiliar voice, this time male, got on the line and asked for my company name. I gave him the name I had used for the safe deposit box but he repeated, "Company name please." After another repetition of the same words, I realized the game he was playing. He wanted me back in my old bullshit Roca Group self. He wanted my codename. I didn't want to give that much, not yet, so I said, "I'll play your stupid game. Belinda, okay? It's Belinda."

"Please state your company name slowly and clearly."

I knew that he was wanting Jelinda, my code name, not Belinda, but that was as far as my pride was prepared to go. I said innocently, "My memory is a little shaky. You know how it is being a helpless woman just burned out of house and home and discovering that I have no money. It's Belinda isn't it?"

"Please state your company name slowly and clearly."

Typical Roca Group bullshit. "Jelinda, okay? Now put that asshole Manny on the phone!"

"One moment."

" . . . You there Pepper?"

I knew it was Manny because he was the only person who ever called me Pepper. I had made the mistake of telling him about my curious collecting habit and he never let me forget it. Maybe it wasn't really a mistake. In that impersonal world that we shared, at least we had a nickname between us that was personal.

"Another bank robbery for your resume Manny? You must be next in line for the executive board."

"This is no kid stuff Pepper. We haven't gotten our mail in a couple of weeks and you know he would never let that happen. He's been in and out of 90M four times since you left and this time he's in deep." Ninety M was our codename for Cuba, it being 90 miles from Florida.

"You're bluffing, Manny. Postman's a swimmer and if by some slim chance he was down, why would you have to take my money? You think I would leave him there?"

"Ninety M is one of the hottest spots on the planet right now," Manny insisted. "I can't tell you any more on the phone. There's a ticket waiting for you at the Albuquerque Airport. Phone the 800 number when you get to The Beach." The Beach was Roca codename for Miami.

Manny hung up without waiting for a response. That was typical. He acts as if it's a *fait accompli* and then I'm supposed to do the same. They wanted me to think that Eric was in trouble. The Postman was their main man for hot spots, and since I got out of it there was no one else who could operate in Cuba. That is, unless they had recruited someone new, and a rookie wouldn't be ready for a weighty assignment for another year or so. Ninety M wasn't a particularly dangerous assignment, unless of course

20

something special was up. Then anything was possible. The way Manny operated, he presented everything as truth, even though whoever was listening knew it was only a matter of assessing how much of a lie it was. But I had no place to go and I knew I couldn't get the money back unless I went to Miami. There wasn't much to think about. An idealist might have said no at any cost, but that wasn't me. I got in the Bronco and headed south to Albuquerque.

I switched my ticket and flew into Miami through Minneapolis. It wasn't the most direct route, but I knew that they would be clocking flights from Houston, New Orleans, and Dallas. If I came in on any expected route, I wouldn't have to call the 800 number and I knew it. It didn't take a Mossad agent to know that they had someone checking flights and would be waiting for me. Not that I wasn't going to make contact, but it seemed important that I not lay down and roll over.

I wasn't much company for the lady on the aisle, unless she was lonely enough to appreciate my nodding head hitting her shoulder from time to time. The food was the only thing I sat completely upright for and that might have been a mistake, because my digestive track ended up feeling like it was paying for something it couldn't afford.

There was no pretending that the time away hadn't clouded my memory. It had. But one thing was clear. It wasn't about ideals. It was about money. So much money that people got idealistic about what it could do. Of course the people who figured to get their hands on it weren't going to do anything idealistic with it. But that's the world, and I sure wasn't trying to change it. I just wanted to find a nice spot to plant my tomatoes. The Roca Group had a code of ethics, but

I never knew one of us that believed in any of it. We were recruited and brought along slowly, given small injections of intrigue, drama, excitement, and glamour, until we were habituated. Then it was only a matter of time before the doses were escalated and finally we were hooked. As cool a customer as he was, the Postman was as much a junkie as any of us. We were all addicted to the action.

It was only recently that I had begun to renovate my attitude toward my fellow Earth inhabitants. By the time I had gotten away from the Roca Group and to the cabin, it had gotten to the point that humans looked to me like the sorriest species on the planet. Most of them had to generate problems to occupy their minds. That can be hard work, and the problems are usually low-level petty. When you worked for the Roca Group, every moment was a problem, every interaction had cover-blowing potential, or worse. Sometimes I felt like the Pink Panther and the rest of the world was sitting out in the theater missing their mouths with their incoming popcorn.

Chapter 4

Miami International is the hub for the leap into the Latin American world. The flight from Minneapolis was full of Anglos, but with my first hit of the terminal it was clear that the Spanish-speaking world was just a takeoff and a landing away. That is, the part of it that wasn't already under my feet.

What a difference a day makes. Twenty-four little hours ago. Sure, song lyrics, but there I had been, sitting on my porch overlooking the Sangre De Christo. Behind me were all the cheap and expensive tricks I had pulled in the name of . . . Why bullshit myself? Usually in the name of nothing. Now it was all in front of me again – Eric, Manny, the Roca Group . . . too fuckin' weird.

"I spotted you outside the bank, so I can't say, *Long time no see*," Manny called over from in front of the Avis counter. "Back in Santa Fe I was patched in on a cellular while you were on that pay phone."

No matter how many reverses a spook pulls – reverse on top of reverse on top of reverse, some other spook will guess the point of arrival. We all think like that, and forgetting it is a sign of rust. I guess I was rusty. I noted it, I'm sure Manny noted it, but nobody gloated.

I walked over to him and he gave me a hug. I had reason to hate the bastard for more than the money snatching, but he was a big teddy bear. No, he was more like a grizzly, and I hadn't been wrapped up by anyone for a long time. I let myself believe that he meant a fraction of it, but only a fraction. I knew the rest was con.

"You'll need a rental car Pepper. You got a license?" Manny asked.

I shook my head and he put down a fake license and a credit card to match. "I don't feel like driving, Manny. As pissed-off as I am I'd rather go with you."

"Can't do it kid. You're going to have to make a stop first, and I can't make this one with you." He slid over an open spiral notebook with an address on it and an envelope with a small stack of twenties. He told me to check into the Fort Lauderdale Hilton after I made the stop and he would come by in the morning.

"Is this what's left from the heist?" I wisecracked.

The Avis guy heard my last remark and we all laughed like it was a joke. It was a stupid thing to say but I didn't care. I knew I would be Roca before long and I was getting as many of my *ya-yas* out before I would have to get serious.

Manny got me a white Lincoln Continental. After I was committed it would be a Chevy. I remembered the rules of the game. The air in the Miami summer was about as different from Taos as Venus is from Earth. Even with the fire smoke it was fresher in New Mexico. I turned up the air-con full blast and put on the radio news. Sometimes droning voices help me to think better than meaningful music. Most of the stuff that I could have popped in the CD player from my tote bag would have hit a little too close to home.

The address was in Plantation, a chock full of senior citizens suburb of Fort Lauderdale, which is a suburb of Miami. Plantation probably had its suburbs too, but I don't know what they call them. I drove north on the Florida Turnpike. It was as empty as the last time I had driven it a couple of years before. It's amazing what people will do to avoid paying fifty cents.

Eric's father was his FSCL, his fail safe communication link. It wasn't Roca Group procedure to have one, but we all knew that the Roca Group was capable of stranding us for its own interests. Most of us worst-cased to a family member who could handle it. I never had one, but Postman had the best. His father was a retired U.S. Navy intelligence lieutenant commander and would know what to do if the shit ever hit the fan.

Eric grew up in New England, on the coast of Rhode Island actually. He came from second-generation European parents, both born in Rhode Island. His dad was Greek and his mom Italian. I went there to meet him once in the early years and got a dose of his whole family. Salt of the earth types, or maybe salt of the sea. I grew up proud of being a big-city girl, and rural folks always threw me a little. Eric was eight years older than I and two inches shorter. It was the only thing I had over him, but it rarely paid off. He wasn't the kind of person that you describe physically and then think, that's him. He was more than the sum of his parts, even though his parts were pretty appealing. He looked like anyone he wanted to look like. That's what made him the best spook around. He was invisible. If you saw him three times you wouldn't recognize him the fourth – that is unless he wanted you to. Not that he used disguises. He just blended. He was best in Latin countries because of his build and dark hair. But he had also operated in Eastern Europe and the Med before I came on the scene.

After retiring from the navy, his dad had bought a fleet of fishing boats and became a very successful business man. He even ran for a congressional seat in Rhode Island and served two years before his health deteriorated (politics can do that). That's how Eric got into Yale. Gus Lynne (Lynacos) helped an influential U.S. Senator from Connecticut get reelected and Senator Abe paid back the favor by helping Eric get into Yale. He had neither the grades, the S.A.T. scores, nor even the desire, but he had a recommendation from a U.S. Senator. As it happened, Eric only lasted two years there. During summer vacation, he found a way to make large amounts of money without a college degree and that was the end of Yale. Where Yale ended, his career began. No, not directly, but drawing a line from Eric's money-making scheme to a career with the Roca Group is certainly not difficult.

At the age of 21, Eric and a classmate nicknamed BC formed a partnership for cashing large denomination parimutuel tickets at the race track for winners who didn't want their winnings reported on their taxes. They would take a 10% commission from the winner and find a down-on-his-luck person at the track to cash the ticket, for which they would give him a cut. This scheme required that Eric and BC carry large amounts of cash with them. Race tracks around the country had begun instituting multi-race bets where a winner of four races in a row could win thousands of dollars for a two dollar bet. Eric's partner decided that carrying a gun was the best way to protect all that cash. When the illegality of the scheme was uncovered and the two were eventually apprehended in the act, so was the illegal firearm.

Back then, the courts would sometimes, in a first offense situation, give the convicted youth the option of joining the military and having all record of the incident expunged. It was an alternative to going to jail and having a criminal record follow him through life. Within two weeks, both boys found themselves at Fort Dix, New Jersey undergoing basic training. Eric eventually ended up in Stuttgart, Germany as a private in the finance division. He never graduated from that institution either.

After a year, his unique capabilities were noticed, and he was recruited by a quasi-government task force as a potential financial operative. The rest, as they say, is history. Eric's creative talents were one of his strongest attributes in Roca Group operations. If there was any subterfuge, and there almost always was, Eric could sniff it out. He had a devious mind and the Roca Group execs were eager to harness it. I actually met Eric on one of those assignments where he was expected to exercise that very talent.

I had finished what you might call my basic training with Manny at the helm. He covered martial arts and target practice even though we both knew I would never have to use those skills. I think it was fun for him to put a five-pound Glock 21 .45 caliber pistol in the hands of a girl, knowing that she could hardly heft it much less fire it. That's when he started calling me Pepper.

For my first assignment, I was to assist Eric Lynne, codename Postman, a veteran agent I had never met but whose reputation had already been established. The assignment required Portuguese language translation for a deal that was being negotiated in Rio. Eric was fine in Spanish but knew no Portuguese. I did. Not only did the deal turn out to be bogus, but it was my first run-in with danger.

Some well-financed businessmen with underworld connections were trying to negotiate a contract with the City of Rio De Janeiro. They were proposing to renovate the hillside slums, known as favelas, for the impoverished inhabitants. There was nothing wrong with the idea or the $200,000 that the businessmen were going to pay the Roca Group. That is, until Eric found out that the slums were not to be renovated, but demolished in advance of construction of luxury high-rise hotels.

Had we facilitated a contract that duped the Brazilian government, they would never have had confidence in the Roca Group again. We would be out of business not only in Brazil, but potentially in the rest of South America. Needless to say, the backers of the defunct deal were not happy with our participation. Their unhappiness manifested itself in the necessity for Eric and me to go underground in Uruguay for a couple of weeks.

That's how it all started between us. Not even close to love at first sight. More like, *This kid is a pain in the ass, and how did I draw the assignment of baby sitter?* That's how it started, and maybe even lasted for a while. But eventually Eric saw that I was quick to pick up the subtleties of a situation, and he was a sucker for subtleties. He introduced me to the phrase, "beneath the surface of things," and clearly liked playing the teacher when it came to exploring hidden anomalies. And though there wasn't much beneath the surface of things during our two weeks hiding from Brazilian gangsters in Uruguay, there was a lot of time with nothing to do. We were in our twenties and of the opposite sex. Not that we fell into bed on the first night, or even the second or third (the fourth I think it was), but we got to know each other and we both liked what we got to know.

Sure Eric was cute, and still is, and could be charming when he thought it fit, but what I remember liking most about him from that time was his confidence. It didn't seem to be based in bravado, more like he was okay with himself. If he wasn't prepared for what might happen, he would find out how to get prepared. My dad never got to meet Eric, but I know he would have liked him. My dad had, as his most honorable category of person and the ones that he would allow to get closest to him, something he called being "a stand-up guy." He called me that once, and I never forgot it. I don't know from where that saying stems, but I do know that Eric was, and is, a stand-up guy.

The Roca Group execs weren't pleased to lose a $200,000 payday, but they were also not so greedy as to be oblivious to what the implications could have been had we *successfully* closed that deal. They were certainly pleased that we eventually got home safely. They saw benefits in what had obviously become a budding relationship – one that they definitely could use to their advantage. Over the following two years, Eric and I were paired in numerous assignments. Our ability to play a believable married couple proved to be quite an asset.

The Roca Group recruited by claiming to be under the U.S. government umbrella. Too inside to even have initials – like some kind of financial Delta Force. But it was bullshit. The Roca Group worked for money and influence – and influence meant more money. We claimed to be available to work for any country that wasn't an explicit enemy of the U.S. or its allies. But sometimes even that restriction wasn't rigorously adhered to. There were nationals of a dozen countries working full time on the payroll and offices in twice as many countries as that. The Roca Group operated by contract. Some were ongoing for years, and others took a few months to fulfill. All the operations that I was ever involved in were focused around financial matters. This wasn't a political or military outfit. It was about money, and like they said in our first training seminar, "When it gets down to it, there are no countries. There are conglomerates and multinationals. There's no Thailand or Argentina. There's only Exxon and Xerox and Sony."

It's not that politics didn't come into Roca Group operations. Governments run on money. So the best way to overthrow a government is to cut off its allowance. It's only when that doesn't work that things turn bloody. Some of the Roca Group executives thought they were world servants – keeping wars at bay by helping to manipulate the world economy. They scared me even more than sleezeballs like Manny.

Wyndham Otnabe was one of those guys. He was not as old as a person with so much power is supposed to be. He was tall, distinguished, and the last time I saw him a little gray was just starting to show. His suits always looked like he wore them one time and then gave them away, and his hands never got dirty. As smart as his dress was, he was even smarter. In all the time I knew him, I only remember one miscalculation. Sure it was a costly one, but that's still quite an average. He was a Turkish/British mutt and too sophisticated for the average schmoe to resist. I was one of those average shmoes my first year, but after my Roca Group initiation, I made certain not to let it happen again.

Otnabe cleared all the operations for my group. When he gave the okay, you could be pretty confident that you had all the best going for you. I learned to depend on his plans and his contacts but not believe a word he said. That was how Eric lasted so long in the open. He took whatever they gave him like it was gospel and verified it all over again.

Postman taught me to become my own operative – not a pawn of the Roca Group. As far as he was concerned, he was the boss and he hired the Roca Group to hire him. It took a long time for me to believe in myself enough to think that way, and a longer time to really feel it – but it happened. By the end, I had my own organization, my own operatives, my own sources, and I could climb most ropes without having to use the Roca's knots.

That's how the notebook came about. I started building my insurance policy after a sticky operation in Kuwait. When any of our people got their pictures in the press, it was bad news. Our clients hated it and we hated it even more. That's what happened in Kuwait, and our client was big enough that two of our agents were forced into the open and out of the game.

One of the biggest insurance companies in the world cut a deal with Saddam Hussein. If he would set the oil fields on fire, they would pay him what they wouldn't have to pay the Kuwaitis because their policy exempted acts of war. Then they tripled the rates to the multinationals that owned the wells. The underwriters would recoup their money in two years and get triple premiums throughout the Middle East from then on. Exxon and Shell suspected something when the insurance company balked at paying off the claim. They hired us and we uncovered the scheme, but there was too much press around during the Gulf War and our people got blown. Saddam set the fields on fire anyway, but he never got his money. If I had cut his deal he would have gotten half up front.

From then on, I broke one of the Roca Group's primary directives. Nothing goes down on paper unless authorized by the execs, with nothing under any circumstances retained as personal records. Well my notebooks surely weren't okayed, and personal records were exactly what they were. So I was on my own, and that's the way I wanted it. Even Eric wouldn't have approved. I think in his guts he was more Roca Group than I was.

Chapter 5

I was ten miles up the Florida Turnpike before I realized that I had passed the Sunrise Highway exit to Plantation. I circled around at the next off-ramp and headed the two exits south to where I was supposed to get off in the first place. I didn't remember Plantation from the last time, but it looked like just about every other franchise-studded boulevard in America. Mr. Lynne lived in a retirement community that probably was a normal progression to cap a life that included thirty years in the military. His ex-wife had stayed in Rhode Island, so he found a new regiment. From what I remembered of my last visit, he was very active in organizing activities there and even contributed to their newspaper.

There was no phone number written on the paper along with the address, and anyway Manny didn't say to call first. I knew what the visit was about, and in hi-pri matters you just show up. That's expected. The only time that the Roca Group would ever have contact with an FSCL was in what we called "dire straits." It used to be called something else, but one of the execs was a big rock n' roll fan. Manny wanted me to hear the story directly from Eric's dad. That would save him the trouble of having to convince me. He was right. If it came from the Commander, I would believe it.

Most times when you don't see an older person for a while, they look even further on than you'd expect. When the door opened, I was frozen for a moment. Mr. Lynne looked more like a slightly older Eric than an age-extended version of the man I had seen three years before. He recognized me right away and gave me a hug to match. This second one in as many hours was family and there was no mistaking it. He knew that I was once in love with Eric, and since he loved Eric, the algebraic principal applied.

His apartment was retirement efficient – fifties furniture, shag carpet, small chandelier over an oblong dining table. The only inconsistencies were the books. No T.V., but books everywhere, lining the walls and stacked on every horizontal surface. Anyone who fathered the Postman couldn't be too straight. I felt good about all those books.

We sat at the breakfast table in the corner of the kitchen. He made some coffee, splashed in some brandy, and I told him about the last 48 hours. I wasn't in a hurry to hear his story because there was nothing I could do yet. Anyway, he probably needed to be reacquainted with the person who might have to save his son's ass. My recent history was the best I had to give to further the cause.

It was getting late for me and I figured it was the same for Commander Lynne. He was anxious to tell me what he knew, but I was too tired to process the information clearly. The man reminded me of my father, whom I dearly missed. Formalities seemed ridiculous in the situation. I asked if I could sleep on his couch and we could resume in the morning. I liked the idea doubly because it would fuck up Manny's plans. That made me feel more on top of things. When he went to the Hilton he would figure out where I was

– *he* would have to wait for *me*. As far as I was concerned, that's the way it was supposed to be.

The Commander was delighted to have me as his guest, and the couch was the softest thing to caress my body in as long as I could remember. Before I fell asleep I fixed on a plan for my meeting with Manny. He might not go for it, but I worked best when I had a plan to start with.

The window air conditioner was a few feet from my left ear and the cool breeze fed me dreams of the Sangre de Christo. When the Florida sun came in through the window, I was walking in the woods behind the cabin. My eyes now open, I moved through the denial stage rapidly and sat up to prep myself for my talk with the Commander, and then with Manny.

The Commander was already in the kitchen, cracking, flipping, and toasting. He waited for me to call over to him. I guess he had lived alone long enough to know that one waits till one's guest is ready for the human to human portion of the day to begin.

As we ate, I got the story of his communication with Eric. Four days before, the secretary at the Commander's retirement community newspaper got a call from a local business that dealt in mailing services. They were checking rates for a three-column ad to run in nine consecutive issues. The businessman said that a Mr. Lynne had phoned their location and had recommended that they look into advertising in the Omega News. When the secretary tried to return the call with the rate information, the 800 number that she had been given seemed to be the wrong number. She thought she had copied it down incorrectly so she asked the Commander.

He knew immediately who it was. Not only had he not recommended advertising to anybody recently, but the combination of a reference to a postal business and the numbers three and nine, components of their pre-arranged emergency signal, made it obvious that it was his son. The secretary passed on what she thought was an incorrect 800 number. Mr. Lynne called it and was put through to Manny.

I cleared the dishes from the table and carried a cup of coffee into the living room. I plopped down on my previous night's nesting spot while the Commander went back into his bedroom to get some papers that he wanted me to see. He came back empty-handed and sat down at a small desk in the living room and began shuffling through some documents in the bottom drawer.

I asked him to explain his FSCL set-up in as much detail as he could. I needed to know anything that would give me something more explicit than "emergency signal." He pulled out a blue-gray piece of paper and started reading it to me. I got up and walked over to the desk so that I could look over his shoulder while he was reading. Their system was basic and easy to interpret: two rows of one-digit numbers, 1-9. The first related to a statement of physical condition and the second to an urgency level. The 3 in "three news paper columns" meant he was in harm's way but had not been injured, and the 9 in "an ad to run for nine consecutive issues" represented maximum urgency for sending assistance.

Mr. Lynne told me he had only once before gotten an FSCL call from Eric, and that was a 2-2, which meant no present physical danger and no need to send help yet. "That time, he was notifying me that everything was okay for now, but if I didn't hear from him voice to voice within seven days

I should call the Roca Group. He called me two days later, and over all these years that's been our only use of the FSCL."

The Commander had no idea what the Postman had been working on, nor did he know where the call to the newspaper had come from. He had no more useful information. Still, I didn't want to bolt out of there and meet Manny in the lobby of the Hilton just yet. As I perused the pictures on the apartment walls, we chatted about the past – my dad and his Cuba stories, Eric, Rhode Island, family stuff. I needed it and maybe he did too. The Commander was a big Hemingway fan, so he was fascinated to hear about my visit to his home, La Vigia, out in the countryside east of Havana. It had been preserved as a museum, and my father, as a friend of the family, had access to the grounds. Some years after Hemingway's death, he took me to visit the estate. For some reason all I remembered was a closet with dozens of pairs of shoes and a huge poster advertising an upcoming bull fight.

I stalled around for a while getting a couple of doses more of the family feeling till I knew it was time to go. I think I would have liked this guy even if he weren't connected to Eric. There's something magnetic about having someone accept you for what you are and not for the impression you're making. Maybe it was the missing dad thing, or maybe it was something else. I didn't have time to get introspective about it now. My meeting with Manny at the hotel was next and I didn't want to have to rush to get there.

Chapter 6

Carmen Miranda had the same name as the lady who made Chiquita Bananas famous, but that's where the similarity ended. As the Roca Group's only woman exec, she was not a random choice for head of the New York office of Career Management Associates Incorporated – which was neither incorporated, nor did it have anything to do with career management. The offices occupied the entire 22nd floor of the building at 50 Broad Street. Its proximity to Wall Street was not coincidental.

Miranda, the only name to which she responded, was in her early forties. It was a tossup whether her brains, her looks, or her steely nerves were her strong suit. If she had a weakness, it was her inability to delegate authority. In her eight years as both the boss of the N.Y. office and head of Latin American operations, she seemed to be able to juggle as many balls as were thrown to her. Usually she had a free hand left to juggle a few that weren't her own, and the guys who owned them rarely recovered from the exercise.

The Roca Group avoided assignments that required one of its operatives to commit a violent act. But Miranda was not the voice of temperance that was responsible for maintaining that policy. She was ruthless with a treacherous twist and everybody who worked for her knew what she was capable of. The Latin American section was perfect for her. She didn't have the patience for dealings with either Middle Eastern or Asian interests, but patience was rarely needed anywhere south of the border. Mostly it called for bold strokes and taking advantage of spur-of-the-moment opportunities.

She came into the office every morning – every single morning, but she spent her afternoons around home. Home was her New York apartment on 46th Street between First and Second Avenues. The United Nations building was the picture outside of her picture window. Roca group people rarely came to her roost – only clients and contacts. That's how she got to be an exec and Roca Group's top saleswoman. She was all business. Half the contracts that were active at any given time were procured by Miranda.

Most of the agents disliked working for her but they all had to anyway sometime or other. Miranda was brought into the Roca Group by the Postman, but since she had worked her way upstairs, there was no love lost between them. In the weeks before the fire, Manny had spent more time with Miranda than made him comfortable. Manny was always looking for the easy way. Miranda had a *just get it done* style. He had forwarded her the first news of contact between the Postman and his FSCL, and she ordered him up to New York that same night.

Business came first, but she still had a little bit of the "woman scorned" thing, so the Postman was perpetually on her shit list. She took every opportunity to knock him down a few notches, but in order to do that he had to be operational. If he was in trouble, she wanted him liberated as much as anybody. That is, except for Jelinda of course, once she found out.

Neither Manny nor Miranda took the news that the Postman was inoperative as a fact. First of all, Roca Group policy was to confirm and re-confirm anything that came by way of an FSCL. Carrying even more weight than that, the Postman had always been in solid with the Cuban authorities. But on the other side, two weeks without communication was unheard of. One week was a lot, and in the case of Postman's current assignment, five days had been pre-arranged as the outside limit.

Roca Group procedure in the case of a potentially downed operative was for Miranda to notify Otnabe. He was in charge of overseeing all operations around the globe. He got the call from Miranda after she got the call from Manny. Everyone had been acting a little jittery ever since. The Roca Group operated on a system of mutual distrust. Within the organization, most operatives and all the execs had their own moles, informants, and favor-owing secretaries. The principal was that if everybody checked up on everyone else, then nothing clandestine could last for too long. Both Miranda and Otnabe tapped their personal information resources to find out if there were any subtleties or counter subtleties not previously revealed about the Postman's present assignment.

It had been put forth as a straightforward, what the Roca Group called, "turnover." Three major U.S. tobacco companies were consorting to approach Cuba with a deal that would be considered illegal according to the U.S. government's trade embargo. The consortium had already notified the appropriate Cuban officials that they wanted to talk deal and both they and the Cuban government approved Roca as an intermediary.

They wanted Roca to present an offer of 250 million dollars to be paid to the Castro Government through a European subsidiary. The payment was to secure a 15-year option to sell highly sought-after Cuban cigars as "American Made" to the U.S. market and around the world, if and when the embargo was lifted. It was a gamble that the tobacco consortium was comfortable making. In each of the past three years, the United Nations General Assembly had voted that the U.S. embargo against Cuba was a violation of international law. The likelihood that the embargo could last much longer was small. Outside of the Cuban expat community in Miami, there was little support for it. In its 30 plus years, the embargo had little to show for its efforts.

American tobacco had dealt with Castro before through the Roca Group. Years ago, using a European front company, they had secretly invested in the tobacco fields of the Vuelta Abajo region on the western tip of the island. This was where the highest export quality cigar tobacco was grown. A deal like this new one could greatly increase Cuba's market for its cigars and tobacco. On the other end, it would revive the American tobacco companies' cash flow, which was hurting from years of negative cigarette media. They were actually silent partners already, so this was the obvious next step. A one percent commission for the Roca Group would be 2.5 million. It would not be an easy assignment – not with Castro involved – but a good payday if the Postman could pull it off.

After Lynne left for Cuba, Wyndam Otnabe, at the personal request of Raoul Castro, agreed to negotiate an add-on to the agreement. No one but Otnabe knew about the extension in perpetuity clause that might be added onto the deal. It required that the tripartite tobacco consortium approve returning their interest in the Vuelta Abajo fields. If the embargo were lifted during the 15-year option, the perpetuity clause would kick in and the tobacco companies would be looking at billions in profits. The Roca Group would be in for one percent in perpetuity.

Postman got his codename from his ability to deliver. He had handled numerous similar operations. Although they didn't always end successfully, they rarely involved any jeopardy to the Postman himself. Miranda needed to find out if the basic tobacco deal was a smoke screen. Otnabe might know, but that didn't mean he would tell her. She was the exec who originally procured the deal, but there still might be another element hidden beneath the surface of the "turnover." After all, information about operations in the Roca Group descended on a need-to-know basis.

Cuba was one of the most lucrative activity centers for the Roca Group. Aside from North Korea, which was rapidly becoming one also, it was one of the few places that discreet, clandestine, non-official intermediaries with connections in high places were needed on a regular basis. Over the last eight years, the Roca Group's business in Cuba grew to become a substantial portion of its gross revenues. There was no overlooking that the reason for this windfall was a talented female operative, Callie, short for Caroline Barton – codename Jelinda.

Explanations of her influence in Cuba ranged from illicit relationships with Fidel and/or Raoul, to unconfirmed rumors about her now deceased father. Harris Barton, her father, had been involved with Meyer Lansky in the gambling and entertainment industry in pre-Castro times when Batista was president. Batista not only invited gambling czars from the U.S. to develop hotels and casinos in Cuba, he enticed their involvement and patronage with favorable regulations and eased restrictions. Eventually, the casinos rivaled others anywhere in the world, and their profits were shared generously with Batista himself. Tourists from the U.S. were assured not only of beautiful beaches, but of honest casinos and a safe environment. Even the likes of Mafia bosses Santo Trafficante and Joe Silesi realized that there was more money in running an honest casino than a crooked one. Harris Barton was one of those "honest casino" executives.

But unlike all the other Batista supported elements, Barton managed to maintain a unique relationship with the revolutionaries. It had never been verified, but some said that he had played an instrumental part in financing El Comandente's *coup d'état* and had made numerous secret trips back to Cuba until the late 1980s. In the winter of 1988, he made his only acknowledged post-revolution trip to Cuba with an invited group of professors from New York University. He died in a tragic traffic accident in Havana with two other elderly academics.

Six months ago, Callie Barton was released from the employ of the Roca Group under cloaked circumstances and had not been heard from since. Her whereabouts were considered unknown. Counter to Roca Group procedure, the matter was not handled by consensus of the entire executive board, but was the product of a private arrangement with Wyndham Otnabe. As director of global operations, Otnabe had the authority to act thusly in matters of his choosing.

Cuban operations had been hampered from that point. Several new operatives had been recruited and were presently being developed for that market. Regardless of his seniority and impeccable reputation as an operative, Eric Lynne, who had taken over all high-level operations in Cuba, was not able to compensate for the departure of Jelinda. Miranda wanted Jelinda back, but all her attempts thus far at convincing Otnabe to re-sign her yielded no results.

Miranda recognized the possibility that Otnabe was finally going to act on her request to get Jelinda. Perhaps he had either involved the Postman in collusion or set him up to get her back. That was a remote theory, but Miranda's favorite. It might result in regaining Jelinda's services and increasing the percentage of women at or near the top of the Roca hierarchy. There had been no corroboration of this hypothesis and there was little likelihood of its accuracy. If that's what was happening, why would Miranda be kept in the dark? Of course it was possible that Otnabe didn't know any more than she did. Until she knew, she would follow procedures in a downed agent situation, and that's why Manny was in New York.

Chapter 7

It was Sunday and the roads were empty, save for the few cars that were heading to or from Sunrise Highway's best known attraction – the largest swap meet in the world. I guess there wasn't a big church-going population in Plantation either, because on the way to the Hilton I only passed a few other cars going east on Sunrise, and their passengers didn't look like they were heading to church.

Manny was sitting on a wingback chair in the corner of the Hilton lobby on the border of the free breakfast buffet for overnighters. He had a fat copy of the Sunday Miami Herald on the coffee table in front of him and was obviously prepared to wait however long it took. When I walked up, he had a mouthful of bagel so we just looked at each other for an awkward moment or two.

As I sat down I smiled, having caught a glimpse of a kid stuffing his pockets for a later snack. When I traveled with the swim team, we would carry ziplocks for the purpose. I wondered if this kid was that prepared. That kind of larceny had probably been part of my agent training. I wondered about his future.

I had rehearsed my opening, so there was no reason to sit down till I got my performance over with. "Whatever it is you want me to do, if I say go, I want four times the amount you took. I want it in cash so I can put it in a Swiss numbered account where your clammy hands can't reach it."

Manny laughed a few bagel crumbs my way and said, "Hey, would you sit down please? You want something to eat, some coffee?"

I sat on the small couch that right angled Manny's wing back chair. It faced a window that looked out on the parking lot. There was a group of school kids packing up a van, probably heading to some athletic competition. Better days . . . "No Manny, the Commander fed me fine."

"Quite a guy. I never met him but Eric's told me some pretty outrageous stories."

"So what do you say?" I wanted to stay on track. Manny was pretty smooth with business, but I knew he also liked to shmooze. At another time I could have done it, but not now. I knew it wasn't his idea to pull the money from my box, but I wanted him to think I was still pissed at him personally. It might give me an edge.

"Listen Pepper, my clammy hands don't get around anywhere near as much as Otnabe's do. You should know that better than most. If it were up to me I'd give you a mil. You're the best. There's nobody I ever let the line out as far I did with you. Well, maybe the Postman, but with him I usually didn't have a choice."

Manny was easy to categorize but it never stuck. That's what I liked about him. Most people saw him as some kind of an errand-man/thug hybrid, but Manny was none of these and all of these. He was given most of the dirty jobs Roca handed out, but he usually handled them with that little bit of extra class that wasn't required by anyone but Manny himself. When it didn't conflict with his assignment, he treated me like a daughter, and that was chocolate for me since losing my dad. It's not that he treated me like a little girl or anything. There was respect there, not condescension, but the teasing and the "Pepper" stuff felt like fatherly affection. He also liked setting me straight when he thought that I had the wrong take on an assignment. In the beginning that was really important for me. I never left that appreciation behind. That's not to say that I trusted him. Trust was something that depended on truth, and truth was not like appreciation. It was a variable depending on expediency and certainly not a constant. Trust definitely had to be left behind.

"Do I get my 200K in cash or not?" I snapped.

"If it's okay with Wyndam, it's okay with me," Manny countered.

That was a lot of cash to me, but I knew it wasn't much to the Roca Group. I got plenty of benefits over the years but most of them were in lifestyle, not in security. Otnabe would have cleared Manny to make the decision and I knew it. "One more time . . . do I get my 200K or not?"

Manny didn't miss a beat in answering, "Done."

"Okay, so what do you want me to do?" I said after an inhale.

Before he answered, I told him what I thought he needed to know about the FSCL, figuring that I'd better leave out the details of their code. He told me about Postman's assignment in Ninety M. It was obvious that I was only getting the surface level of the operation, but it was also possible that was all Manny was in on. And maybe that's all there was. I needed to know more. I needed to talk to Miranda. Eventually I knew I had to talk to Otnabe, but nothing good could come from that. He'd only tell me what he thought he had to – anything to get me to do whatever he wanted me to do. I would have to find out for myself whether it was true or not. I may have been naive, but I thought that there was something real between Miranda and me. Two women high up in a man's world can feel drawn to each other, and we did, at least from my side.

Manny wanted me to go to Havana that night on the scheduled charter plane. Very few people know that there are official flights from Miami to Havana from Miami International. They're subject to tons of security and not available to the general public. They leave after midnight when the fewest possible people will be around the airport. The Roca Group had the kind of influence it took to avoid being considered part of the "general public." Sometimes it was necessary for our operatives to slide in invisibly, but sometimes it was okay to walk in the front door. So far, I had always been welcome in Cuba, so whenever I went, I took the charter flight.

Most people think that the Cuban government has placed restrictions on travel for U.S. citizens, but that's not the case. The U.S. government has placed the ban as part of its trade embargo. Even though an overwhelming percentage of Americans would prefer not to be banned from traveling to Cuba, the restriction remains in place. No other country has restrictions for Cuban travel. It's actually the number one tourist destination for Canadians. Even the United Nations has condemned the embargo as a violation of international law. In order for an ordinary U.S. citizen to visit Cuba, he or she must travel there secretly, either through Canada or Mexico. Cuba doesn't stamp the passports of Americans, so on their return they can avoid saying where they've been.

However I was going to get there, I wasn't going to jump in before I got some of my own people digging around for the real story. I had been out of it for six months, but good connections are good connections. Then there was Miranda. I told Manny that I needed to talk to her before I made another move. He said that she would come down to Miami later that afternoon if he passed it on that I would meet with her.

That was the moment I knew for certain that something really big was going down. Miranda never left New York. Not for anything . . . never. She was an office exec, not field. She jockeyed from Wall Street to the U.N. and between. That was her world. If she was coming to Miami, we were talking about a whole different dimension of priority. My bet was that Otnabe would be close behind.

Manny told me he was going off to use the pay phone to call Miranda. He could have used his cellular, but I'm sure he didn't want to make the call with me listening. I lost track of how long he was gone. I had gotten used to daydreaming on the porch of the cabin. It was a sweet way to spend the time looking out over the Sangre de Christo. Now that I was in shark-infested waters it would be counter-productive, to say the least.

When Manny returned, he told me Miranda would meet me in the bar at the *Bleau* at 5:00 p.m. The Fontainebleau Hotel was a frequent meeting place for financial deals, and the two of us meeting in the open there wouldn't arouse any suspicion – no matter who saw us. There used to be a lot of underworld activity around the luxury hotels, but it had moved downtown where the Latino drug dealers owned the streets. I asked Manny if he would be there. He said it was up to Miranda but that he guessed he probably would. I started to ask if anyone else was expected but thought better of letting on that I knew we were into something big.

Since I had to be at the beach at 5:00 p.m, I figured that I would go directly over there and chill out – or warm up. Sundays can be pretty crowded on the sand, but up in the north end around Hollywood it would be relatively quiet. I don't know which Hollywood came first, but there was absolutely no physical resemblance. I could pick up a bathing suit in one of the suntan lotion shops. All the regular stores would be closed. As I drove to the eastern end of Sunrise where it meets the Atlantic, a thunder shower soaked the Lincoln and the street in front of me. Behind me the sun was shining. When I got to the beach the sun was out again. That's the way the weather is in south Florida. I bought a striped towel and a black two-piece and used the shop's bathroom to slip it on under my clothes. After I walked out I realized that I'd better pick up a tube of SPF25. I had olive skin which rarely burned, but it had been a while since I had been in the tropics.

There is a stretch of sand and water starting in Hollywood, Florida and continuing north through Fort Lauderdale to Pompano that rivals any beach in the world – even the secret beaches of Gulf Shores, Alabama – maybe even the South Pacific. Swimming for half an hour in the warm ocean felt like balm. It soothed my body, but more importantly it put into perspective my most recent monkey-cage agitated life.

When I walked out of the surf and looked in the direction of my striped towel, I noticed a man in a swimsuit sitting at its perimeter. In New Mexico I was a mountain woman, but in Miami I was Roca, so I rolled through the possibilities of who this interloper might be. Renewing my professional paranoia may have been good for practice, but as it was, I was only being visited by a tourist from Boston. He was staying in the hotel that was attached to the beach and must have seen me enter the ocean from the deck. We small talked for a while and he offered to buy me a drink at the hotel bar. A drink was not what I needed four hours before my meeting with Miranda and who knows who else, but some harmless company could take my mind off recent happenings.

Until I got some new information, any more thinking I did about the subject would just be repetition. I considered using the time before the meeting to reach some of my old contacts but thought better of it. After I met Miranda I'd have a clearer picture of what it was I wanted to verify, so I would put my calls off till after that.

Leaving enough time to drive to the *Bleau* left me with a little less than four hours. I accepted the offer, accompanied him to the hotel bar, ordered tea, and made friends with the contractor from Boston. He was an extremely masculine guy. He had big hands and wrists that must have developed swinging a framing hammer. Either that, or people with big hands and wrists usually go into that kind of work. We talked about Boston, the construction business, Arthur Fiedler and Robert Frost. He had been living in the woods alone too, and the more we talked, the more I liked him.

I could tell he was too polite to act abruptly but probably would eventually invite me to dinner. Dinner, or anything between 3:45p.m. and the rest of our lives was impossible. So anything that happened between us was going to have to happen in the next three hours. I knew if I wanted things to go that route it was up to me. It had been too long for me, and this guy seemed as nice as anyone I might casually meet. I knew eventually I would be running into the Postman, and I didn't want to feel desperate when I did. I figured I'd go for it.

I told him I had a family obligation later in the day that I couldn't avoid, but that maybe we could spend the time up in his room where we could talk until I had to leave. Since the bar was beginning to get pretty crowded, the suggestion was direct, but at least it wasn't crude. Sure I knew it was bold, but bold was nothing new for me. He seemed to take my request in stride, and soon we were riding the elevator up to the ninth floor.

He had a great touch. His hands were big and strong but they were gentle as well. It was a gentleness that I deeply appreciated. It took me a while to recall my sexuality. It only found its way to the surface when I was able to imagine that I was with Eric. Then it was like a deep massage, very deep. I could have gone to the health club at the Fontainebleau for a rub-down, but this was more my style. I wasn't all that attentive to *his* needs, but he seemed to be okay with the one-sided arrangement. Maybe he figured that I'd reciprocate next time. Too bad there'd be no next time. As we lay there, closer together than strangers are otherwise capable, part of me wished that I could find a guy like this and make a life of it. Of course it wasn't that simple because I had already found a guy. He may not have been like this one, but . . . The *but* was what I needed to find out, and I was being pointed in that direction.

Chapter 8

Collins Avenue wasn't what it used to be, but it still represented the model from which every luxury high rise beach resort in the world was copied. The Fontainebleau was the first giant beach hotel built with modern extravagance, and even though it had been refurbished a couple of times, it still reeked of the 1950s. The croissant-shaped main building held court over Collins Avenue until the early 1960s when money flooded the Miami Beach real estate market. After that, every year the new hotels were bigger and better.

My father had dealings in the hotel business here, but I never really found out any of the details. Whenever I walked into any of these giants, whether in Miami or Vegas or Monte Carlo, I had a few thoughts of him. Today was no different as I walked under the thirty-foot-tall crystal chandelier that floated ostentatiously above the main lobby.

I remembered that the entrance to the bar was off the far corner of the lobby before it spread out toward the beach. I went downstairs to the long hallway lined with shops that led under the building to the sand and the ocean. I figured I'd come into the bar from the beach-side entrance and be able to scope out the scene I was about to walk into before they spotted my approach.

I was glad I did. Sitting at an oblong table opposite a small unused stage were four recognizable faces; Carmen Miranda, Wyndam Otnabe, Paul somebody or other who was Otnabe's security guy, and Manny. They were all faced around in the opposite direction so they didn't see me seeing them. I backed away from the glass doors and walked toward the benches on the edge of the sand. I wanted to take a minute or two to assess the situation. Otnabe was there, so I couldn't get down to it with Miranda, and that was my main aim. I'd have to find some way to arrange to see her later, but that wouldn't be easy with Otnabe there. Nothing was going to happen sitting there on the bench, and I couldn't play the whole scene out in my head – not really anyway – so I made my entrance.

The green marble floor made a popping sound in defiance to my silent approach. Manny spotted me first and jumped up like he was the host at a family reunion. He cut me off before I got to the table and whispered to me that Otnabe wanted to have me checked for electronics. I ignored the absurdity and walked around Manny to the table, but Paul the hulk blocked me from sitting down. He was actually pretty low key about it, and being frisked was nothing new to me – just not by my own people.

"Please Caroline, humor me on this one," Otnabe said in his professionally ingratiating manner.

"What is it exactly we're looking for?" I said with maximum sarcasm.

As Paul did his job, I noticed that Miranda was looking down and away. I sensed that she was displeased with something, or at least uneasy. It could have been the security ritual, but it could have been something else as well.

Paul nodded that I passed. He was in a position to know; he was very thorough. He even dumped out my sling bag on the next table and sorted through the junk in it. I guess that was his function at the party, because after that he walked over to the bar about twenty feet from us and sat on a stool facing the other way.

"Manny, would you call and make a reservation for Caroline and me for dinner at Michelle's."

Michelle's may have been the most expensive French restaurant in Miami but that didn't stop me from recoiling at Otnabe's presumption. I lost a little of my cool. "This is the only meeting I agreed to," I snapped.

Otnabe ignored my remark and nodded to Manny that he should go anyway. I knew the dinner reservation talk was bullshit. This was between the three of us and it was time to get down to it.

"It's good to see you Callie," Miranda said, with that little extra bit of sincerity that a person puts forth when they really mean it.

"You look good Miranda. How's New York?"

Miranda smiled. She was aware I knew that her leaving the roost must be for a good reason.

"So where are we on this one?" Otnabe opened.

"Where we are is that *I'm* going to be 200K richer. No, actually 150K richer. The other 50K is just a return of what you stole." I knew I had to play this one strong. I was in the land of the dragons and not of the *Puff the Magic* variety.

"Why don't you brief Caroline on what we know," Otnabe suggested to Miranda, ignoring my remark. "Bring her up to date." Paul came over with three glasses of Perrier, left one of them on the table in front of each of us and returned to the bar. This was standard procedure, so that no hotel servers would overhear our conversation. I sniffed the glass and gave Otnabe a nod for remembering that I never drank alcohol at business meetings.

Some European men have to wear that scarf causally draped artfully about their necks to remind you of their continentality, but that was not Wyndam Otnabe. His confidence was never in doubt. It was in the way he looked at people – not in his concern for the way they looked at him. No, he wasn't aloof at all. Actually, he was affable in an almost homey way, but not as an American would be. There was always a formality behind it that seemed to leak out saying, *I am from an ancient culture and if you aren't, you'd better adopt the appropriate attitude.* Speaking half a dozen languages like a native didn't hurt either, nor did having his suits made in Saville Row.

We had a few moments of silence and a few gulps, deep breaths, and sighs around the table before Miranda started talking. She explained the tobacco deal and how she got the contract. The rest was nothing new, but I pretended that I was listening to every word. I knew that I was getting the abridged version so I put more energy into reading their facial gestures than I did listening to this bunch of crap that I would have to sort through later anyway. I had seen this show so many times before that I probably could have done a cross word puzzle too.

"Manny told us what he knew of the FSCL. Not much help there," Otnabe added casually. "Anything else we should know, Caroline?"

I shook my head in the negative. If I wasn't going to give Eric's FSCL code to Manny, I sure wasn't going to give it to Otnabe. "So I'm going to Cuba . . . and then what?" I asked. I was waiting for him to mention my notebooks, or at least my habit of writing down details of my operations, but he seemed to be looking past them – to what I didn't know.

"This is going to be your operation Caroline," Otnabe said as he reached for my hand. "We haven't a clue on this end. You know as well as I do that we have to entertain the possibility that Eric might be crossing over, but for what?"

I instinctively pulled my hand back and turned the discussion toward the arrangements for my money. The idea that Eric would dump was absurd – at least the Eric that I knew. Also, it was rare that the Postman ever had to be lifted out after an operation. He just hung around till it was over and left when he was ready. I was the opposite. The fact that I was a woman was usually a prime factor of my edge, but after it was all over my cover was usually blown. That is except for Cuba – in Cuba it was different. I could go back there anytime I wanted and pick up where I had left off. If I was proud of anything about those eight years, it was how smoothly I left 90M. When I went out on my first solo, they wanted me to shake my ass to make things happen. Sometimes it went that way, but I never felt good about it. I knew I had the brains to operate above the neck, and eventually that's how most of my assignments went down.

Otnabe was doing his best to pretend like our parting six months before had been amicable when it definitely hadn't been. There was no mention of our fallout over the Burma deal, the one that pushed me over the edge, and certainly no mention of my holy book of secrets, my notebook.

For years the country known as Myanmar (Burma) had been operating as a secluded entity with little or no connection to any family of nations. The female Burmese peace activist, Aung San Suu Kyi, had just won the Nobel Peace Prize, and it was rumored that the military government was moderating and looking to move toward embracing international acceptance. Some multinationals, mainly oil companies, actually one of the largest oil companies, took notice and saw some future potential for investment. To openly negotiate with a repressive military junta was not viable for a company that had to maintain an image while doing most of its business in democratic countries. This led to the Roca Group being contracted to do what it did best – operate in secrecy.

Roca had no Burmese-speaking operatives, but Roca had me and my reputation for being a quick learner of languages. I hired a tutor and spent two months cramming all the Burmese I possibly could into my head and out of my mouth, until I could communicate most generalities, but certainly no subtleties. After being briefed thoroughly by the oil company's execs as to their aims there, Otnabe decided that I was to perform the whole operation solo. This would eliminate any possibility of it leaking that they were courting business in Myanmar.

I spent a month in Yangon (Rangoon) and traveling up and down the Irawaddy River to areas of the country that were not considered off-limits to foreigners. My attempts to communicate with dissident groups and individuals including Aung San Suu Kyi were unsuccessful, but I was given full access to what was considered the "legitimate" government. I was able to come away from negotiations with a basic agreement that would allow our client to begin researching oil drilling sights and investment potential. It was a considerable success and coup on my part. I was due a reward.

I considered some extended vacation time definitely in order, and decided that before returning to the U.S. I would cross over into Thailand and spend some time on the beach. The accepted way of crossing would have been by air from Yangon to Bangkok, but I wanted to go the slower route and try some overland travel. I took advantage of the highly placed connections I had made with the military and got permission to cross over at Myawaddi.

Mae Sot is a Thai border town across the Moie River from Myawaddi, about 300 miles north of Bangkok. My border crossing experience was cumbersome as few foreigners, if any, ever cross there. Eventually a phone call to Yangon was needed to let me exit the country and enter Thailand. My original plan was to get a bus heading south and bypass this border town, but I was tired and it was getting dark when I took my first steps on Thai soil. It was not hard to find a guesthouse in Mae Sot and it turned out to be a delightful one.

In the morning, over breakfast of noodles and tea, my host agreed to arrange a ride south for me, but insisted that first I must visit with her friend Cynthia, a local Burmese refugee. Having no fixed schedule and finding myself captivated by this charming woman, I agreed, as long as the visit could be that day. Later that morning she drove me to a compound on the edge of town with a sign above denoting the place as the Mae Tao Clinic.

Her friend Cynthia was Dr. Cynthia Maung, a physician who had established this extensive medical facility for Burmese who had no access to medical care in their own country and had to escape across the border to get treatment. Dr. Maung escorted me around the clinic and educated me as to both the present actual conditions in Burma, and the future tragic prognosis for the Karen hill tribe people. The Karen, who make up a considerable portion of the 150,000 patients she treated each year, are an ethnic minority who have been persecuted for years.

I did not leave Mae Sot that day or even the next. I returned to the clinic not only to continue my education with Dr. Cynthia, but to talk with the refugees there about life in Burma. It was my first experience of awakening of conscience. To see what my actions in helping to bolster up this repressive regime could manifest was shocking, and opened up voices of conflict within me that had been previously silent.

On my first day back at Roca HQ in New York, I announced my refusal to allow the agreement I had brokered to be presented to the oil company. Revealing my conflicting thoughts and feelings evoked an expected response in the Roca execs – Wyndam Otnabe in particular. I further proclaimed to him personally that if he were to force the issue, I would make public the details of some past operations, including our dealings with Saddam. I assured him that I had written documentation to verify my revelations. I was in such a state of confusion over my past possibly damaging deeds, ones that unbeknownst to me might have had similar repercussions to those in Burma, that I threatened to make all my notes public.....period.

With that kind of weight hanging over Otnabe's head, he had to either work with me or try another tactic. His other tactic was to enlist Eric's help in convincing me that my actions were rash and unprofessional. Eric agreed to see if he could sway me, but I was not of a mind to be receptive to any view other than my own. These discussions were a main component of our relating verbally, and after a while I knew I needed some space not only from the Roca Group but from Eric as well. I eventually made a deal with Otnabe that Burma would be on hold, and I would take an extended leave of absence and receive a substantial chunk of money for my silence. It was blackmail, but I didn't care. I just wanted out.

Now I was back in the game. . . I reached down to finish my Perrier while listening to Manny getting all my Cuba details worked out. "You probably won't need a cover, but if you do, you're a trade rep for a Swiss drug company called Grayley Pharmaceuticals. They're in phase three clinical trials with a new M.S. drug. It's all in this file with some other data," Manny said, as he handed me a manila envelope. After that, he looked down at the floor for a few seconds like he was trying to think of what he might have forgotten. "Oh yeah," he looked up and continued. "They're actually one of Miranda's clients, so it wouldn't hurt if you showed up at their event in Havana. You know, just for PR.

When I was finished with Manny, I asked Miranda if she'd drive me to the Miami airport and Manny or Paul could return the Lincoln. That would give me my opportunity with Miranda. I was also having some cramping, and driving a car wasn't an attractive option. I guess it had been a while and my body wasn't used to visitors.

Chapter 9

The summer humidity was high, but the trees absorbed most of it and the altitude tempered the balance. At 2,000 feet, the Sierra de Los Órganos mountains weren't as high as the Sierra Maestra on the eastern end of the island. The remote caves that pockmarked their surface better served the purposes of a man who was burning his candle full on at both ends with a smolder beginning in the middle. Che Guevara had set the precedent when in 1962, during the missile crisis, he used Los Portales cave for the headquarters of the western army that he commanded. Even though the Postman chose a smaller cave for his use, Che would probably not have been pleased with his purpose.

Magelinos brewed the coffee as he had done for the last few mornings. The hot syrupy liquid was a staple of the island and a ritual of his recently adopted service. He had worked with Lynne several times before, but this time he sensed an urgency in his co-worker's assignment. Magelinos was tall and sinewy with thinning light brown hair and a chiseled profile. His eyes were dark and wide set, and his brow had a permanent questioning wrinkle causing people to wonder if he was hearing what they said. His skin was as light as Eric's, as was that of many Cubans of more Spanish than African descent. He was wounded at the Bay of Pigs, and though the leg wound was superficial, it never properly healed. When he had to accelerate his pace, a slight limp showed.

Before Lynne, Magelinos worked as a full-time agent of the DSE, the Departamento de Seguridad del Estado, and before that the DGI, the Dirección General de Inteligencia, both branches of the Cuban secret service. His current assignment to aid the Postman was not from the DSE but was a direct request of the commander of all Cuban forces, Raoul Castro. His dual allegiance was no secret to Lynne, and they managed the association above board and with the humor and perspective of two professionals.

It was not that the Postman was being sought after by anyone, nor was he in any danger, but now he needed a place where he would be incommunicado. Staying at the old Brazillian embassy would no longer serve his purposes. It was one of the deserted ruined mansions of Cubanacan, an area of Havana known for its old and stately past. A week ago, he left the embassy with its patio surrounded by a score of multi-colored marble columns. While there, Lynne camped out in the main dining room under a massive painting on canvas of Columbus' exploits, which wrapped around the entire room. The compound had a chained driveway and only a couple of workmen were ever around. It had been perfect once he had obtained permission from a Brazillian official who owed him a favor – a leftover from an assignment in Rio. It wouldn't be perfect any more. According to his plan, Jelinda would soon be on her way to Cuba. Magelinos knew the countryside of his native Pinar Del Rio. The caves that overlooked the Viñales valley would be perfect. They had served a very different kind of clandestine operation before, and they would serve one now.

Once Jelinda arrived in Cuba she would certainly approach the U.S. Interests Section for information. Learning that operatives from Eric's own agency were concerned about his whereabouts would likely arouse their suspicion. If they knew that Eric was accounted for, they wouldn't have any reason to try to pressure Jelinda into giving up details of the operation – details whose revelation would be untimely. Once he left the city he would be essentially out of touch, but it was a bit premature for that necessity. A short stay at the U.S. Interests Section residence located at the Swiss Embassy before he headed for the mountains would work nicely.

Most Americans didn't know that there was an active U.S. presence on the island – that is, other than Guantanamo Naval Base. The chief of the U.S. Mission was responsible for representing long-term U.S. interests, maintaining contact with government officials, and keeping the Miami Cubans placated – the last was indisputably the most difficult. After Cuba's withdrawal from the civil war in Angola, the U.S. increased its diplomatic relations by opening what was discretely called an *interests section* in Havana and vice versa in Washington D.C. The U.S. mission was technically part of the Swiss embassy, and the Cuban contingent part of the Czech embassy in D.C. It turned out to be a good idea because through dialogues made possible by the exchanged *interests sections*, Castro was influenced to release some 50,000 political prisoners over the years.

The Swiss Embassy was nearby and Barnes Connert was the only American presently residing at the U.S. Interest Section. Though not having seen each other in 15 years and having no such official authority, Connert decided to take it upon himself to approve his old college friend's sequester in the mansion on the basis that they were cooperating on a mutually beneficial project. His only condition was that Eric let him know about his assignment in Cuba.

Unlike Eric, BC had completed his stint in the army, and finished what he started at Yale, graduating with the illustrious reputation of campus bookie and loan shark. He considered going to law school as a stepping stone to politics, but even corrupt lawyers, of which there are many, usually begin their quest with some regard for the law. BC had none. With the connections he had made at Yale, he eventually found a spot with a lobbying firm that represented various commercial interests. One of their clients was a company developing experimental pharmaceuticals in Cuba. Getting to Havana became his new goal, but not to further his client's objectives. Representing experimental drug interests had little attraction for him. His plan was to first meet and then develop a mutually beneficial relationship with one of his heroes, the infamous Wall Street swindler Roger Brisco. Barnes Connert had no idea that he was going to cross paths with his old college friend and co-conspirator in the process.

Eric had misgivings about divulging anything to Barnes, even if their history was more than 15 years old. Any premature involvement of U.S. company representatives would be contra-indicated. They just couldn't be counted on to keep a secret, and Connert, for one, might not be insightful enough to appreciate the need for discretion. After all, it was his gun.

Eric overcame his reluctance by rationalizing that it might prove to be advantageous to have an ally who might be privy to U.S. State Department inside information. Anyway, he would only divulge the basic tobacco deal, and there were few secrets there. After all, an option to be exercised when the object of the option became legal could hardly be considered against the law in the present. And the payment angle was covered by using a European front company.

Connert was fairly well paid as a consultant for U.S. business interests, but that was a salary. His theory was that the big bucks came from finding a middle. Eric's deal had one with good potential. The tobacco companies were putting hundreds of millions into this deal, but it wasn't for cigars, and more importantly it wasn't the first time. It was for participation once the embargo was dropped. To approach a high roller like Brisco, he needed to be involved in something major. Now, he thought he may have found it.

Connert's next move was to contact Brisco. His whereabouts in Cuba were no secret as he was in little, if any, danger of apprehension there. A perk of access to the U.S. Interests Section was its files on American citizens and others who were of interest to the U.S. government. Brisco was certainly of very substantial interest, and both his present telephone and address were prominently located at the top of the page in the files under the category of fugitives.

Connert presented both his exaggerated credentials and his interest in discussing pharmaceuticals to Brisco in their first phone conversation. It was enough to secure a meeting between the two, and they agreed on a place and a time. Connert's plan was to restrict their first conversation to medical issues, while casually mentioning some other huge deal to be discussed in the future. Connert was anxious, but he was not so naïve as to ignore the need for patience.

Chapter 10

Months earlier, when Raoul found out about Fidel's potentially terminal illness, he began to set the stage for a plan that might ironically only come to life upon his brother's eventual death. However Raoul might have perceived the events since the year Soviet support faltered, he would never condone any repudiation of Fidel. Now it might no longer be necessary. Fidel seemed to be fading. The cancer began in his liver but had not yet spread into the marrow of his bones, so there was still hope of a remission. Whatever the outcome would be, it was time for Raoul to assume the reigns of power.

The revolution had been a magnificent experiment. But a research laboratory needs subsidy, and the Soviet Union, enthusiastic patron of the Cuban dream, was no more. In another fifty or a hundred years, Cuba might have proved its premise to the world. But as gallant as they were, the people were not strong enough to support a plan that required such extended deprivation.

When it was clear that El Comandante might not survive what could be his final battle, Raoul sought council from a close friend of Fidel – a man whom Fidel affectionately called El Jugador. He was a North American, long a supporter of Castro, who lived on the south coast of Cuba in retirement. Since the death of Che Guevara, other than his brothers, El Jugador was as close as any man had ever gotten to Fidel. But he too saw the intractability of El Comandante's ways. El Jugador loved Fidel, but he had grown to love Cuba more. It was time to moderate for the sake of the people. He respected both the revolution and the experiment in equality so much that he had separated himself from his family in North America to be part of it.

El Jugador could council Raoul Castro, but when it came to the fortitude required to bend the curve of the revolution toward moderation, he knew it would take men and women of strong constitution. They would have to be capable and knowledgeable in international monetary brokering. He had closely followed and often been consulted about Fidel's attempts to both circumvent the blockade and develop relationships that would relieve Cuba of its financial burden. Over the years, though he was never in the forefront, El Jugador came to know the skills and performance of the foreign financial operatives who competed for the Cuban market. It was clear to him that no Cuban he knew could negotiate so sophisticated an arrangement. There were Cubans who were both brilliant and competent, but the island had been isolated from the international community for too many years for its nationals to maintain the necessary financial sophistication, not to mention the high level contacts.

Two North Americans, both working for the same agency, seemed to have the credentials and abilities to broker the deal. One had minimal allegiance to the Cuban predicament, and the other was not likely to be attracted by any altruistic motives. Their agency, the Roca Group, had operated successfully for the Cuban government before. The close connection between the two agents was well-known in Cuban financial and diplomatic circles, and it might be used as an asset. El Jugador was familiar with the history of both the man, who had a reputation of always delivering, and the female former Olympic athlete, who had evolved into one of the most respected financial operatives in Latin America.

Raoul needed a team with the competence to broker a deal between Cuba and the rest of the free-market multinationals. El Jugador was asked for his recommendation. The only way to find out was to get these two to Cuba and see just how talented they were, and how much loyalty could be expected of them.

When the offer came from the tobacco consortium, it was time to proceed. Both El Jugador and Raoul agreed that the director of the Roca Group, Wyndam Otnabe, would probably be the weak link. He had no loyalties and was untrustworthy. His word was subject to the most recent expediency, and his commitments were always contingent upon a higher bid. That's how he had become so successful. He was a financial sociopath. The bait of the 1% commission on a 250 million dollar turnover brought Otnabe scurrying around less than 24 hours from the time the Roca Group's Latin American director of Operations, Carmen Miranda, was approached outside of the United Nations building.

It was important that Otnabe know that the basic tobacco deal might be approved with the addition of the "in perpetuity" add-on. But it was more important that he didn't know about Raoul's plan and Fidel's health. Otnabe had to be in on this second level of the tobacco deal, so that when

Raoul's plan became operational, Otnabe wouldn't try to find a more lucrative middle. He already knew of the millions that were invested in the 1980s. The Roca Group had handled the transaction. El Jugador and Raoul needed him to hope that the tobacco companies would wave their rights to the original 500 million dollar investment by returning ownership of the Vuelta Abajo fields. That might be attractive to them if Castro fit them into the international Cuban cigar and tobacco marketing loop in perpetuity. It could mean many millions more in commissions for Roca over the years – enough of an incentive to keep Otnabe in line and away from Cuba.

Raoul agreed with El Jugador that with that kind of payday, the only person that Otnabe might have enough confidence in to keep him away from Cuba was Eric Lynne. He was only an operative, but in his way he had more influence in financial circles around the world than Otnabe could muster from his office. They had worked together for years, and Lynne never let Otnabe down – he always delivered. The only hitch was that Lynne would have to know everything in advance . . . everything. Raoul had worked with the Postman before, so he was only slightly concerned, but El Jugador was not as confident. Where were Lynne's loyalties? What would he do when the chips were down?

El Jugador was scheduled to make a visit to Fidel, perhaps his last. El Comandante had sent for him and asked that he come toward the end of the week. Everything had to be in place by then. Fidel was clearly no longer capable of running the government, so whether or not he fell victim to the cancer Raoul would become the next president. At that point, the tobacco companies would announce their one billion dollar investment like it was a new occurrence. Instead of finding out that tobacco had made three-quarters of that investment eight years ago in an illegal transaction, it would look to the multinationals like tobacco was giving its vote of confidence to the new moderate free-market Raoul Castro Government. After that, all the major corporations would jump in with support, and the new Cuba would be off to a well-financed beginning.

There would be no necessity of a power struggle after Fidel was gone from office. No coup, no takeover, no insurgency. Money would establish the necessary priorities. When the pledges of support from the multinationals reached a total of fifty billion dollars, no faction of the government could resist the affluence that this would represent – not the executive committee of the Council of Ministers, not the Fuerzas Armadas Revolucionarias (the armed forces), not the Partido Comunista de Cuba, not even the people. The only prerequisite for the investment would be the promise of a free-market Cuba, and the result would be a *fait accompli*.

Author's note: There is no Chapter 11, as I have skipped my numbering from Chapter 10 to Chapter 12. As anyone familiar with finance knows: Chapter 11 is only used when all other options fail.

Chapter 12

Once El Jugador accepted that he would have to meet personally with Eric Lynne, he had Magelinos convey the message. It was arranged that Lynne and El Jugador would meet in Cienfuegos. Eric agreed to be a guest on his sailboat for the day. A face-to-face meeting was the only way that El Jugador was going to assure himself that including Lynne in the details of the grand plan would further its becoming a reality.

Eric had not been on a sailboat since his days at Yale. He was then a frequent guest of one of his wealthier classmate's parents who had a sailboat moored on the Quinnipiac River in New Haven. Long Island Sound was an excellent training ground for learning to sail. Eric seemed to have a natural knack for harnessing the balance of wind and water. He certainly had been on his father's fishing boats many times before, but they were all driven by engines, very different from dependence on the breeze.

They met at the Cienfuegos Marina coffee bar. It was once a bustling place, both in the days of Batista and the wealthy gamblers from the north, and later when the Russian fleet was in. Now, there were few private pleasure boats, and the marina was relegated to servicing many small, dilapidated fishing boats along with their captains and crews.

It would not be hard to spot a gringo in a crowd of Cubans, but spotting was not necessary. El Jugador was the only one sitting at the few tables scattered in front of the coffee bar counter. As Eric stood in front of the seated El Jugador, the words with which he was greeted notified him that this would be no ordinary business meeting.

"So," El Jugador paused just a bit longer than would be comfortably expected before he went on, "You are Eric Lynne, and your codename is Postman, and I am El Jugador, that is my codename." He laughed so heartily at his own joke that Eric was infected and joined in the lightness of the moment. They walked together down the ramp to where the boat was moored. Eric noticed an unexpected bounce in the step of this man who was probably, by the grey in his beard and his receding hairline, in his late sixties. El Jugador was of medium height, had a hawk-like nose that made his gaze appear even more forceful, and had the belly of a man who was either reticent to exercise, or a beer aficionado.

The sailing came back to Eric quickly, and they worked well together to negotiate the 40-foot Cheoy Lee out of the harbor into the open bay without the use of the inboard diesel. The breeze was up, and with the raising and lowering of genoa and spinnaker, there was hardly time for a word or two other than the usual pre-tack, "Coming about, helm's alee." After a couple of hours, they let out the anchor in a calm bay of crystal clear Caribbean water about 200 yards from shore.

"May I call you Eric?" were the first words spoken between them since the anchor was set. "Since we may have something that I consider of great consequence to discuss, it might be best if we leave formalities behind. Out here in the water it seems more natural anyway. Don't you agree?"

"And what should I call you?" Eric countered.

"You can call me Captain. At least while we are on my boat," he said, with both a laugh and a hand to his belly to accentuate that he was making a joke. "May we talk business now Eric?" El Jugador said, changing gears.

"Of course, Captain," Eric responded.

"Ms. Barton is central to Raoul's plan," Jugador began, giving credit to Raoul for the plan rather than including himself. "He has considerable confidence in her, but is unsure about you. Of course your competence is not in question. It is your respect for Cuba's future that we must assess," El Jugador said, including himself. "We would not be contracting your services to assist Ms. Barton only in matters of finance. To a certain degree, the future of Cuba will be in your hands, so we must know that you have regard for our plan and our goal. When I say we would be hiring you and Ms. Barton, I mean that literally. I understand that you work for the Roca Group, but to trust Wyndam Otnabe for something with such far-reaching consequences to so many people would only be necessary if you were not available. Then we would have to accept Mr. Otnabe's help in assisting Ms. Barton. We have contracted the Roca Group for the tobacco deal and we will honor that commitment. Our desire is that you and Ms. Barton act independently from both Mr. Otnabe and the Roca Group to represent Cuba to the financial powers of the world during our transition."

Over the next hours, the two men got to know as much of each other as can be known in so short a time. They clearly liked one another. The affection El Jugador began to feel, which bordered on fatherly, opened the doors that allowed him to disclose the plan in which Eric was to be included. The passion for his cause was so disarming that Eric became fascinated by this altruism. It was a quality that he rarely saw manifest and was generally uncomfortable with. El Jugador held nothing of the plan back. He confided that the need for secrecy required that even members of the military, like Enrique Magelinos, were being kept unaware of the extent of the plan. It was possible that they might have a hard-line attitude toward liberalization. By the end of their discussion, Eric was not only comfortable with aiding him, but enthusiastic about his newfound concern for the fate of the Cuban metamorphosis.

"I know that you must discuss this matter with Ms. Barton, and you have my approval to tell her, and *only* her, everything that I have told you." El Jugador paused to let the word *only* sink in. "If you both agree to our arrangement, we can proceed accordingly. If not, I trust that all that you have heard today will be kept in the strictest confidence."

As they parted at the coffee bar where they first met, Eric felt that he needed to ask the question that was unanswered amidst all the details that El Jugador had divulged.

"How is it that an Anglo from the United States becomes an intimate of both Fidel and Raoul Castro and gets to architect such a high-level plan?"

El Jugador looked pleased that Eric saw fit to disclose his curiosity, but chose not to satisfy it . . . yet.

"That is a story for another day. A day that I am confident will come – and not too far in the future I suspect."

Chapter 13

I'd been known to come down with an occasional cold, but other than that I was unused to feeling under the weather. Having eaten questionable foods over the years in a slew of Third-World countries, I had developed an iron stomach that was basically immune to upset.

I told Miranda that I would be skipping dinner and would be out on the beach between the Fontainebleau and the ocean when she was ready to go to the airport. After the meeting, I walked out onto the sand and staked out a chaise lounge with a slightly soggy mat on it. I was dozing within a few minutes. I had two hours of the best rest I had had since before the fire. When I awoke, my physical discomfort had passed and in some curious way I felt very at home.

Miranda called from the deck of the hotel that it was time to go. I grabbed my satchel and followed her out to her car. I told her we had to stop on route so that I could get some things for the trip. It was Sunday night, but the shopping mall stores would be open, and that was good enough for what I needed. Cuba is more than a little short on retail goods, and I didn't want to waste time searching and shopping after I had arrived. There would be too much to do. I also needed an hour on my own to make phone calls to my informants before

I took off. That was a must. The rest of the time I could spend with Miranda.

I knew I had to pick her brain as much as possible, but that wasn't my only interest in Miranda. During my years with the Roca Group, she was my model of what a woman could become. She was powerful, assertive, and influential without using masculine muscle-flexing techniques. Six months on the mountain had altered my perspective of life somewhat, but just how much I wasn't sure. I suspected I was smarter than Miranda, but she had a decisive quality that I greatly respected. She could make crucial decisions while her peers were still juggling the variables. That was an incredible asset in Roca operations, and it was probably the one that first shot her up onto the executive board. She was about ten years older than I, and I think there was something of big sister affection there. We were both fiery types though, and we clashed on almost every assignment I worked on for her. If I was going into an unknown situation in Cuba, I needed an ally on the executive board, and Miranda was my best shot – probably my only shot.

We girled around the department store clothing section for a while, and I got what I needed for whatever might come down in Cuba. I hadn't done anything like that for a long time. Doing normal things in a wacko life can sometimes feel lifesaving. Miranda always wore short, I mean really short, dresses and skirts. I never asked why. I mean, she had great legs, but so do a lot of women who don't want everybody to take note of that. I didn't have her legs, but mine could have handled that style if I didn't have the attitude that I wanted to be accepted for something more than my body. She certainly had gotten long past that, having been accepted for the exec she was. I guess flaunting her assets pleased her without the self-consciousness that goes along with being *not so sure*.

I knew that sooner or later we had to get down to business. I was sure Miranda knew that it wasn't only a ride to the airport that I wanted from her. She liked to drive sports cars, but I personally hated the squirrelly little bastards. Actually, in this case, it probably was helpful to have the extra activity of whipping around through traffic. I found that I could ask her weighty questions while the ride in the company BMW sports coupe created a light background around them.

"What do you think he's up to?" I said, not specifying if I meant Otnabe or Eric, but figuring it would give her the opening to tell me whichever was on her mind.

"Which *he* are you asking about?" We had been shopping partners, but she was Roca Group. Of that there was no doubt.

"Let's start with Otnabe," I said.

"Well," Miranda explained, "I was the one that got the contract from the tobacco cartel. So unless that was a setup, which is possible, anything he might know that I don't would have to have been an add-on."

"How about the Postman?" I countered.

"If there's anything more than the bare deal that I worked out, he's got to be on the inside of it – maybe even in the middle of it – and just maybe right at the top of it," Miranda speculated.

We pulled into the short-term airport parking lot and Miranda turned off the motor. In the quiet of the concrete, I turned around to face her and started recounting what I knew out loud. "Okay, so Postman offers Castro $250 million for a deal, and then disappears – why? It doesn't figure. Postman isn't carrying any money. Castro's dealt with big tobacco before, so that's nothing new. Sure Castro's got enemies, but what would they want with Eric? Maybe the *gusanos* are trying to get the 250 for themselves? But how could snatching Eric help them to do that?"

Miranda was with me at every step. She laughed at my use of the Castroist expression "gusanos," which literally means worms, to refer to the counter-revolutionaries. This had always been my favorite part of Roca Group procedure. I felt like I might have a teammate in Miranda. She waited till my brain stopped storming and then picked up the ball.

"Otnabe's got to know something," Miranda stated with certainty. "If he suspected Eric, he wouldn't be sending you down. He'd send Manny. If Eric was bailing on the Roca Group, what could *you* do? Eric must want you down there or he wouldn't have called the Commander. But why would *Otnabe* want you in 90M – just to find Eric?" She looked over toward me but not at me, like she was thinking about something else. I thought it might be that I knew she and Eric were on the decline when I first showed up at the Roca Group. I don't think she ever held it against me personally, but a little of that has got to hang around – at least for awhile.

"Maybe that's it," I said. "Eric's not in trouble and he's not bailing on Roca. Otnabe and he have cooked up something big, and for some reason Eric insisted that I be in the formula. So Otnabe is sending me down there to keep Eric happy. The Roca Group's commission on the deal *you* brokered was 2.5 million, so whatever they're working on must add up to a lot more than that. Otnabe must be drooling over the biggest payday of his life."

"Possible, but not likely," Miranda countered. "Eric and Wyndam holding hands on this one? I don't think so. I got the goddamn deal but . . . I can't figure this one out – not yet."

Miranda had her reasons and I had mine, but the result was that we made an agreement to work together. We would keep in communication by way of an indirect telephone link-up that I had used from time to time over the years in 90M. This would allow us to send messages to each other without Otnabe or anyone else knowing their content. Otnabe would be expecting me to communicate to his office through coded telegram. He would reply to me via a scrambled signal on the regular short wave programming of La Voz de la Fundación – the station that the Miami Cuban community beams into Cuba under the auspices of the Cuban American National Foundation (CANF).

Miranda told me how much she wanted me back with the Roca Group. I never got to tell her why I left last time around. She said that not knowing what happened gave her some trouble. She had usually played it straight with me over the years, and we had some pretty good mutual respect going. It wasn't her style to be warm, so she was obviously pushing the edge to make a personal gesture toward me. I wanted to have a friend about now, but I wasn't naive enough to rule out Miranda's going back to Otnabe and telling him our entire conversation. I just hoped she wouldn't go that route.

The plane was scheduled to leave just after midnight, and there was always a lot of red-tape before the flight. I still had plenty of time to make my phone calls if I got going, so it was time to split. I had an urge to hug Miranda, and the look in her eyes might have been telling me that she felt it too. I wasn't sure. Best to play it conservative on this one. The stakes might be very high.

I went through the first phase of check-in and then found a private spot to phone my list of contacts – none of whom I had spoken to for six months. But first I called the Commander, and we arranged for him to be both my FSCL and an intermediary for any information that my U.S. contacts might dig up. He wanted to know if there were any further developments. I didn't tell him my theory, but I did put forth that from what I saw so far, Eric was okay. He seemed to take my response in stride like a past navy intelligence officer would.

I gave him my contact in Cienfuegos, a beautiful coastal Cuban town on the southern side of the island. He was a radio repairman who had access to shortwave telephone receiving equipment. He often helped out his friends by sending or receiving messages to and from the U.S. I gave the Commander instructions on how to leave a message there for me if he heard anything that I should know.

"Okay, I got to go now, wish me luck," I said, imitating how I used to break off phone contact with Eric in similar situations.

"Well, the mail is late, but I trust that the Postman will deliver eventually," he said as he hung up the phone.

I was left with the phone in my hand and a queasy feeling in my stomach – one not related to the discomfort caused by my indiscretion at the beach. It was a strange thing for a father to say about his disappeared son. And the word *trust* – why would he say, *I trust*, rather than, *I hope*, or *I know*? And why would he call his son by his codename? Was he deliberately telling me something, or did it slip that he knew something that I didn't? I would have time to ponder that one on the 45-minute flight to Havana. Now I had half a dozen phone calls to make.

Chapter 14

It may have been six months since I had been there, but the coat of paint that José Martí Airport's international terminal needed the day I left was still needed. Manny had gotten me a visa, and I remembered the immigration drill well enough that within an hour I was through with the *aduana* and out into the middle of the humid Cuban night. I found a taxi driver who was willing to take me to the Hemingway Marina, a spiffy real estate development about ten miles outside of Havana on the "Great Blue River," the appellation that the marina's namesake used to refer to the Gulf of Mexico. One of the Roca Group's clients kept a year-round condo there. As my tiredness rose, the cramps I had back at Miami resumed. I told myself that all I needed was a good night's . . . or now it would be day's sleep. Health problems were the last thing I needed on this one.

The townhouse was even more luxurious than I remembered. I didn't recall everything being so white – the carpet, the drapes, the couches, everything. The air conditioning was turned up so high that I had to open the doors and windows and wait for the temperatures to equalize. Eventually I dumped myself on the couch. I never made it to the bedroom.

In a few hours it was daylight, and the living room was so bright that I dragged myself into the bedroom. After that, the next thing I remember is being awakened by the telephone, and it was just beginning to get dark outside.

The voice on the phone belonged to a man named Enrique Magelinos. I vaguely remembered the name, but his voice was not recognizable to me at all. I was familiar enough with Cuban Spanish to sometimes be able to place an accent. His contained the unique staccato slur of the campesino – probably from the western provinces. It was an area I was particularly familiar with. One of my sweetest memories of Cuba was a vacation that I spent with my father in Soroa, with its orchid gardens and waterfalls. Of all my father's favorite spots, he chose to take me walking in the rolling hills of Pinar del Río. I think because those gardens were built by a man for his daughter – a daughter who was never to be born as she died in childbirth.

"I am calling for an old friend who is anxiously awaiting your arrival," Magelinos said in the formal vernacular.

"What friend is that?" I asked. "I have many friends here in Cuba."

"I can arrange for you to meet him whenever you are ready," he answered, ignoring my question.

I wasn't prepared to meet anyone, including Eric, if that's who this guy was repping. I knew the business well enough to know that I needed all the information I could get on my own. Eventually I would be exposed to the conflicting stories that are sure to flow whenever large sums of money are involved. I pretended to Magelinos that I needed a day or so to rest up after my long flight (actually only 45 minutes). I would be glad to meet this "old friend" after that and taking care of some other business.

"I won't meet anyone unless I know in advance who it is I'm going to meet. You understand Señor Magelinos?" I said, trying to sound as determined as possible. "Names aren't necessary, just something to verify who it is. Give me a number and I'll call you when I'm ready."

"When should I call you señorita?" he said.

Maybe it was the style in which he included the word "señorita" in his question. Or maybe it was the way he dealt with questions that he didn't want to answer – by ignoring that I had asked them. But suddenly I knew who I was talking to. It was the DSE, better known as the Cuban secret police. Magelinos was an agent from the early days when the DSE was known as DGI, even before I had ever come to Cuba. I remembered him as a quiet, older man who was always a storehouse of information. He knew everything that was going on, whether it was part of his current assignment or not. As long as I knew who he was working for, there was no reason for me to play the hard-ass.

"Call me here, tomorrow. I have a meeting to go to during the day, so I won't be around till late afternoon or early evening." After a quick thought I added, "Call, don't come over . . . got it? I don't want any surprises."

"Hasta luego señorita, I am sure that your friend will be very pleased to hear that you are anxious to see him too."

I didn't feel like decoding his last statement so I decided to forget it. I knew what I had to do. It was evening in Havana and a good time to start. I didn't have to spend time going over my list of Cuban contacts. Considering where I was, there was only one place for me to begin.

Chapter 15

Roger Brisco was an American. I say "was," because he was not only wanted for numerous crimes in the U.S., he was *persona-non-grata* in every country of the free world. He was accused of having stolen two billion dollars from an investment fund that he managed. Since that time, he had been a fugitive living in various countries in Central America and the Caribbean. He had come to Cuba some years ago and managed to find a haven here ever since. From time to time, there had been rumors that he was under house arrest, had fallen out of favor with Castro, and in a matter of days would be traded to the United States for some reciprocal easing of sanctions. The eventuality of such a trade was not likely to take place, probably because no one was more adept at circumventing the blockade in order to get certain needed goods and services into Cuba.

We had met numerous times and even worked together on one deal, but I never really got the feeling that he knew as much as he liked people to believe. Anyway, it was not Brisco that I planned to seek out, but his daughter.

Fawn Brisco and I were almost the same age. We had met at St. Claire's School – a girls' school in Costa Rica where my mother had sent me as a last ditch effort to get me away from what she called my "lazy unmotivated existence" (she was right). The Brisco family was living in Costa Rica at the time, and I knew no one at all there. I visited with the family on several occasions, and Fawn and I found we had much in common. We had maintained sporadic contact through the years, but the logistics became more and more difficult with her father's circumstances. Now she lived part of the time in Miami and part in Havana. She didn't have much to do with her father's dealings, but she knew everyone who wielded influence in Havana. Unlike her father, people trusted her, and she was very easy to talk to.

Mr. Brisco had lived at the Hemingway Marina for a few years until too many people started to recognize him, especially at Papa's and Cojimar, two of the Marina's best restaurants. He was presently living in Atabey but still owned a condo at the marina where his daughter spent a good deal of time. Atabey is one of the more fashionable suburbs of Havana, and the one that coincidently was the current neighborhood of Cuba's illustrious leader.

Her father knew my line of work, so it was sure that Fawn did also. I don't remember ever directly talking about business with her, but I always came away from our get-togethers with a few useful tidbits. She was smart enough to know that I wasn't really that interested in her socially. But as long as I wasn't looking to make trouble for her dad (which I never was), we could talk about Cuba and the U.S. with a perspective unlike most other people who were familiar with both places. That was usually magnet enough to draw us together for a visit when we found ourselves in the same location.

I called down to the reception desk at the main office of the complex and asked for the number of Fawn's condo. The clerk understandably was reluctant to give out the number. Instead of making a big to-do on the phone, I decided to walk down to the lobby. I knew that if I showed up in person I could find out.

I waltzed through my recent acquisitions, found a sarong dress and borrowed a pair of sandals from my anonymous hosts. My hair needed washing badly, so I stuffed it up under a broad-brimmed straw hat that probably belonged to the owner of the shoes. I checked the mirror for acceptability and walked out the sliding glass doors that led to the central pool and beyond it, the office.

The last of the daylight had faded, and the dark red sky was reflected in the pool. No one was swimming, but there were a few people sitting on chairs and chaise lounges mesmerized by the sight of so much deep red wine. I had a mission, but even *I* stopped to take in the anomaly until the fading light of the sun resurrected the dark blue of the water. The multicolored electric lights went on in the pool, and although pretty, the hypnotic quality had evaporated, and people resumed their conversations. I walked into the lobby.

I hadn't seen Roger Brisco for several years, but even from a one-quarter profile I recognized him instantly. Knowing his past difficulties, I was aware that walking up behind him and startling him with a *hello* was not the way to introduce myself. He was right in front of me though, and I sure as hell was going to try to get to talk to him. So I stood in the doorway about fifteen feet away and called out, "Hello, Mr. Brisco, it's Callie Barton."

At first he didn't react, and I thought that he might not have heard me. But as it turned out, he had become experienced at not wheeling around when people called his name until he had identified the voice. He slowly turned his head to face me without turning his body. When he recognized me, a big smile came across his face and he turned full around. I never thought of us as long lost friends, but his smile said that we were, so I played out the string. He had known me first as a teenager, and I think that made it hard for him to take me seriously as a high-level financial operative.

He told me that he had come up to visit Fawnie, but had just found out she wouldn't be getting in until the day after tomorrow. Without asking me if I had already eaten, he invited me to have dinner with him at the Fiesta. It was his favorite of the three main restaurants on the Marina. I accepted, and after arranging to meet there in an hour, he excused himself to take care of some business.

Dinner with Roger Brisco on my first . . . no, actually my second night in Havana, might possibly be a windfall. Could he know what I was doing in Cuba? Was the smile of a seasoned operator like Brisco the smile of an old friend, or of an opportunist who instantly assessed what I was doing there? It surprised me that I was as excited as I was – not to meet an international celebrity – but to be back in the thick of the intrigue.

I had first learned the details of Brisco's chicanery years before. I didn't have the standard judgments about him because the Roca Group wasn't averse to dancing around the fringes of the laws that restricted financial manipulation. In any case, all he did was get caught. Dealing with individuals' money was always more dangerous. Sophisticated financial entities usually, if not always, know the implications of their actions, but individual investors can get squirrelly when things don't go their way or they think they've been lied to. International financial dealings allow for a lot more flexibility because there is rarely an oversight authority with absolute sovereignty. Within the U.S., the law enforcement presence can come from almost any angle – though it's usually too little and too late for the victims.

During my indoctrination period with the Roca Group, we were schooled in every aspect of financial manipulation so as to sophisticate ourselves about the environment. Below, I have included the notes I took at the time on Ponzi schemes and some of their most notorious practitioners, which coincidently included the name of my present dinner companion.

(1) Charles Ponzi didn't begin it all, but he certainly made enough of a splash in the 1920s to have his name linked in perpetuity with the illegal pyramid concept. He stole $15 million, promising investors 50% return on investments in the postal system.

(2) Reed Slatkin, one of the originators of Earthlink, solicited investments from wealthy show business people and executives. He was creatively thorough with documentation for his clients while cheating them out of $600 million. Other than benefitting himself, The Church of Scientology, to which he was intimately connected, was the other beneficiary of his pyramid scheme.

(3) Gerald Payne, minister of The Greater Ministries International Church of Florida, managed to take $500 million from his fellow churchgoers using gold coins and precious metals in his Ponzi scheme.

(4) One of the most fascinating, and probably my favorite, was Lou Pearlman, already a millionaire and manager of a couple of very successful rock bands. He set up something he called Trans Continental Savings Program, claimed it was FDIC insured (which it wasn't) and managed to bilk $500 million from his investors.

(5) Michael Kelly found older people, the easiest on which to prey. His scheme used time-shares at its center, and that Ponzi gained this real estate developer almost $500 million. He knew how to over spend his ill-gotten gains better than most of his contemporary con artists, buying yachts and racetracks.

(6) Roger Brisco earned the title of record holder for having stolen the most money ever in a Ponzi scheme – two billion dollars. Of course, he hoped to keep it going with winning investments, but after 15 years the market turned on him, and his ability to share in the wealth dried up. His moral defense was that he never took money from anyone who couldn't afford to lose it. Though that perspective gained my sympathy, it did nothing to mellow the jury that convicted him

to 25 years in jail and a fine equal to what he stole. He fled the country before the sentence was to be enforced.

There also was a woman in the late 1800s whose name I don't remember. She had a women's-only scheme that I neglected to include in my notes back then because of some gender loyalty I felt, and a concept (which has been altered with the passing of time, and my exposure to Carmen Miranda) that only men did that kind of thing.

I went back to the apartment to gather my wits in preparation to meet a man with a reputation for being one of the most successful con men ever to walk the earth. I had a lot of confidence in my ability to scope out a con, but dealing with Brisco, especially if he knew why I was here, was going to be a challenge to my skills.

Having only recently entered his sixties, Brisco would not yet be immune to the attentions of a younger woman. Not that I was considering anything flirtatious, but the right costume could only help my cause. I used the available hour to resurrect my hair and adorn myself with apparel consistent with my aim. On the way out, I consulted the same mirror that revealed a tousled ragamuffin less than a couple of hours before. I remembered an incident back in school, and was grateful for the input of the guys on the swimming team.

The Fiesta Restaurant could have been in the upscale quarter of any Caribbean port. It was staffed by Cubans but was out of reach financially for any other than a few highly-placed officials. I spotted Brisco before he noticed me. He was talking to the bartender at the mirrored bar at the far end of the room. As I approached him, he saw me in the mirror and greeted my image without turning around. He had a reputation for appearing casual and was not about to tarnish it with me. I was obviously meeting another facet of the man who was so pleased to see me in the lobby just a couple of hours before. I entertained the possibility that he had gotten some information about my mission in Cuba in the interim and was now on guard. I decided to suspend my analysis of his behavior until we had spent a little more time together.

"Are you one of those women who think, *In Cuba, it's gotta be daquiris*"? he said, finally turning around to face me. "You know, daiquiris were invented by Constante, the island's most famous bartender."

Brisco playing the tour guide was a little hard to take. Especially since my father had first told me the story while introducing me to Constante at the Floridita, Ernest Hemingway's favorite bar. I was seven years old. "I'll have a Perrier, Mr. Brisco," I said, noticing that he actually *could* have passed for a Cuban tour guide, or at least an older version of Richard Gere in *The Cotton Club* – pencil-thin mustache included.

"My name is Roger . . . and yours is Caroline, Caroline Barton. Are you hungry Caroline?"

"Roger, I'm nothing if I'm not hungry," I said, laughing at my own wiseacre tone.

I was remembering the time I had crossed paths with him a few years before. It was over an aborted Cuban sugar deal – with Switzerland I think. I knew it was important for him to feel like he was calling the shots, and I had no reason not to play along. After all, I was looking for information, not financing.

What can you say about Roger Brisco, the quintessential sharpy? Not a sincere bone in his body. His appearance, his delivery, his manner – all contrived for the appropriate affect. He was one of those people who would never reveal what's behind that façade, if anything. Maybe he'll never find that out either. He was entertaining, however, and I guess there's even a place for shallow in this world. There was at this moment anyway. Over dinner I asked him what his thoughts were about what kind of guy Andrew Grove, founder of Intel, was. I knew that Brisco had been in on semiconductors early and knew Grove. About the best he could come up with was, "He was a sharp dresser," – a current reminder of how deep Roger Brisco ran.

The bartender, obviously a long-time acquaintance, came out from behind the bar and led us over to a table on the side of the restaurant that overlooked the harbor. The view was pleasant enough to be distracting, but nothing spectacular. Brisco animatedly introduced me to the routine of the Fiesta Restaurant. There was no menu, so you simply told the waiter whatever it was you wanted to eat in as much detail as you saw fit. Some people might find the procedure too demanding. In such cases the waiter would make suggestions. Brisco, of course, knew exactly what he wanted. I decided to enjoy the ritual by giving a detailed account of how I wanted a fresh salad prepared. I asked for lobster and crab meat all arranged in a very large bowl with carrot spears sticking out of a half of a baked potato placed in the center of the salad.

I could tell that he enjoyed my sense of humor. We spent the next several minutes talking about the "old days" in Costa Rica where we had first met, and the well-being of both his family and what was left of mine. He was surprisingly free from the bitterness that one would expect of a man who was the subject of an international campaign of harassment. He mentioned the necessity of carefulness almost casually. His main concern was that the Marines from Guantanamo would try to kidnap him for extradition to the U.S. He pointed out his security man near the doorway of the restaurant and commented on how accustomed to the ritual he had become.

"So what are you working on Caroline? Besides me, that is."

I smiled at his directness. I liked it. "Money, Mr. . . . I mean Roger. I always seem to be working on money. This time it's only routine . . . courier service, nothing original or exciting. How about you Roger, what are you working on?" I didn't see any reason to either talk about what I was doing there or fabricate something that I wasn't. I needed to know if he knew anything that could be useful to me. That meant he do the talking, not I.

Just as he began to answer, the waiter showed up with a huge bowl that reflected that the chef had a sense of humor equal to my request. Under my dinner, he wheeled a preparation tray that allowed cooking at table-side. On it the waiter proceeded to perform the Cuban version of a hibachi ritual, resulting in what Brisco ordered – a plate of assorted grilled sea food and various vegetables. The orange antennae in my face and the waiter's slicing antics created a jovial mood – perfect for the type of exploratory surgery I had in mind.

"So you were telling me what you were working on," I returned us to the subject.

"Have you ever met Barnes Connert? He's with the U.S. State Department down here," Brisco offered, exaggerating Connert's actual connection to the government as something other than a temporary consultant using the U.S. mission as office space.

"The name sounds familiar, but no, not that I remember," I said, wondering where he was leading.

He went on to tell me that he had just met with him and described the project in which Connert was currently involved. It revolved around alternative medicines – always a big item in Cuba considering Castro's penchant for wonder drugs. He told me a little of the history of pharmaceutical production in Cuba, beginning with a drug called Interferon, another anti-cholesterol medication called PPG, and now this one that Connert was pushing. Connert hadn't yet found much of a reception with U.S. drug companies for this new anti-cancer drug derived from the Citronella plant, so he had approached Brisco. The drug was called Trioxidal, and Connert said he was trying to negotiate a deal with Fidel's brother Raoul granting free use of the drug for the Cuban population in exchange for the production and marketing resources of the government.

I listened with genuine interest for the first few minutes and, not coincidentally, until I had eaten as much as I wanted of the impossibly large portion of food I was presented with. Around the fifteen minute point I began to drift. Even though I supplied the appropriate nods and "uh-huhs," I was thinking to myself that anyone so wrapped up in whatever it was he was talking about couldn't possibly know anything that could be of use to me.

"You have any interest in meeting Connert? Once he gets things set up here you might be able to work something out for him with one of the U.S. pharmaceutical houses," Brisco offered, interrupting my drifting away.

Now I was sure. If Brisco was promoting me for business contacts then he certainly had no idea what I was doing in Cuba. It was time to exit. I avoided answering his question directly and said that I had to make a delivery early the next morning. I told him that I was hoping to visit with Fawn, and that I would appreciate it if he would mention to her that I was in town. We said good night. As I left the restaurant I looked back and saw that he had returned to the bar and resumed whatever dialogue our dinner had interrupted. The food was good, but Brisco wasn't going to be able to answer any of my questions – maybe his daughter.

The privacy and quiet of the condo was welcome. I had a lot of strategy to plan before my meeting with Enrique Magelinos of the DSE and my *old friend*.

Chapter 16

"She told me to call her late this afternoon or tonight. She said she had a meeting today," Magelinos reported upon his arrival back to camp. The nearest phone was in La Esperanza, a small fishing village on the north shore. Going from the mountains to the sea on a primitive road was an arduous undertaking, and Magelinos had just accomplished a round trip.

"She was very insistent – very strong," Magelinos continued. "I don't know how she knew that I intended not to call and just show up the next time, but she insisted that I not do that."

Eric smiled at the memory of Callie's strength. She had a knack for spotting a double reverse, even when she was young and first introduced to the world of subterfuge. She was capable of helping him pull this one off, of that the Postman had no doubts. He wasn't sure if the romantic connection would have survived, but he was confident that they could work together.

"She said there would be no meeting unless she knew who you were. I think she recognized my name, or maybe my voice, but I'm not sure of that. If she did, she might think that her 'friend' is my superior at the DSE, General Gomez. They had financial dealings in the past."

Eric was sure she knew that he wasn't in trouble. There was no reason to maintain the ruse – unless, of course, she proved to have allegiances he wasn't aware of. The Callie he remembered would love the deal once she heard the details. She'd love the intricacy, the humor, the intensity. That was part of the love that they had shared – one that might even be equal to any personal feelings or passion that they had for each other. In Eric's view, in matters of business at least, they were brother and sister, and their mother and father were intrigue and subtle manipulation.

"What do we do now? Should we get in touch with El Jugador?" Magelinos needed a resolution as to how to proceed.

Eric's mind was only partially on the political and financial entanglements of the plan devised by El Jugador and Raoul. He knew he would be preoccupied until he had seen Callie. Though there might be shortcomings in procrastinating, he wouldn't be able to get down to business unless some personal questions were addressed. Not so much in words, but merely by physical proximity would he know just how much he was wanting her involved in the plan, and just how much he was wanting her.

They agreed on how to proceed. The next morning Magelinos would take their car to Havana and call Callie from there. He would tell her that there was mail for her that he had to deliver in person. She would ask, "What kind of mail?" and he would say, "A parcel, and it is small and fragile." She would then know by their code that the "friend" was the Postman. It would not be a good idea for Magelinos to pick her up at the marina because of the risk of them being spotted together. He would arrange to meet her in Havana the next day and drive her into the mountains to their camp. It would be a long drive, so Magelinos would have to maintain vigilance with his answers to Callie's probing. She was sure to be probing.

Eric wondered if when Callie eventually found out that the plan that brought her to Cuba had intricacies she could never have expected, it might be a challenge for her to sustain involvement in the operation. If the possibility existed that they could establish a mutual commitment, either to the operation or to each other, or preferably both, then any vacillation she experienced could be held in perspective. At any rate, Callie had to be dealt with first. There would be plenty of time to communicate with El Jugador. He would have his hands full with Raoul and his meeting with Fidel. In any case, this first meeting with Callie would not be business – at least that was the Postman's wish.

It didn't come naturally for Eric to spend extended periods of time with decreased activity. He was not at home in the mountains, nor had he ever really felt at home in Cuba. He had operated in most of the Latin American countries, but Cuba had been his least favorite. The enthusiasm of the people for their Fidel and his revolution made him uncomfortable. It was the ingenuous positivity in the face of adversity that he found the biggest challenge. His adult life had been spent with the power brokers of the world. His valuation for ordinary people and the strength of their essential aspirations was very remote to him.

Since Callie's departure from the Roca Group, he had been thrust into the role of principal operative for Cuban operations. Before that, he had functioned as a financial intermediary during armed conflicts in Nicaragua and El

Salvador and had a role in the interplay between Britain and the Falkland Islands. These situations were more clear-cut. The self-interest of the opposing groups was easily recognized and identified.

But in Cuba there was no armed indigenous force, nor had there been for years. Yes, there were human rights abuses, and limitations on individual expression if one departed from accepted dogma. There certainly was no semblance of democracy, and the ruse of it being a benevolent dictatorship was just that, a ruse. It was a totalitarian dictatorship, period. Any benevolence was isolated to the privileged few. Brutal treatment of those who persisted in demanding reforms was commonplace, and dissenters often disappeared in the middle of the night, some never to be heard from again. It was far from the promised workers' paradise with equality for all.

Still, the only battle that the government struggled with was the one to maintain fortitude for a unique experiment – an experiment that had already produced undeniable gains in education and medical care. Many types of crime and most extreme poverty had also been all but eliminated. Eric wanted to be done with this operation and leave Cuba to the Cubans. He liked working for the multinationals. With them there were no ideals, only money.

But a professional gave his best to each assignment, and the Postman always delivered. He would have to read the books that he brought with him. He had postponed the research project, but now he would have to use his remaining seclusion to peruse them for any subtleties that he might learn concerning Fidel, Raoul, the revolution – whatever background might be of use. Once Callie arrived, time for reading would have to be stolen. He knew, since he would be both the perpetrator and the victim of that misdemeanor, it would prove to be a near impossible heist.

Eric already knew the basic facts about recent Cuban history: that Castro had been a practicing attorney and a candidate for the House of Representatives in the election aborted by Batista's coup. Castro vowed to force Batista from office by any means necessary and was imprisoned in a military attempt at doing just that. After release from prison, he went to Mexico, joined with Che Guevara, and prepared for his eventual return. In 1956, he landed the ship Granma in Oriente province with 82 men. After three years of coordinating the insurrection from a hideaway in the Sierra Maestra Mountains, he forced Batista to relinquish control. Eric found it interesting that there were never more than 3,000 guerrillas in the mountains under the command of Fidel, Raoul, and Che, but the popular support among the peasants in the countryside was overwhelming enough for them to gain their objectives.

Going back further into the history of Cuba, Eric stumbled on some new information. During the Spanish rebellions, many of the intelligentsia were included in the refugees who migrated from Spain to Cuba. The current inhabitants of the country were descendants of unions between those educated refugees and African slaves conscripted after settling in Cuba. The refugees from the rebellions in Jamaica, Haiti, and Santo Domingo were reluctant to seek refuge in Cuba for fear that another rebellion might occur there. So the elements in control of the Cuban government became more and more conservative through isolation. This was evidenced by the fact that it was not until

1886 that the African slaves were liberated – the last in North America. After Cuba's independence from Spain around the turn of the century, there was a popular movement in Cuba to join the United States, but of course that never came to pass.

Eric read late into the night, first by firelight, then by the light of his lantern. At dawn, when Magelinos started the engine of the car, it sounded to Eric like one of the voices of the night had been amplified to rouse him from his dreams. He looked over and saw the car departing, glad to have been awakened for a chance to smile. He knew that on its return it would be carrying what he had gotten used to looking on as a lost possibility.

Chapter 17

With a bed under me instead of a couch, I didn't have any trouble sleeping until mid-morning. I awoke to the sound of halyards slapping on the aluminum masts of sail boats. The wind orchestrated the pings into such a harmonious chorus that I drifted off again and was not ready to initiate my inquiries until slightly before noon. I had a few hours before the drug convention, or whatever it was I was supposed to attend for both PR purposes and a cover story if I needed one. I settled down with the telephone and whatever the previous inhabitants left in the refrigerator and eventually dialed the number for DSE headquarters.

I gave a fictitious name and asked for Enrique Magelinos. After being transferred several times, I found myself on the phone with someone I had had dealings with before. There was no reason to conceal my identity from General Gomez, so I told him who I was. I said I heard that Magelinos came from Pinar Del Rio and might be familiar with the organizers of the tobacco cooperatives there. To make him feel like he was on the inside, I told him I was here to broker a confidential deal between El Comandante and some large U.S. tobacco companies that could bring considerable financial benefits to Cuba. Having had dealings with me in the past, Gomez knew that negotiating an arrangement of this kind was certainly within my capacity.

I recognized the possibility that he knew about Magelinos' call and about the Postman's situation. Telling him the surface level of the tobacco deal couldn't possibly cause any problems. Maybe he'd slip and give me something that I didn't have. He told me, with what seemed to be a genuine tone, that Magelinos had left the service last year because of poor health and that he hadn't seen him for some time. He suggested another of his officers who came from Pinar. I pretended to take an interest in who it might be and how I could make contact with him. At the close of our conversation, he offered any assistance possible to help facilitate my project. I kept the door open to collecting on that offer. I knew that by the time I might need his help, my project could have less to do with tobacco and more to do with something else – a something else of which I was not yet aware.

So . . . Magelinos was no longer with the secret police – at least not officially. Could he be working for the Postman? *Doubtful, but possible.* Could he be working with Eric in a DSE capacity? *Too complicated to theorize about.* At least I knew that the "friend" wasn't likely to be another DSE officer. It would either be Eric, or conceivably someone high up in the government for whom Magelinos was working. The clandestine nature of Magelinos' phone call pointed to Eric. It wouldn't be long till I found out.

The hotel where the drug meeting was to be held was in the middle of Havana's newest business district. Certainly not impressive by western standards or even eastern ones, but the best that the city had to offer. I easily found the listing for the gathering on a board with push-on letters planted obtrusively in the path of anyone who entered the hotel. There were two or three other happenings that day at the Metropolis and each was listed with most of the letters required for recognition. Mine said Pharmaceuticals, Habitación Rosa 301.

I had chosen the appropriate business attire for what I thought was going to be a convention of sorts, but had I showed up with shorts and a tee shirt it probably wouldn't have made too many waves. There were fifteen or twenty men standing around talking to each other with drinks in their hands. My appearance would be breaking the gender monopoly, but that was nothing new to me. I didn't recognize any of the players, so I went over to the table that held glasses half-full of something fruity and waited for someone to approach me, or not. I didn't know if the gig was a business opportunity for the others there, but for me it was strictly PR and worth about an hour, tops. Even though I was wearing a business suit, I represented an obvious diversion to anyone who was bored with the gathering.

It took less than three minutes for the magnet of amusement to take effect, after which I became the centerpiece of a four-person conversation. As long as I was going to be around for a while, I figured I would establish my business credentials for the meeting. I contributed the few facts I knew about the company we were representing and the drug it was producing. The enthusiasm, feigned or otherwise, was modest, and that saved me from the necessity of any further contributions. Since I didn't do any research and hardly even read the file that Manny gave me, I was relieved that my part in the show was completed.

I eventually extricated myself from the circle that had formed around me and took up a heading for the restroom as a stopover on route to the exit. A man from over at the drink table obviously knew geometry and found the hypotenuse to cut me off before I reached the door. He had a drink in each hand, and when he got close enough he pushed the left one forward in my direction. He introduced himself as Barnes Connert of the U.S. trade delegation.

If I was the only woman at the gathering, this guy was the only preppie. The semi-formal attire of choice for men in Cuba, and for that matter in the rest of the Caribbean, is a white embossed overshirt made of very light cotton fabric. When I say overshirt, I mean one not tucked into the pants but worn outside as would be a jacket. This guy was wearing a blazer. Not the usual blue, heavy weight yacht-club variety, but one probably custom made for the tropics. It did have the Yale University crest over the breast pocket, signaling the purpose of his unique for Cuba attire. When a man gets into his mid to late thirties there seems to be a cusp. His youthful demeanor can reassert itself, sometimes for a lifetime, or he can surrender to middle age. This was a tall, handsome man clearly of the former variety. His blond hair was obviously cut short by a stylist, and his smile was that of a snake oil salesman.

As dull as my edge had become, it was not so dull as to not recognize a name that I'd heard spoken from the mouth of Roger Brisco the night before, so I reached out in acceptance of the liquid offering. This get together was about medicine, so where more likely to meet a drug rep? No big coincidence there. I was also familiar enough with U.S./Cuba trade relations to know that there was no such thing as a U.S.

trade delegation in this country, but people have tried to impress me before.

I smiled and returned the lie. "I represent Grayley Pharmaceuticals." It was actually a lot less of a lie than I was used to telling. After all, they were Roca clients.

He had a lot to say about the pharmaceutical industry and the drug he was promoting. I listened with a little less than a third of my attention – another third already walking somewhere between the hallway and the door to the street. The last third was grasping for the memory of where and when I had heard this guy's name before Roger Brisco mentioned it. He gave me his business card with a handwritten phone number under the printed stuff. I did take note of the fact that he was living at the U.S. Interest Section residence at the Swiss Embassy. At least that's what he told me.

Later in the day the clouds in my memory parted. They weren't storm clouds, but more like little wispy ones that still have a way of blocking the warmth of the sun. That small parting was enough for me to remember that it was Eric. Eric had mentioned the name to me more than once. One night when we were swapping life story stuff, he told me this wacky one about some scam he ran in college. His partner in crime was his friend Barnes Connert, the same name I had heard from Brisco. Could Eric know that his college buddy BC was here in Cuba? It was doubtful that this guy could know something useful to me, but Brisco, Connert, Eric . . . coincidence?

I was uncomfortable with being so uninformed. My discomfort frequently led to impatience, especially when I had too much time to think, so I had developed the habit of substituting action for patience. That's what I did. I made numerous phone calls with either no response or no results. My last call was to the phone number on the bottom of Barnes Connert's business card.

Our conversation turned out to have a certain entertainment value. Except for Eric's dad, I had never known anyone who knew Eric way back when. As far as useful information about Eric here in Cuba, the call held the expected disappointment. I knew Eric would never confide in an American with ties to bureaucrats, so my expectations were modest. I had to be discreet in my inquiry, so I purposely neglected to mention that the Roca Group had lost contact with one of its operatives. Still, all I could get Connert to acknowledge was that he had contact with Eric recently. It was always a possibility that my questions could help to blow an operation of which I was ignorant, but I felt compelled to pursue the lead.

I tried to get Connert to fill me in on their conversations, but anyone who could walk the tightrope that Brisco told me Connert was walking in Cuba had to have the heart and mind of a spook. Barnes Connert seemed to play the game pretty well. At least his responses were confusing enough for me to come away wondering who and what I was talking to. At worst, all I really accomplished was alerting someone connected to a U.S. government agency that there was something afoot. I suspected that Connert would probably be looking to have a talk with the Postman. Why, I didn't know. Hopefully he would be hard to reach and I wouldn't have caused too much trouble.

My telephoning was only successful at notifying a lot of people that I was back in Cuba. Unfortunately, I knew so little about where this operation was heading that I wasn't sure if that would be helpful or not. My relations with both the military and the civil sections of the government had never been tarnished, so all of my calls to officials were well received and numerous dinner invitations were forthcoming. I had never stopped loving both Cuba and its people. Part of me wished that I could accept those proposals in the open, friendly, and social way that they were presented. Maybe someday . . . but probably not.

I only had one more call to make and that was to my contact in Cienfuegos, to see if Eric's father had left me a message. I decided to postpone that call till later, giving the Commander as much time as possible to find out *something . . . anything* that I could use.

The pool was bathtub clear and the sun was still a few hours away from creating its nightly biblical miracle. After splashing around for a while, I pulled in an inflatable rubber-ducky, the kind with a holder for a daiquiri, and floated on into the early evening. I had told Magelinos to call me that night without specifying a time. I still had to find out if the Commander had come up with anything. Reluctantly I aborted my cruise and went back to the condo.

There was nothing from the Commander, but my stomach was reminding me of its presence. I was trying not to think about it, but every once in a while I would have a twinge that I called hunger, but it seemed more a relative of the cramping I experienced in Miami than anything to do with missing any meals. Hoping it was the former, I called down to the Fiesta, asked to speak to the chef, reminded him of my creation, and asked him to deliver its twin, sans antennae.

The condo was equipped with a T.V., and I switched it on for the dual purposes of passing the time and catching up on the latest in Cuban culture. In comparison to U.S. standards, T.V. in Cuba is somewhat limited, but closed circuit Sun Channel is usually available in tourist venues showing movies and traveler information. In addition, there are two Cuban stations in Havana. Channel 6 is the educational station broadcasting classes in an assortment of academic and cultural subjects, and Channel 2 carries entertainment programming in addition to programs similar to the ones on Channel 6. I read in the weekly *Cartelera* that the percentage of educational television was higher in Cuba than in any other country in the western hemisphere. The food came, and after switching channels for about half an hour while I ate, I think I can attest to the accuracy of that claim.

The phone rang at ten minutes past eight. It was Magelinos.

"There is mail for you that I must deliver in person," he said.

"What kind of mail?" I asked.

"A parcel, and it is small and fragile," was his response. Those words threw my recently fed metabolism into overdrive.

I thought of saying, "*Whatever he wants me to do, I'll do*," but I dug down for some extra self-control. It was a little early in the game to give up the farm after one coded message. Lord knows part of me wanted to. I finally said, "Where and when can we meet? I am very busy and have many other matters to attend to." After the words came out I was glad that I had chosen the more professional option.

"Señorita, do you know the place where you last picked up a letter that the postman delivered to you in Havana?"

It didn't even take me a second to remember. "Yes, I know that place."

"Can we meet there tomorrow morning at eight?"

"Let's make it ten. That would be more convenient for me."

"I'm sorry señorita. I know that eight o'clock is early, but the package comes from far away, and I must bring back word before dark that it has been delivered. I will be driving a blue and white Oldsmobile."

"Very well, I'll meet you at eight. Goodbye Enrique, and I'm glad your health has improved," I said as I hung up, letting him know that I didn't buy the story that he had retired because of his health. One-upmanship can be an addiction, but in my line of work it was a necessity.

Chapter 18

Jelinda had kept Miranda abreast of current developments, but as far as Jelinda was concerned, Otnabe was not going to get much until she decided he would have to be placated. What Jelinda didn't know was that whatever Miranda knew, Otnabe would soon find out. They were members of the Roca Group board of directors, and no personal connection would superimpose itself on Miranda's commitment to her life's work. Miranda would play any part necessary to further the aims of the Roca Group and facilitate the accomplishment of whatever mission to which it was committed.

"She's made the second contact with Magelinos and they'll be going to meet Lynne shortly," Miranda reported. "She seems willing to pass on information to me. Not that she's anxious to confide in me, but more that she likes the idea of keeping it from you. We're still depending on her for information. She's our only source but she won't tell us what she doesn't want us to know. She's been in Cuba for 48 hours Wyndam. We have to get that transmitter operational."

Otnabe had the transmitter in place but no way to monitor its receptions once she was in Cuba. He needed a confederate in Cuba who had the freedom to move unimpeded about the country, and he had none. It would have to be someone with government connections, because a private citizen in Cuba would never have that kind of flexibility. No legitimate government personnel would take on such a questionable assignment unless they were susceptible to monetary compensation as an incentive. Although the Roca Group had worked in Cuba before, Otnabe himself had no such contact. He did, however, know a man who might.

Years before, Roca had received a substantial retainer to act as the representative of a man who was in danger of being convicted of numerous crimes. He was looking for assistance in sheltering stolen money in Swiss bank accounts. That man was Roger Brisco. As anyone who read newspapers knew, Roger Brisco found refuge in Cuba. Otnabe assigned Miranda to make the contact.

Their eventual phone conversation was brief and to the point. Did Brisco know someone, perhaps in the police force or military, who would be interested in a healthy payday? When Brisco responded that he did, Otnabe, knowing that the last thing Brisco needed was money, asked the obvious question, "And what can I do for you?" Brisco postponed that subject by assuring Otnabe that they would work something out later. That was good enough for Otnabe, and *voila!* Roger Brisco brought a man with both the time and the available audio receiving technology aboard – General Arturo Gomez of the DSE. Gomez would know nothing of the operation other than that he was sending monitored transcriptions to Brisco.

The only missing piece, for both Brisco and Otnabe, was the method of contact. How would Otnabe get the information from Gomez through Brisco back to himself? He certainly couldn't have direct contact with either a convicted felon or a Cuban military officer that he was bribing. They needed a legitimate intermediary and once again, Brisco had just the man. A trade representative accredited by the U.S. government and actually living at the Interest Section residence would do nicely. Brisco told Otnabe that he had Barnes Connert in his pocket, and he would do whatever he told him to do.

Brisco had met with Connert just the night before. Although all they spoke of was pharmacuiticles and Connert's casual mention of "a big deal," Brisco knew an aspiring huckster when he saw one.

Chapter 19

I had arranged to meet Magelinos outside of the El
Patio Restaurant on Chorro Alley, directly across the square
from the Education Museum. I arrived early. Since the
museum had not yet opened, I spent the time till eight o'clock
walking through the Experimental Graphics Workshop next
door.

The Education Museum was in Old Havana, or as it
was originally called, San Cristobal de La Habana. The
narrow streets around Cathedral Square were always packed
with tourists. Meetings between Cubans and North
Americans could go relatively unnoticed – at least as well as
anywhere in the city. Before the revolution, the museum had
been a bistro, and before that, the mansion of the well-known
Lombillo family. The exhibits in the museum are displayed in
rooms with white walls and blue beams supporting the
ceiling. They are dedicated to the literacy campaign that
Castro initiated in 1961, when he sent thousands of teachers
out into the countryside.

It was a normal sight to see a full-sized 1956
Oldsmobile in Havana. Here such cars were not considered
classics but were maintained out of necessity. The last U.S.
autos to make it onto the island were during Batista's final
years and most of them were still running, and running well.

Many of the streets in the old quarter of the city are so narrow that big cars rarely venture into them. So the Olds that Magelinos described to me would be easy to spot.

The aquamarine color popular in the "boats" of the late fifties cruised by slowly, and from the front steps of the museum I recognized the driver. At a distance he seemed younger than I remembered, maybe a benefit of his "retirement." I noticed that he wasn't craning his neck in an effort to spot me, but leaving it for me to spot him. I smiled at the tactics of an experienced intelligence officer. I walked down to the curb, and on his second pass around the block he stopped in front of me. There was no reason to trade passwords. We recognized each other and his smile reflected his pleasure. Whether that pleasure was in seeing me, or that his assignment was on schedule, I didn't know.

He started to get out of the car to come around and open the door for me, but I was sitting in the front seat before he got the chance. He smiled again, this time at my confidence I think, as I said, "*Vámanos, señor.*"

We drove down Obispo Street and past the Parque Central and out San Raphael toward the University of Havana. We skirted the campus and swung north toward the Malecón – the famous boulevard that greets the Gulf of Mexico as it first embraces the island. We had not exchanged even a word for the first ten minutes when I realized that he must be under instructions to divulge the minimum. His way of doing this was to avoid talking to me at all.

"How is he?" I asked, as I looked out over the water as we drove along the Malecón.

"He is well, señorita."

"Is he being detained?"

"Not at all, señorita."

The next obvious question was either, "Where are we going?" or "Why are you doing errands for Eric Lynne?" But I felt that neither was the place to begin. At least not if I expected to learn anything from Enrique Magelinos. Eventually he turned south, away from the coast, and soon we were on the Ocho Vías (the Cuban Thruway).

"We will be traveling on this road to Pinar del Río and then we will head into the mountains. I expect us to arrive at our destination in four hours *mas o menos*," Magelinos contributed. "There is coffee in the thermos on the back seat and some fruit in the *bolsa*. Please feel free to sleep if you like. Perhaps you remember that I drove you once before some years ago? You may recall that I am a very good driver."

I was sure that Magelinos would have liked to possess the skills of a hypnotist to protect whatever information he had, because we both knew that voluntary sleeping was not on my agenda. I laughed and reached for the knobs on the radio, glancing over at him to get his approval for the inclusion of music into our environment. If we were going to be driving for as long as he said, I would have plenty of opportunities to ask questions. Later, when we were more relaxed together, would probably be better.

In the interim, I would spend the time reacquainting myself with Cuba. My many sojourns on the island had taken me from the Sierra Maestra and Guantánamo on the east end to the tobacco fields of Vuelta Abajo in the west. Though I had spent most of my time in Havana, I had also lived for an extended period of time on Isla de la Juventud, a magnificent island off the south-western coast.

My eagerness to see Eric was juxtaposed with my affinity for the landscape and the names of the villages I remembered. Part of me wanted to go faster on the thruway, and another part get off and take the local roads so as to more richly relive incidents from both my childhood with my father and work with the Roca Group.

We passed Soroa with its mineral baths, the hunting reserves of Maspoton, the hot springs at San Diego de Los Baños, and the La Güira wilderness. Eventually we arrived in the town of Pinar del Rio, the provincial capital of the province of the same name. The town is rowed with the wooden houses with columned porches popular around the turn of the century. All I could remember from the only other time I was in Pinar was the cork palm in the local museum that belonged to a 250 million-year-old species.

We stopped for a break at a café on Martí Street. We ordered two *guayabita del pinars*, a local drink made from fermented fruits and rum with a dash of creme de menthe. I excused myself to use the restroom and added a side-trip to the telephone to call my contact in Cienfuegos. I was anxious to hear from the Commander in Miami, but there was nothing. He was my access to information from sources in the U.S., and until I got some I was flying blind. I would try again in a day or so. When I came back to the table, the waiter was still there talking to Enrique. I initiated some small talk of my own with the waiter, and when he left, some larger talk with Magelinos.

"Eric Lynne and Enrique Magelinos, not a combination one would expect."

"Señorita, at my age there are few combinations that I haven't seen."

"What are the two of you up to in the mountains?"

"It is a very restful place and we are well off the traveled road there. When you were in the U.S. señorita, did you ever think of Cuba?" Magelinos asked, in an attempt to stem the tide of my questions.

"I was living in a cabin in mountains called the Sangre de Christo. Their name, when I thought of it, often reminded me of Cuba," I answered sincerely. "But Enrique, I would think a man of your age and accomplishments would be pleased to be retired and fishing in the gulf. Your work with Lynne must be very important."

"I have worked on so many assignments señorita, and I have tried to think of each of them as important," he answered, with the polite and casual manor he had adopted for dealing with me. "You know, of course, that it is not for me to give you any information. That is for the señor to do. But I can tell you that although we have only met each other once or twice, I have followed your career with interest and have the greatest regard for your abilities."

Some years before, Magelinos had picked me up for questioning and driven me to the offices of the DSE. That was the time he was referring to when he was reminding me of his driving skills. On that occasion, he had reason to interrogate me about some dealings I'd had. He was polite and respectful and seemed to try to make an otherwise unpleasant situation more tolerable for me. I remember his explaining to me that the reason for the manner he had adopted grew from his past experience. Years before, when he was suspected of being a rebel sympathizer, he had been taken prisoner and questioned by the SIM, Batista's military intelligence. The torture they subjected him to created a profound impression on him regarding the humane treatment of fellow countrymen, whatever their politics.

Not only did I not want to compromise Magelinos' confidential agreement with Eric, but I didn't think he would give up anything of consequence anyway. For the rest of the ride I would be a sightseer. We finished our drinks, which tasted to me like they had been fermented a bit too long, and headed north into the Viñales Valley.

The Sierra de los Órganos is supposed to be the oldest chain on the island. The Viñales Valley that runs between its ridges is distinguished by numerous *mogotes*, or juts that abruptly pierce the surface and rise several hundred feet. There is a place on this road that I had heard of but had never seen. It is a huge mural painted on the side of one of the bluffs overlooking the valley. It was the creation of a student of Diego Rivera and depicts the prehistoric creatures that once inhabited the area.

"Will we pass the mural?" I asked, as we ascended and the temperature began to show the affects of the altitude. It had not taken me long to acclimatize to the humid heaviness of the air in the lowlands, but the increased freshness that I was now being introduced to reminded me of my preference.

"Yes señorita, it is around the next curve. We will turn off the road shortly after and head into the hills on a dirt road. It will be very bumpy I'm afraid, but it is the only way."

The mural must have been restored, because the colors were more vivid than one would expect to see on painted rocks. Whoever did the painting and restoration must have hung on ropes suspended from the top of the ridge. The dimension of the mural was startling, really quite impressive, like Lascaux caves painted by one of its gigantic dinosaur inhabitants instead of the humans that followed them.

The road was bumpy, but by New Mexico standards it was average for one that was unmaintained. We traveled through magnificent scenery, mountains on both sides of the track with caves stippling their flanks. We hadn't seen another vehicle since turning onto the dirt road. I knew that this type of seclusion was not Eric's natural habitat. It must have been an important component of his operation, whatever it was. My butt was beginning its plea for mercy when Magelinos pointed up ahead and informed me that we would be parking in a grove of trees. We would have only a few minutes walk from there to a cave that overlooked the other side of the valley.

After we stopped, I grabbed my shoulder duffel from the back seat. While walking after Magelinos, I took a long look and a longer deep breath of the mountain air. The path was wide at first, but as we turned the corner of the hill narrowed. Eventually, we were facing the entrance to twin caves that appeared to be raised up on a platform of rocks. They looked as most caves do when the sunlight is not on them – like dark round blotches stained on the side of the mountain. Out of the black circle on the right emerged a figure. He was about 50 yards away, but the look was unmistakable. Eric had a muscularly athletic build throughout all of his compact frame. His hair was dark and curly at the back of his neck. His eyes, even from that distance, were a disarmingly very light blue – *as the blue in the Greek flag,* his father would say.

Chapter 20

For the first hour we sat opposite each other. There was an amount of awkwardness, but it was not overwhelming. I knew that Eric had difficulty hearing out of his left ear from having had it in close proximity to a minor explosion. Sometimes he gave the impression that he was perpetually posing, when actually he was facing people in semi-profile in order to hear them better. He asked about my family and how life in New Mexico suited me. I told him I had seen his father, and of his concern for Eric's well-being.

I knew that the words we were trading were only acting as a vehicle for the thoughts and feelings that were beneath the surface. Both of us were looking inside of ourselves as much as we were looking at each other – looking for signs of affection, recognition, and of course passion.

The twin caves appeared to have been used many times over the years. They both recessed some 50 feet into the side of the hill and were endowed with the cool air that was denied the valley. Eric and Magelinos had their separate apartments in the first cave, and the second was to be for my use. Each was furnished with old cots and wooden tables and chairs left over from previous inhabitants. Magelinos' cave had an opening to the sky that afforded ventilation for their cooking fire. Pure water ran down the back wall and could be easily gathered. Rustic bathroom facilities could be found anywhere outside on the forested slopes that came within 100 feet of the caves.

The obvious next step was to find out what was going on, but I wasn't quite ready for that one yet. I suggested Eric show me around the area and he gladly agreed. He went next-cave to tell Magelinos that we would be gone for awhile. I started to wander over toward some other smaller caves that skirted the side of the same hill. Eric caught up to me and we walked briskly through the winding path created by the chaparral that covered the hillside. We mounted some rocks to better view a cave across the valley. Eric was in the midst of telling me how it was used as headquarters by Che Guevara in the 1950s when he broke off from the story.

"Remember Bolivia?" he asked, looking not at me but out to the horizon.

"Sure," I said, thinking he was referring to the place where Che met his end.

"No, I mean you and me . . . Bolivia," Eric said, maybe thinking that reminiscing would help break the ice if there was any.

Some years before, we were assigned to broker a financial agreement between the government of Bolivia and a private sector company. The company owned a process for removing the impurities in wolfram, commonly known as tungsten ore. It was a commodity that Bolivia had in considerable quantities but was unable to mine economically. The president of Bolivia was a man, but his position was more or less ceremonial. His wife, on the other hand, was the prime minister, and was the boss. The company that had developed the process knew they had a monopoly, which put them in a powerful bargaining position. This was a problem in negotiations. Bolivia, being an impoverished country, was not in a financial position to make the huge cash payment that the developers were requiring.

Curiously enough and certainly unusual, the CEO of the company was a man (not the unusual part), but his wife was the president, and also the boss. I managed to get the two women together without their husbands. The three of us hashed out an amicable deal involving profit sharing and deferred payments in a bargaining session interspersed with laughter and commiseration about all of us working with a husband as partner.

It was a proud one for me because it was the first time that my services were clearly indispensable. I emerged as more than a number two of two, but as an agent in my own right. It would have been otherwise had Eric not had the confidence to let me take the lead that time. I have never forgotten that gesture of confidence and respect. For the next couple of years my services were recognized as paramount whenever a female in a position of power had to be dealt with. Eventually, Cuba became my territory. After proving that I could operate at the highest level on my own there, I was no longer defined by that limitation.

We had an intimate laugh about the event from our past and after a few moments of silence got up to walk back to the cave. On my first step down, I caught my ankle between two rocks and twisted my left knee.

I had sprained that same knee on the last morning of the Olympic team's workout in Seoul years before. I think I had been diving off the three-meter board. For the next few years, whenever I involved myself in strenuous activities, I wore one of those elastic braces with the little hole for the kneecap. It was reversible, with red on one side and black on the other. I remember considering which color I wanted to display to better accent my current outfit. It always seemed foolish, but I did it anyway. Athletics had been at a minimum for me of late, and I had lost track of that elastic band and had never missed it.

After I rested for a while, Eric put his shoulder under my arm and supported me as we walked to a nearby cave. It had also been used as a living space before, but was apparently deserted. I sat down on the edge of a ledge in the cave and Eric found some pieces of cloth in his daypack to wrap around my knee as a support for the hike back down. My knee hurt like hell, but I liked the feeling of his hands on my leg. They seemed very confident. He wrapped from under my knee to over it. When he got to the top, I asked him if that was as far up as the bandage needed to go. He looked up at me from his kneeling position on the ground and slid his hand up my thigh until it was just under my hiking shorts.

I liked it when he touched me in the usual places, but that wasn't the best of it. He loved to stroke the small of my back, and I loved that he loved it. His hands would float north and south along my back like he was climbing up a ski jump and then running down it. It felt like we had this unspoken agreement of touch. He discovered a place above my breast and below my shoulder that he said was his favorite, and the way he caressed it, I believed him. When I passed behind him, whatever the circumstances, I would have the urge to wrap my hand gently around the back of his neck, and I often did. We both coveted waking up together in the morning time. It was when I could study his face the best from close range. There was a place below his right eye where his smile began. Sometimes I would touch that place gently with my lips in an effort to awaken him. I could close my eyes and disappear into the feel of him under my hands or against my body. I could do that for a long time. Those were the only times that I lost all restlessness, and more importantly, all selfishness. I wanted nothing more than to give him pleasure. When that happened, I wanted those moments to go on and on and on. It felt like I had come home for a while.

I remember his laugh and my surprise as he took his hand away, stood up, helped me up, and we started to walk down the mountain. He told me he didn't mind that I wanted to pick the time and the place, but that my timing was premature. He was right about both my wanting to call the shots, and the other as well. We had business to attend to – business about which I was still uninformed. *Why did he want me there? What were he and Magelinos up to? Why was he keeping information from Miranda and Otnabe? Were the execs really in the dark, or was I the only one in that position?* It was time to find out. As I hobbled along at his side, thinking about those questions anesthetized the pain of my twisted knee. I collected, itemized, and prioritized them in my head. I would have to be organized at the inquisition over which I planned to preside upon arrival back at our granite apartments.

Magelinos saw us coming and rushed over to bolster up my good side. I courteously brushed his assistance aside and made my way to the nearest sitting place. It was an old crate with a boulder for a backrest. As I took a couple of deep breaths, they both sat on the ground opposite me and began to make a big to-do about my knee. I suspected that their concern was only partially genuine. First of all, it wasn't that severe a sprain, and beyond that, I was sure that discussing my knee was their subject of choice – obviously knowing the topic that I was on the verge of broaching.

"Sooner or later you're going to have to tell me why you're way the fuck out here," I said, looking down at the two of them, each with a hand on my knee busily in search of a swelling.

Magelinos smiled and immediately backed off to a sitting position a few feet away. I liked his manner. As my father would have said, "That guy is a *mensch*."

Eric was still hoping – not for a severe injury, but for a postponement of the inevitable. I asked again, "So what's going on?"

Eric got the message and scooted back a few feet and sat down creating a triangle. He smiled his resignation and after looking in the dirt for a few seconds said, "I need your help Callie. I don't think I can pull this off without you."

Enrique broke in and asked if Eric would prefer talking to me in private. With a nod of his head Eric acknowledged that it probably would be best. Enrique got up and excused himself till later, saying that he would prepare coffee in the cave for whenever we were ready. Preparing coffee could seem to be a casual offer, but to be able to make acceptable Café Cubano (which generally required an espresso machine) on a camp stove was an art form of which Enrique Magelinos was extremely proud. He later explained that in order to create the *crema*, he had to add just a few drops of espresso to the sugar and mix thoroughly. This makes a creamy, brown paste. He would then add the rest of the espresso to the paste making a light brown foam layer, or *espumita*, on the coffee.

When Enrique was out of range I said, "I'm listening," while taking over the knee massage myself.

"It's a turnover, but that's not the whole deal. Not even close," Eric responded.

"Tell me something I don't already know Mr. Postman." I paused, looked him squarely in the eyes, and then continued. "Listen Eric, maybe we're destined to play post office and maybe we're not, but if you bullshit me on business, I'll be out of here even if I have to limp all the way down the mountain."

"You haven't taken long to remind me, have you? There's nobody like Callie Barton is there? She's one of a kind."

"That's very flattering Eric. So one more time, what's the deal?"

After expressing his willingness, he suggested that I first fill him in on what I had been told by Miranda and Otnabe. I did so. After I finished, he also wanted to know if I had found out anything beyond that, but I insisted that now it was his turn.

"Raoul Castro hired Roca to broker a tobacco deal – nothing new, just more of the same. They asked for both of us, and Wyndam told them that you weren't available but I could come down. He told Raoul that I could do it alone. Raoul pushed the point of getting you also, but Wyndam assured them that was impossible. Before I left to come down, Wyndam briefed me about the deal. He added that he absolutely didn't want you involved in any Roca business until you turned over your notes, and for now that was not going to happen. I assured him I could do the deal."

"What do you mean, 'more of the same'? Is this connected to the other tobacco deal? The one we did a few years ago?" I asked, trying to make sure I wasn't missing anything.

"I'll get there, Callie. I promise. There's a lot going on here so let me tell it my way, okay?"

I was a little more than a little impatient but I nodded my *okay* anyway.

Eric continued, "So, when I first came down, I sensed something weird. Otnabe sent me down to offer Fidel some big bucks. I pulled all the strings I knew to get in to see him or Raoul, but no matter what I tried they weren't available. Not available for 250 million dollars? It didn't make sense. Instead they sent me to Raoul's assistant, but all she wanted to talk about was getting you here. I knew that I could do the tobacco turnover myself – maybe not as well as you could, but who could?" Eric joked as he gave me a wink.

"Eventually they hooked me up with Magelinos as a go-between. The first time I talked to him, he also asked me if there was any way to get you here. I made a joke that the only way you would come down was if you thought I was kidnapped."

"Nice joke," I interrupted.

"I hear you. Well anyway, the next day Magelinos asked me what if I went MIA? Would that get you here, and if it would, how would I go about it? It didn't make sense. Something else was obviously going on. What could be important enough for me to pretend I was missing in action? There had to be some other reason, but I couldn't find out what it was. That is, not until the other day when they hooked me up with someone called El Jugador. You ever heard of him?"

"The player?" I translated muttering to myself out loud. "I don't think so."

"Yeah, the player," Eric continued. "Well, I thought I was meeting a negotiator, but it turned out this guy is a gringo from the U.S. who's been living in Cuba and is one of Fidel's best friends. I spent a day sailing around Cienfuegos Bay on his boat and eventually I agreed to help him – them I mean.

"The guy really got to me. He wants the country to take care of its people. He told me that he feels like a hypocrite most of the time. He lives pretty well in comparison to the people and doesn't feel so good about it. He's not proud of his affluence, he's actually kind of ashamed of it. He said idealistic stuff like, *the fortunate people should take care of the country so the less fortunate can be taken care of by the country. The healthy should take care of the sick,* things like that. And you know what, he wasn't bullshitting. I've heard enough bullshitting to know the difference.

"He said Fidel is one of the smartest people he's ever met, but even he can't figure how to make it happen without subduing dissent. El Jugador has big trouble with the human rights violations and admits that there are plenty of them. It's gotten me thinking about some of the stuff we do. We never take the effect on the people into account. It's only about the money – like it's a Monopoly game. Like what you were saying when you got back from Burma. Oh yeah, and something else. You know my dad is a Republican and a big small government, free enterprise guy. Well this guy is just the opposite, but he still reminds me of dad. I can't help thinking that they would really like each other. Weird, huh?"

I'd never heard Eric talk like that, and I really didn't know what to say. So I said nothing. After a minute or so of silence, he went on.

"After I made the FSCL call, Magelinos and I spent the next week lying low and driving around the island together looking at tobacco fields and talking to planters. I didn't report in to Roca and nobody there knew where I was.

"I never talked to anyone up north except the FSCL message to my dad. What you didn't know was that I sent my dad the all clear the next day and asked that he keep that to himself. I didn't know the details of how they got you. I didn't know they raided your cash. I'm sorry about that, but I'm sure glad you're here. I'm not sure how much Magelinos knows or even who he's really working for, but with all the time we spent together, I got to like him and even trust him. We became sort of partners, which is ridiculous because he's probably only here to spy on me. So you never ran into an old guy called El Jugador?" Eric asked as an afterthought.

"Wait a second!" I came out with, still back there with the FSCL. "So you got back to the Commander and gave him the all clear. Riiiiight . . . I thought there was something off when he said goodbye to me. Something like, *I trust the postman will deliver eventually*. What a guy! He wanted to obey your instructions but he didn't want me to worry. Hey, you know what? Maybe I got involved with the wrong Lynne?"

"So, did you ever hear of El Jugador?" Eric repeated, wanting me to see that he was frustrated with my interruption.

"With a name like that I think I'd remember. So, no," I answered, feeling satisfied enough with my sarcasm to leave my last comments behind.

"I want to tell you what's going on – all of it," Eric announced as though it was time to get down to business. "El Jugador is working with Raoul on . . . " Eric went on to tell me the entire plan – Fidel's illness, the tobacco money, Otnabe's secret perpetuity add-on, and the finesse into a free-market Cuba. He finished with explaining that as far as he knew, the Roca Group brass didn't know about any of it aside from the tobacco deal. "They certainly didn't know that they were being cut out of the free-market negotiations and that was going to be our private deal – yours and mine."

"Tell me again. Does Magelinos know any of this?" I asked, trying to tie this whole thing together in my mind. It was a lot to grok, so I grasped at an obvious loose end.

"Only the tobacco deal," Eric answered. "At least I'm pretty sure."

So far it seemed to make as much sense, or nonsense, as other ops I'd been in on – but one part didn't. I couldn't figure out why they let Eric get so far inside. Why was he told so much more than Otnabe? I didn't know how to ask that one, so I didn't. I figured I'd find out along the way.

"So you agreed to help them. What does helping them involve?" I asked.

Eric leaned forward and continued as though he was about to give me the most important part. "They need a top-flight negotiator to handle the multinationals. I was flattered because I thought at first they meant *me* – but they meant *you*. This El Jugador wants *me* to assist *you*. We set up this disappearance so that Otnabe would have to send you down and you would have to come," Eric said looking sheepishly. "Sorry babe, I had to do it."

"What's this *had to* shit? And if my ego is supposed to be soaring, it isn't. Okay, so what else?" I asked, not being sure where I wanted to go with all this.

"It involves doubling on Otnabe," he continued. "Not the money part. He'll get his money – probably even more than he contracted for. It means not letting him know, because there could be a much bigger middle if he knew about Fidel and the free-market plan. It means keeping Otnabe out of Cuba till it's all over. It means getting you down here to work the deal with me. And it means getting a big enough piece off the top so that I can get out of this business and join you on that mountain top in New Mexico."

Now I knew what the *had to* was about – and it wasn't shit. This El Jugador must have really gotten to Eric. If what he was telling me was so, then Miranda and Otnabe were partially right. He was finally going to put his own well-being ahead of the Roca Group. He hadn't gone over. He had just realized what some of us realized years before. So he found a deal where he could allow the Roca Group to make their payday and still have some left for one of his own. The mountaintop in New Mexico was a thing of the past, and maybe we'd find out that Eric and I were too, but whatever happened, his attempt to get free of the Roca Group was going to get my whole-hearted support.

It was near dark and I had enough input for one day. My leg was throbbing, so I limped over to the cot in my cave in an attempt to get some rest. Magelinos came in after a while with a plate of food and I asked him to leave it on the crate next to me.

Chapter 21

The food was still there in the morning when the sun began to make shadows on the dirt floor of my bedroom. When I first looked around I didn't relate to much more than my urge to find a place to pee. It wasn't till I swung my legs onto the ground and tried to lift my bones into a standing position that I realized that there was a problem. My knee wouldn't hold any weight. I grabbed the leg of a broken stool, and using it for support gimped my way to the nearest bush. I wasn't feeling heavy on modesty, but I was glad there was no one around. I needed privacy, but not only for my bathroom needs. I needed to figure out what to do about my leg. I knew that whatever I decided I would still need help, but jeopardizing an operation with Eric's future at stake was out of the question. I managed to get back to the cot with heavy breathing my only payment. I was lying there on my back when Eric knocked on the rock and came in.

I didn't tell him about my knee right away and he didn't ask. I guess he had a lot on his mind. He started talking about my meeting El Jugador and maybe even Raoul. I figured I'd better let him in on my disability and we could both hope it was temporary together. He felt around the swelling and I had to squelch my inner expression of pleasure in having that intimacy with him. I guess we both knew that it was only a matter of time before we tested the present against the past. For now I was in no rush.

The possibility of that test happening right then and there evaporated when Magelinos came in and made it three for playing doctor. He seemed the most knowledgeable of us in medical options and insisted that he take me to the polyclinic in Pinar del Río. Although it was more reassurance than I needed, Magelinos' confidence in the Cuban medical system was contagious. As he reminded us, "We have unquestionably the finest doctors and hospitals in Latin America."

Eric would stay at the cave and we would be back before dark. It meant that nothing would be furthered with arrangements for me to meet the other players, but Eric seemed to think that there was no rush. If I had a day off, this was definitely not how I would choose to spend it, but there was no choice. I had to get operational. If Magelinos knew someone who could help me onto my feet – then that was that.

Eric offered to carry me to the car, but I opted for a shoulder under the armpit. It was a more fitting posture for co-workers and would probably better serve to establish the position I wanted to maintain under the circumstances. As we drove off I felt a missing. Funny, less than twenty-four hours together and I was already feeling a missing.

As we descended the mountain, Magelinos enthusiastically reassured me that although we were not headed to the CIMEQ Hospital, Havana's finest, nor the Frank País orthopedic hospital where Francois Mitterrand, Muamar Gaddaffi, and Saddam Hussein all were treated by the world-famous Dr. Rodrigo Cambras, I would be in the finest provincial medical facility in Cuba – thus, according to him, one of finest in the world. I hoped that merely having a sprained knee would not disappoint this state of the art establishment. I knew from a minor injury that I had sustained on an earlier trip that medical care in Cuba was free for residents and that there is no charge to foreigners for their first hospital visit. I had always found it interesting that Cuba had managed to match the life expectancy rate of the U.S. Actually, for their small population, they also had an inordinate number of doctors working in other underdeveloped nations.

The ride down the mountain was very taxing. In addition to the pain in my knee, which actually had decreased considerably, I was feeling both nauseous and a return of the cramping that I thought had left me to plague another host. Magelinos offered to go into the clinic and bring out a wheelchair, but I pridefully put the nix on that idea. I had him pull up as close to the entrance as possible and he helped me the rest of the way. My first impression was that the building looked well-kept, but the inside temperature and humidity seemed to equal that of the outside. Unfortunately, without the moving air of the car ride to make it tolerable, I started to get dizzy.

As I approached the counter, I felt the pains in my gut increase. As the nurse's face began to blur, I headed voluntarily for the tile floor before it came up to meet me. Magelinos' voice was loud and clear, but so much perspiration was running down into my eyes that I couldn't see him. The nurse was restraining me from getting up and I heard her giving instructions to get a doctor. With Magelinos' help, I worked my way into a sitting position and leaned against the counter. I was barely even aware of any problem with my knee, but there was a pain halfway between my naval and my pelvis that was excruciating. I was more concerned with avoiding vomiting than anything else, so I focused on taking deep breaths. It was a trick I'd learned from sailing. The doctor finally showed up, but the last voice I remember was Magelinos'. I passed out without hearing what he said.

My eyes fixed on a statue of the Virgin Mary. It was difficult to judge its scale. It could have been very large and far away, or very small and close up. It would take two eyes to make that assessment, and as yet only one was open. As the other joined it, I realized that I was looking at a statue on a shelf attached to the far wall of a room – a hospital room. When my other senses clicked in, I noticed the smell of oranges. There was no one around and I found the smell comforting. I checked my body, and though it felt tired I couldn't locate any problems with its functioning. Even my knee felt flexible and almost without pain. I did have some soreness in the area of my uterus, but it was far decreased from the episode at the counter – an episode I had no trouble remembering.

I didn't feel moved to call anyone and spent the next hour or so nodding in and out of sleep until a female doctor came into the room and stood by my bed.

"What happened?" It seemed as intelligent as anything else I could say.

"You fainted grasping your abdomen, so we took you to X-ray to find out what was happening in there. Your friend said he brought you in for your knee, but that was clearly not the cause of your passing out. I myself thought you had an ectopic pregnancy, but our X-rays showed something quite different."

By now I was alert enough to remember the events on the beach in Miami and had no doubt that there was a connection. I certainly wasn't pregnant, ectopically or otherwise. "What is it? Is it serious?" I asked.

"Not any more it isn't," she said with a smile meant to be contagious. "There was a piece of your birth control IUD coil that adhered to the wall of the cervix. It had dug itself in. It's a wonder that you could even walk. You must have passed the rest of the coil without knowing it – or possibly you did know it. You know, you should always check that it's complete when it comes out. *Strange things can happen when foreign bodies are left where they don't belong.*"

Her first two sentences were clear, but the rest of her doctoring voice disappeared beneath a torrent of voices only audible to me. That is, until her last sentence, which mantrafied itself in my brain. I had no IUD. coil. I never had a coil. It happened at the beach. The man from Boston was probably a fuckin' gynecologist. I almost laughed out loud at the accuracy of the phrase – a fuckin' gynecologist.

As I was piecing together what had happened, I remembered something that I had heard the year before I left the Roca Group. It was a description of a minute stainless steel microwave diode transponder capable of accurately transmitting sound to a receiver up to a few miles away. It was being promoted as the ultimate eavesdropping device. It was usually carried in a brace in the mouth but always with the host's knowledge. My indiscretion had transformed me into a human bug. Who was that bastard working for? I knew my own people wouldn't do that . . . would they? Someone else must have that technology, but who, and why?

I knew that before I went ahead to try to figure out that one, I'd better cover any loose ends. "Could I see the piece of metal?" I asked the doctor innocently.

"I think it was thrown away," she answered casually. "It certainly was of no use to anyone anymore."

"Is the man who brought me still here?"

"No, he left late last night. It was after we removed the object. He seemed greatly relieved."

"So you told him what you found?"

"Oh yes, I think my assistant actually showed it to him before it was thrown away."

I had so many thoughts of self-dislike that all I could do was close my eyes and pretend I was going back to sleep. I needed to be alone. Not only to beat myself up for being so stupid, but to recount everything that I had said and was said to me since that bastard bugged me. Who did he work for? If I thought about that long enough, at least I could replace self-dislike with anger. But that wasn't good enough. I knew I needed to get my thoughts organized and get some perspective quickly. I often used humor to separate myself from an otherwise untenable attitude. I scoured my retinue of any wiseacrings that might relate to my naiveté at the beach. I came up with a pretty good one. *At least I wasn't pregnant.*

Chapter 22

The bay at Cienfuegos was what the Canadians came for. In the winter, the buses waited for the charter planes and whisked the Canucks off to the city known in Cuba as the *Pearl of the South*. Those that didn't come in on the charters found their way to the beach by train from Havana's Tulipan station. For a five peso fare, the air-conditioned train rambled through the numerous stops on its eight-hour delivery assignment to the sea.

These days El Jugador was an infrequent passenger on the return train to the capitol. His one-time position of anonymous influence had been on the decline for the past few years. It was a welcome withdrawal, but not without a component that could only be described as melancholy.

He had first met Fidel during the revolution, when his had been a position of influence of a very different kind. As a representative of the large sums of money cascading down from U.S. gaming interests, he was often consulted by representatives of Batista, and once by Batista himself. Part of his job had been to keep abreast of the potentially volatile political maneuverings that were ever-present on the island since Fidel's return from Mexico.

Another part of El Jugador's responsibilities had been the gambling operation at the Jagua Hotel in Cienfuegos, so the flight between Havana and the south was a monthly ritual. In those days, it was common knowledge that the hotel was not the only place on the bay where games of chance were taking place. Fidel had many supporters in the province, and they were known to risk more than money. They were using the harbor for smuggling in supplies for the troops under the command of his brother Raoul – troops that were encamped in the central highlands of the island.

It was the end of the second day of a regular trip for El Jugador that evening in 1958. He had already spent a couple of days walking the floor, talking to the supervisors, the pit-bosses, and of course reviewing the books. Then came the ferry ride over the channel to the village of Perche, with its red tile roof houses, where he had a monthly dinner with friends. The night was unusually humid for the coast, and the sea breeze afforded little relief. El Jugador spent the return ferry ride at the rail, attempting to foil the air into a moving current to alleviate his discomfort.

It was midway between the dock at Perche and Cienfuegos harbor that he spotted four launches, each with a lantern in its bow. The captain of the ferry saw them also and trained his large spotlight on the mini-flotilla. El Jugador thought that the light was to prevent an inadvertent collision, but Batista's SIM was a lot better organized than that. Ferryboat captains were all well paid to spot and report any unusual night traffic on the channel. Protocol was to keep the crafts in question illuminated while calling the secret police headquarters at the Cienfuegos naval base.

On that particular night, the rebels were carrying a cargo of weapons in their launches. Seeing the lights and knowing the eventuality they predicted, they motored directly toward the ferry. When the automatic weapons fire began, El Jugador dove to a position of safety, crouching behind one of the four row boats secured on deck. The volley of bullets whizzed over his head and found the glass of the two lights that had been installed on the ferry by SIM. As the lights popped and went out, the gun fire stopped and eight khaki-clad figures scrambled up the forward starboard ladder onto the deck.

They appeared highly agitated and moved about the deck with their weapons poised for action. The passengers and crew were herded toward the forward deck. It seemed obvious that there was no one on the ferry to either return fire or present any threat to the six men and two women who had come aboard. One of the commandos shouted something unintelligible from the raised wheel house, followed by the sound of two shots.

A bearded rebel came down, escorting the captain of the ferry at gunpoint. The captain was deposited on a bench across the deck from the rest, all the while repeating denials that he had sent any radio messages. He kept saying the same words over and over. *No mandé un mensaje.* The rebel reported to several others that he had destroyed the radio. But when he came through the door of the wheelhouse, he was sure the captain was broadcasting location coordinates.

One of the women leaned over the side of the ferry and called down to the other boats. A minute or so later, two more men came up the forward ladder. One carried an automatic weapon, the other was unarmed. The two walked through the assemblage of passengers and crew. The taller unarmed man was obviously in charge. He explained that everyone was to either get into the rowboats quickly or get blown up with the ferry.

Being the only North American aboard, El Jugador knew that anonymity would not be available to him. He also knew it was only a matter of time before the discovery of the small pistol that he carried in his jacket pocket would thrust him into an even less advantageous category. He decided to act before he was acted upon. He walked toward the tall man, but as he approached, the armed companion blocked his path. El Jugador put up his arms in a gesture of surrender and called out past the rebel to the one who was obviously their commander.

"My position is somewhat awkward. I keep a pistol in my pocket for protection, but at the moment it seems like having it could cause a problem."

Hearing the word *pistol,* half a dozen rebels rushed to surround El Jugador, separating him from their commander. They found the four-inch Beretta and brought it over to the man they called Comandante. His response instantly changed the mood of the proceedings. He laughed. It was neither a smirk, nor was it a sarcastic snort, but more of a full-on belly laugh. Everyone, the passengers, the crew and the soldiers began laughing along with him. Even the ferry captain managed a hopeful grin.

The mood reverted when the Comandante shouted, "SIM will be coming. Everyone over the side into the boats. We are going to blow up this ferry."

The scrambling lasted a few minutes. After each of the four boats collected its share, they motored off toward the western end of the bay. After the last boat departed, the lights of several larger vessels appeared in the distance behind. The deserted ferry was in the path between the motor launches and what were obviously police vessels, so when it exploded, vision of the pursuing ships was obscured. When the diesel tanks created a secondary explosion, the flames shot 50 or 60 feet in the air, illuminating the distant vessels. They were navy gunboats, still far away, but quickly closing on the burning ferry.

It was only about half a mile to shore and the small motor launches, though heavily laden, were moving quickly through the water. It became obvious that not only would they not be overtaken, but that they wouldn't even be spotted. The woman called instructions out to the other boats, at which point they separated, each heading toward a different landing destination on the beach.

El Jugador sat in the rear of the launch that also carried the tall bearded commander. When they reached shore, the ten or twelve passengers and ferry crew were informed that they were being released. They were told that they had been guests of the Fuerzas Armadas Revolucionarias, and their support would be needed in the coming months when the authority of the illegal government was going to be challenged.

The speech came from the tall thin woman. As she spoke, El Jugador noticed that the man they referred to as Comandante paid attention to every word she said, even though he must have heard the same speech given many times before. As they began moving two by two quickly up the beach toward the palms, the bearded revolutionary reached out his arm and blocked the path of El Jugador.

"I would like you to accompany me," he requested, as he relaxed his arm. "You are not a prisoner, but there is something I wish to show you. I will not force you to do so, but I ask you as an equal, because we are all equals."

The request coming from the commander of an armed force, however small, seemed curious to El Jugador. After all, he had the guns. El Jugador didn't know whether it was the look in the commander's eyes or the speech of the woman that proceeded it. What he did know was that he would go along. He was no longer afraid, and he was not yet curious. He was drawn.

In the 24 hours that followed, El Comandante explained his position to this man who he decided was worth his time. They walked and ate and sat quietly together, and in that first day, the name El Jugador found its birth. As difficult as it is for a revolutionary commander to afford friendship in the midst of an insurrection, still it happened. They became friends.

What Fidel didn't know, and what El Jugador refrained from divulging during that time, was that he was acting as what the CIA called *an external information gathering operative*. He was an independent contractor who was allowed special privileges in exchange for keeping the U.S. government apprised of the current political situation. It was not so much a profession for El Jugador, but a necessity in his chosen line of work. As a liaison man in the hotel and gaming industry, it was required that he maintain good relations with both his natural government as well as that of his host.

In keeping with the responsibilities he accepted from the CIA, El Jugador reported the incident on the ferry. He surprised himself when he deliberately left out one significant detail. From the day of that report, his allegiances began to alter. El Jugador never became a double agent, and El Comandante never pressed him for information that would compromise the U.S. Nevertheless, the reports sent to Langley, Virginia were never again as accurate as they had previously been.

After the transfer of power in 1959 and through the years that followed, El Jugador traveled clandestinely to Cuba numerous times, but it was not for the CIA. It was in the mid-1980s that his trips were discovered by U.S. authorities. Anonymous information led to his being suspected of lending sympathy and support to the Cuban Government.

He knew that he would have to act decisively in order to avoid eventual apprehension. Within ten days of the leak that jeopardized him, El Jugador became a Cuban.

Chapter 23

The top right half of the rising sun was cresting over the United Nations building. From Miranda's bedroom window, she could see the majesty of nature's life-giving agent as it backlit the symbol of man's aspirations for peace on earth. It was enough to temporarily take her mind off the situation that had begun less than two months before, when she had met two tobacco company representatives on the marble steps at the foot of her view. When the sun cleared the top of the Secretariat building, the ability of the panorama to distract her was obliterated by the glare. Miranda closed the curtains and left her bedroom to meet with her co-conspirator, who was in the living room anxiously awaiting her report.

Before the implant monitoring arrangement with Brisco and Gomez had become operational, the information Otnabe had gotten directly from Jelinda since her arrival two days before in 90M was ambiguous and unsatisfying. Miranda entered the living room with a copy of the first transmission from Cuba. "All information that we get from Jelinda will now be verified by our secondary source," Miranda reported to Otnabe. "Its lack of fidelity makes it inefficient for primary information, but for confirmation it will work nicely. There is the expected distortion. But

149

enough words are intelligible that we can use it to corroborate information that we've already received from other sources. The sound lab is working on isolating extraneous noises, of which you can imagine there are many."

As she presented the report to Otnabe, Miranda referred in a businesslike way to the notes that were given to her by the lab technicians. Originally, when Miranda was informed that Callie would be resuming operational status and that the experimental ICS would be implemented, allegiance to her gender made her somewhat sensitive to the modality in question. Now, the direct access that it afforded made it clear that it was too valuable to let emotions interfere.

Otnabe was very pleased with himself. Now that he had access to Jelinda's conversations through the implant, the chain of Brisco, Gomez, and Connert would put him on the inside. Otnabe was in his favorite position. Everyone had part of the picture, but he was the only one who was privy to it all.

"We'll continue to use Barnes Connert to communicate with Brisco," Otnabe said aloud, mainly to remind himself. "Brisco says Connert will be available in any way that we need him. If it leaked that we were using a fugitive in our operation, there could be reverberations, so we're safe as long as Connert acts as a cover. Brisco is our key access to information in Cuba, so that General what's his name will . . ."

"Gomez," Miranda added.

"Yes, General Gomez will be monitoring Jelinda's activities," Otnabe concluded, realizing he was nearing the edge of his competency at juggling variables.

It was in these moments that Miranda acutely experienced the limitations placed on her. Even though she was the first and only female to have ever attained board of director status, it would be unlikely that she could ever depose Otnabe. She was confident of her superiority in every category of Roca Group procedure, but that wouldn't tip the scales unless she could place more women on the board. It was Miranda's view that she and Caroline Barton could make quite a team.

Chapter 24

After Gomez delivered the latest transponder tape, Brisco locked himself in his study and listened to it. The contents caused his brain to illuminate. He knew the next move was to notify Otnabe, but first he had to stake out a position for himself. The information he received might be held in common with a few Cubans, but as far as anyone 90 miles to the north was concerned, he had an exclusive. Brisco knew that he had to deal directly with Otnabe on this one. Barnes Connert would have to be kept out of the loop. Otnabe would not be pleased to receive any communication directly from Brisco, but this was too big to use a middleman.

Later that morning, Brisco drove into Havana and through the tunnel under the Almendares River to Miramar, a beach community of fashionable shops and offices. The communications link he had used many times before was located in the back of one of the booths at La Flora, an artisans' workshop for designer clothes and objects d'art. Relatively secure phone service was available to almost every other country in the world, but not to the U.S. For that, you needed connections. You also needed to pay $25 per minute.

Brisco's calls to Career Management Associates were refused three times before he was finally patched into Wyndam Otnabe. Before he allowed Brisco to begin talking,

Otnabe scrambled the message for maximum security and privacy.

"I have some interesting news," Brisco began.

"I thought we were clear on the necessity for indirect communications, Mr. Brisco," Otnabe interrupted.

"Listen, I'm not one of your Roca operatives Mr. Otnabe. I make decisions according to my assessment of the situation, not according to your procedure manual. Anyway, I think when you hear what I have to tell you, your perspective may very well change," Brisco deliberately spoke with authority. He knew the news could bring Otnabe down to Cuba. That might curtail his ability to manipulate the situation. He needed to present a strong profile that Otnabe could depend on. That is, if Otnabe agreed to his conditions.

Otnabe had no idea what could be of such great consequence. After he heard Brisco's news, he wanted to make sure Miranda was available for consultation in case he needed her input. "Call me in ten minutes on *44-46-#33. That's my private satellite hook-up. Even when scrambled, the line we're on is not secure. I'll expect your call in exactly ten minutes."

Ten minutes later, Otnabe and Brisco were on opposite ends of a Comsat 12 top security private patch.

"What have you got?" Otnabe opened.

"First, the ICS implant is no longer in service." Brisco stalled for maximum effect. "Before it went out of service though, it recorded a conversation that would definitely interest you."

Otnabe was disappointed that no further transmissions would be forthcoming but was much more interested in what Brisco had.

"Go on. You have something worth breaching security procedures I trust?" he asked, feigning casualness but feeling quite the opposite.

"I'm afraid our previous arrangement is no longer going to be satisfactory Mr. Otnabe. That is under the circumstances I'm about to reveal to you," Brisco said, establishing a bargaining posture.

Both Otnabe and Brisco were expedients. They had no loyalties, and could only be trusted not to be trustworthy. This common attribute made them both comfortable dealing with each other. Otnabe knew beforehand who he was dealing with. This call was to be expected. If Brisco had tripped over something, it was probably going to be profitable. Otnabe certainly had more that he could offer Brisco, so he accepted his opening. "I'm a businessman Roger. Give me something of value and I'll be glad to pay for it. What have you got?"

Both of these men had negotiated for millions, and both knew that getting to a first name basis was a step in the right direction.

"I appreciate that Wyndam, but cash is not a problem for me now. Freedom of movement *is*. I know you can't arrange a U.S. visa for me, so I won't saddle you with an impossible request. I would, however, like to spend my next few summers in France. If you use the information I give you wisely, and afford preferential treatment to the French, they will grant your request on my behalf. Do we have a deal?"

"I sympathize with the limitations that the Americans have put on your movements Roger, but even though the French would be the first to stand up to the Americans, they would have to be getting something of considerable value to contemplate such an affront."

There was no longer any need to play negotiatory games. Otnabe would go along once he heard. The only other variable Brisco had to be assured of was that Otnabe couldn't back out. That was easy. Brisco knew too much for Otnabe to reverse on him. Otnabe had to protect the Roca Group, and that protection would be Brisco's insurance.

Brisco recounted the information he had gotten from the tape that Gomez had given him. He confirmed that the source of the information was a conversation between Caroline Barton and Eric Lynne. It had been monitored by the ICS the day before from the General's mobile unit in Pinar del Rio. The transmission not only described Raoul's plan, but disclosed his intention to use Eric and Callie for the most lucrative part of the arrangement, and cut out Roca and Otnabe.

Yes, Otnabe thought, after he cradled his satellite phone and locked it in his desk. Under the circumstances, Brisco was sure to get his French asylum. Being early recipients of the news of Castro's impending demise and his brother's plan for a free-market Cuba, French-based multinationals could be the first to get a foothold on the island. The tradeoff would be well within the parameters of tolerable friction with the U.S. So France would be a winner, and so would Brisco. But what about Wyndam Otnabe – what would *he* get? What *could* he get? Otnabe's answer was simple. The tape revealed that answer. *If Eric Lynne was not available, then Raoul would be forced to use Otnabe.*

Chapter 25

I had to get out of the hospital and away somewhere on my own – at least for a few hours. By mid-afternoon I was feeling relatively normal. My knee was still a little sore and my mid-section even sorer, but nothing I couldn't live with. For starters, I needed to talk to my communication link in Cienfuegos to see if Eric's father had called. He might have heard something from my U.S. informants. If that was a dead-end, I would have to call Miranda and ask her to follow up on the Commander for me. Information is the electricity that powers the operative's light bulb, and I had some of the best gatherers in the business. Why was it not getting through to me? I knew I had to figure out the implications of the monitoring device – basically, what information I gave up, and to whom I gave it. I had no place to go with the *to whom* yet, but I certainly remembered the *what*. In my head it was a list. I wrote it down:

(1) The basic tobacco option deal
(2) The basic tobacco deal with the return of the Vuelta Abajo fields
(3) The free-market entry deal
(4) Fidel's health
(5) Someone called El Jugador working with Raoul
(6) Enrique Magelinos and Eric Lynne working together

I rounded up my few possessions and unobtrusively took my leave of the hospital. That means I left through the back door. The only place I knew in Pinar that definitely had a phone was the cantina I called from on the way to the caves with Magelinos. It was the place where we drank the fermented booze. I found a cab and was sitting at a table at the café within a few minutes. Drinking alcohol was out of the question, so I ordered some combination of fruit juices and a plain roll. I had a feeling the telephone call would be a disappointment, and I was right – no messages. Where was the Commander? Why wasn't he checking in? It didn't make sense. I had to contact Miranda. I went back to the table and over my juice and roll figured out what I had to say to her. I hated to think so, but it was always possible that she was in on the implanted device. I decided to keep it to the basics – just ask her to check on the Commander.

I finished my snack and returned to the telephone. Getting through might be complicated. My contact would have to patch me through from this public phone through his radio-telephone and on to Miranda in the U.S. Hopefully I could get through, but I knew that often even Red-Jack couldn't make it happen.

In the last years of the 20th century, advances in communications technology were proceeding geometrically. The stationary phone with its rotary or keypad dialing system had all but disappeared. In its place appeared a portable handset that could be carried around the office or the home without a wire to encumber the user.

Mobile radio phones for use in cars had been in use for some years, and cellular phones for personal use were becoming more and more available. In 1991, the first digital

GSM (Global System of Mobile Communications) network was established in Finland. Similar networks began to show up around the globe causing personal cell phone use to expand, making these devices the communication mode of choice for an ever-increasing portion of the world. Computers had progressed from too large for anything but immobile office use to desktop varieties for use in both offices and private homes. All this was happening on every continent, but not on the island ninety miles south of Key West, Florida, called Cuba.

Although the hardware for these advancements was available on a limited basis in Cuba, the budget for developing network technologies to facilitate their use was not a priority for the Government. Once the Soviet subsidies were no longer available, funding for improvements in communication technology would not have been available even if it had been a priority.

As the classic autos were the norm in Cuba, so were the antiquated computers and telephones. Traveling to Cuba was like traveling back to a time when technology was in its infancy. Email was barely available, if at all. Even then, it was carefully restricted to communication between highly placed government offices on the island with no international access. The limited communication technology that was available to Cubans was severely restricted, and phone service to the U.S. was all but non-existent. Conventional booths scattered about the island were the mainstay of telephone communications for ordinary citizens. They were frequently monitored, first by SIM in the Batista pre-revolution days, then later by the Castro government's secret services, making them questionable for use in conversations that required privacy.

If Cubans wished to make secure calls, whether domestic or international (including to the U.S.) they had to contract a private party with radio telephone communication equipment – possession of such equipment definitely being illegal.

I had established just such an asset. Rather than having to procure the service by secret inquiry, access to secure communications came to me quite by accident. It was not till much later that I discovered that my contact on the island was a distant relative of my father.

Numbers of Polish Jews had stopped over in Cuba during their migration to the United States and ended up staying. They were known as Polacos in Cuba, the generic name for refugees of Jewish decent. Anyone who spoke German, or in this case Yiddish, was welcomed in the Cuba of the 1920s, as the government was strongly pro-German. Jacob Barton, my father's cousin, never disclosed either our relationship or even his identity, insisting that we never meet. All I knew was that his location was in Cienfuegos. He called his link-up Red-Jack communication. It was a reference to his now thinning red hair and his nickname, Jack. We formed a curious relationship of trust, one that I came to depend on whenever operations took me to Cuba.

"Career Management Associates, company name please?" The connection was terrible, but sufficient.

"This is Jelinda. Put me through to Carmen Miranda."

"Hold please."

"Jelinda, are you there? This is Miranda."

"Yes, Miranda, I need you to contact the Postman's FSCL. He has data for me that I must have. He lives near the Beach (*codename for Miami*). If you have trouble reaching him, his community newspaper office might know his whereabouts. I need a return call ASAP."

I would have had her use my own private communication link, but in order to keep that one a secret, I suggested that Miranda get back to me on the link that Roca had established years before and secure what's called an A.I. – anonymous interlink – with my contact. That way Red-Jack would be calling me when he heard from the U.S. I added, "I'll wait here at this phone," to encourage her to hurry.

"What's happening there? Are there new developments?" she asked, trying to prolong the conversation even as I was about to hang up

"We'll talk when you get back to me," I insisted. "I need that data now. Do you copy?"

Miranda repeated what I wanted her to do and hung up. I remained on the line to tell Red-Jack that a call would be coming through shortly. I remembered what an invaluable asset he had been for me in the past, and here he was playing that part again. I smiled to myself that I still had the same mind picture of him from all the years that I had used his services. Although he had balked at the few attempts I made to meet him in person, it didn't stop me from conjuring a picture from his voice. We used a blind drop for the cash I paid him. It was never all that much in terms of U.S. standards, but I'm sure it went a long way on the island.

I didn't want to wear myself out standing by the phone so I located myself at the nearest table. My appetite was coming back, so I ordered more juice and a *bocadillo*,

Cuba's interpretation of a sandwich, and dug in for the wait. Sometimes it takes more time then you imagine and sometime less – rarely you guess it right. This time it was less, and I was grateful. The phone rang, and it was Red-Jack forwarding the Roca link-up call to me with his usual, "Secure patch is a go."

"Miranda, you there?" The connection was a little fuzzy.

"Yes Jelinda, no luck with the Commander. He must be away. No luck at that office either."

"What do you mean no luck? What did they say?" I barked through the phone venting my frustration.

What followed were a few too many moments of silence. Almost like Miranda was trying to think of something to say because she hadn't really called the Commander or his office. Maybe it was my imagination or maybe it wasn't, but that paranoid thought got to me.

"Did you know about it Miranda? Did you?" I wanted to ask, but it came out more like an accusation.

"Know about what, Callie?" She came back, but not quickly enough. She went on trying to change the subject when she didn't even wait to find out what the subject was.

She knew! She was in on it! My own people! When she stopped talking I was in shock. All I heard was a voice on the other end of the line saying, "Jelinda?" . . . Jelinda? . . . Jelinda, are you still there?"

I left the phone dangling from its cord. I knew I had to sit down. I was feeling dizzy, but this time it was different. I thought I was tough, but I guess I was wrong. *Miranda? Manny? My own people? Maybe the Commander too? If the father, why not his son? Why not everybody colluding to shove an electronic device into my vagina?* Maybe it was the day in the hospital, or maybe it was the time on the mountain, but I guess I had gotten a little more sensitive – or maybe just a little less numb. It was too much. This game that I used to love had gotten out of hand. I couldn't juggle that many variables, and all of a sudden I didn't want to.

Chapter 26

"She's disappeared! There's no sign of her in Pinar Del Rio," Magelinos spurted the words, out of breath from the short jog to the cave from where he left the car under the trees.

"What do you mean disappeared? She left the hospital on her own?" Eric queried in disbelief.

"She left Pinar on her own, and she's not headed this way. She found out . . . I found out," Magelinos answered incredulously.

"Found out what? What did she find out? What did you find out? What are you talking about Enrique? Is she okay? What happened at the hospital?"

Magelinos sat down on the dirt with his legs sprawled out in front of him. He was no longer young but he rarely looked tired. Now he did. Eric stood over him waiting impatiently for an answer.

"Yes, yes, she's fine. There was something other than her knee, but yes, she's fine now. Please sit down," Magelinos prompted. "Listen, my friend, we need to talk."

Eric sensed the gravity of Magelinos' request. Over the years he had spent time with this man, and this was not the petition of the Enrique Magelinos he had known. Enrique's demeanor caused Eric to sit closer than he ordinarily would have. It was the distance of friends, not that of adversaries or even that of associates. "I'm listening Enrique."

"Now I know your secret Mr. Lynne. But I too have a secret, and *that* one you do not yet know. We have both been in this business for a long time. I know we respect each other even though we have been on opposite sides from time to time. Today I learned that we are playing for higher stakes than I was aware. Not since the missiles came have I had such a feeling of concern for my country." Magelinos sighed, and looked through the opening in the cave and off toward the hills before he looked back at Eric and continued.

"When the revolution began, we soldiers were supposed to fight against it. Some of us did and some of us didn't. In those confusing days, Arturo Gomez and I spent many hours discussing politics. That is when our friendship really began in earnest. Even though he was privately very critical of Batista, he was still completely loyal to the army. I was neither that critical nor that loyal. After all, he was a sergeant, but I was merely a private. Eventually, with Arturo's help, I became more aware of the dishonesty and corruption of Batista and those close to him.

"My brother was a supporter of Fidel. As a soldier, I was supposed to expose him or even arrest him, but he was my brother. He tried everything to convince me to leave the army and join Che in the mountains as many did, but I was not the type to be dedicated to a cause. That is, until my brother was killed in a raid on his camp. His death caused me to look more closely at things than I had done before. In mid-November, Arturo and I slipped out of Havana and headed for the Sierra de Cristal mountain stronghold in Oriente

Province, where we planned to join the freedom fighters. It was not as easy as we thought it would be.

"At that time, Raoul was the commander and his policy was that great care should be taken in accepting the help of anyone who had been in Batista's army. We were required to be what he called *repatriated.* That meant two weeks of classes and lectures until it was clear what we were signing on for. Being tired of the corruption wasn't enough to satisfy Raoul. He wanted us to understand what we were *for*, not only what we were against. For the first time in my life, I became very enthusiastic about something other than momentary pleasures of one kind or another. Arturo and I marched into Havana on New Year's Eve along with Fidel and Raoul, and we have been loyal to them ever since." A few seconds after Magelinos stopped talking, he took a deep breath, held it at the top for a moment or two, and then let it out with a long verbal sigh.

"You see," he resumed, "although with Batista I accepted money for favors, since the revolution, everything I have done has been out of love for one man – faith in one man. Now that is going to have to change. Cuba has been in trouble before, but always there was a plan to make things better. I have been aware that in the past few years, since the Soviet collapse, those plans have become more and more unrealistic. The only hope I held was my faith in El Comandante, but I sadly confess that my faith has been waning." Magelinos' eyes cast downward as he said this last sentence.

After a few moments of silence, he continued. "Even though I have been privy to many critical decisions over the years, I have never actually made any of them. It's true, I am not a brilliant man as are some of the others, but I have seen much and I think I know what must be done. I suspect that the circumstances of the next few weeks will lead me to try to influence others in the way that others have always tried to influence me. I know you have different reasons for this undertaking than I, but I respect you. I think we may be able to work together in reality, rather than play this game that we have been playing."

Feigned sincerity was one of the operative's most effective tools, but this was different. Lynne was trained both in the laboratory and the field not to weaken his resolve in the face of human frailty, or even dignity for that matter. The inner struggle showed on Lynne's face as he debated whether to relax his guard and let this man into his confidence. As much as the human being in him had that desire, the covert agent needed more to go on. It needed to know that their aims were complementary, or at the very least parallel. He needed to know Enrique's secret. He needed to lower the lofty tone of the discussion and feed himself on facts. Then maybe the human being in him could be allowed to surface.

"You must understand my position, Enrique. It might be possible for us to join forces, but first I must know what you know and how you see that events should proceed."

"As you know, my friend," Magelinos began, "life has become more difficult here in Cuba since we lost the help of our Soviet allies. Conditions were minimal even before that, but now there are many problems that did not exist before. When a man has a family to care for, he will do things that he would not do otherwise, so I hope that you will not have a harsh judgment when I tell you what I have to."

Eric had no idea where Magelinos was going with this, but he continued to listen, hoping that his friend had not done anything too foolish. "What did you do Enrique? Is it anything that I can help with?"

"I appreciate your offer and your kindness, but I was not talking about myself. It is my superior and my friend Arturo . . . General Gomez. In the Batista years, we all accepted money from the gamblers. It became a habit that lasted even after the revolution, although opportunities became much less frequent. In fact, opportunities either disappeared, or those of us in the Service became much more idealistic about what we were doing. Those with families, especially large families like General Gomez, continued to look for those opportunities. A few years ago he made a connection to supplement his income, but made it clear that he wouldn't do anything that might harm Cuba in any way. He was very adamant about that. This connection was with an American living here in Cuba. His name is Roger Brisco. I'm sure you've heard of him."

Eric nodded that he had heard of Brisco and added that his company even had dealings with him at one time.

"A few days ago, this Brisco offered Arturo a good deal of money to do some surveillance, and guaranteed that it would not be problematic for the Cuban government or its people. Of course Brisco was lying. His kind of person doesn't know the difference between truth and lies, so maybe he even thought he was telling the truth. But he was not.

"Arturo taped conversations that came by way of a transponder. He was not particularly curious about their content, assuming that they were related to a jealous husband, or something like that. Eventually though, he decided that he'd better listen to one or two tapes to make sure of his assumption. The results were startling even to him. He realized that Brisco was lying, and that the information he was forwarding might in fact be harmful to Cuba. He also realized who that startling conversation was between. That conversation, I'm embarrassed to say, was between you and Ms. Barton. Before I tell you more, I want you to know that Arturo came to me for help and advice, and I told him I was going to tell you. He has agreed to help us in any way that he can and is very sorry for his indiscretion. General Gomez will continue to feign that he is working for Brisco, but he will filter information to me."

Magelinos stood up and asked Lynne if he would like some coffee. As he stoked the fire and attended to the coffee, he told Lynne everything he knew. Eric already knew most of what Enrique told him. After all, it was his own voice that had been monitored. But how was it done? Enrique also answered that question by telling him what he discovered at the hospital.

That night, Eric and sleep were no friends of each other. He awoke sometime before dawn, and sat at the opening of the cave looking out over the valley. What must Callie be thinking? He could only guess, and his guesses weren't pleasant. He knew he had to speak to El Jugador in person. He was the one who originated the plan and he would have to call the next shot. Eric would bring Enrique with him – a breach of security, but a vote for something perhaps more important.

Chapter 27

Several years before, I was involved in negotiations between the Cuban and Italian governments. The result of those negotiations was a trade of air-conditioned Fiat buses for a long-term commitment to supply sugar. I had never been much of a bus rider in Cuba, but each time I boarded one of those state-of-the-art cruisers, I had a twinge of pride.

In addition to these super-cruisers, Cuban public transportation included local buses that went west to the Gulf of Guanahacabibes at the tip of the island, but there was no point in heading there. East was really the only direction to go from Pinar, and all those roads led to Havana. I was scheduled to reach there late in the afternoon. I could certainly lose myself in a city of that size, but I was thinking more of using it as a jumping-off point for somewhere else. I hoped that the somewhere else would come to me in an inspiration, as my gift to the Cuban population rolled coolly and quietly down the road.

It was time to put some space between myself and whatever intrigue I had signed on for. I was familiar enough with my volatile temperament to know that, in my case, reverses could not be considered anomalous behavior. Still, I needed some time to think and maybe even relax, although the latter was unrealistic. After all, it took a full three months in the Sangre De Christo before any such experience kicked in.

I had several options in addition to numerous invitations that had precipitated from my earlier telephone conversations. The invitations were unrealistic. Each one could lead back to some player in this drama, whether directly or indirectly. The only option that wouldn't require starting from scratch and have too many strings attached was Fawn Brisco. I had already initiated contact with her, and her father would have delivered the message that I wanted to see her. Originally it was for information, but now I wasn't sure what it was for. I decided to call Fawn at the next stop.

Artemisa is a small town off the thruway, and the last chance to head directly east. The thruway there swings north toward Havana. It was mid-afternoon when the bus pulled in for a ten-minute stop. I wasn't the only passenger who wanted to get off, so I had to wait my turn as we all filed out of the front door. As I advanced from row to row, I occupied myself by gazing out the window. I noticed a phenomenon that I had never recorded in all of my trips to Cuba. The men actually used the rest room at the bus stations. The designated concrete wall that men in all other Latin American countries would normally use for that purpose was unstreaked. I wondered if the addition of upgraded buses also carried with it a commensurate elevation in personal hygiene. However it came about, I would benefit by not having to hold my breath from the time of exit until clear of the area. Anyone who has traveled in Third-World countries, and some not so Third World, would know about that.

The phone was several blocks away in the post office, so I had to jog over to make sure I didn't miss the bus. My knee seemed to have made a nearly full recovery because I didn't even realize that I wasn't having trouble with it until I had reached the post office. The phone was unoccupied and I was on the line with the Hemingway Marina within a few minutes. I said who I was and this time they put me right through to Fawn's apartment.

"Hello," a female voice answered.

"Hello, this is Callie Barton. I hope I'm not disturbing you."

"Disturbing me? No, of course not. I was so disappointed that I missed you. But *you* got to have dinner out with my father. *I* don't even get to do that very often. Where are you anyway?"

"I'm south of Havana and looking for something to do, or someplace to go for a few days. I know I haven't seen you for a while, but I thought you might have an idea."

"This is perfect!" she exclaimed excitedly. "I have just the thing. Do you know where the Ciudad de Los Pioneros is?"

"No, I've never even heard of it. Where is it? What is it?"

"It's a retreat where Cuban kids who need medical care can come and get concentrated attention for a couple of weeks a year. But that's not why I go there. I started volunteering to help with the Chernobyl children about four years ago. I visit for a few days and lend a hand whenever I'm in Cuba. I'm going tomorrow."

"Chernobyl children, what are they doing in Cuba?" I asked.

"I don't know what the politics are, but there are hundreds of them getting free medical care. Some of them are really in bad shape. I just hold hands and play games. Do you speak any Russian?" Fawn asked.

My thoughts were more of the lying on a secluded beach variety, but Fawn's enthusiasm was endemic. It caused me to flash on my experience at the Mae Tao Clinic on the Burma/Thai border. That impression had never left me. Through the years I had picked up a few sentences in Russian, and even if I hadn't, I could certainly do whatever Fawn did. "So when, where, and how?" I asked.

Fawn went on to give me all the logistics and even offered to share her lodgings with me. Knowing her, they would be the best that Cuba had to offer. She suggested I meet her at the Hemingway Marina and we could drive there together. Driving there together sounded fine, but I thought better of showing up at a place where I might be spotted. I might have been playing this one a little more dramatically than it warranted, but I was leaning just a touch to the paranoid side. After all, I was in possession of exclusive information – information that could convert into large sums of money were a creative party to become privy to it.

I could only guess who I had inadvertently shared that information with. The list might include interests who were not against using violence as a tool to eliminate competition. Roca operatives had met violent ends before. Though there were always logical explanations for their demise, we on the inside knew that big money could lead to big trouble. Anyway, even if no one was looking for me, I wanted to put some distance between myself and all that was the Roca Group. Havana and the Marina were too close to that for my current mindset.

We arranged to meet the next day at noon at a café on the main street of San José de Las Lajas, a town on the local route between Havana and Matanzas. She described the car she would be driving, after which any trepidation I may have had over not spotting her was dispelled.

When I opted to use the rest stop for telephoning, I knew there was a chance that the bus would go on without me, and it did. I was traveling light with only my sling bag so there was nothing lost but the comfort of the Fiat Supercruiser. There was a direct route from where I was in Artemisa to where I was to meet Fawn on route to Matanzas, the location of the Children's hospital. Buses would go through Havana, which I wanted to avoid. But buses aren't the only way to travel if you have U.S. dollars in Cuba.

The only decision I had to make was would I find a hotel here in Artemisa and get to San Jose tomorrow, or find a taxi, get on the road, and get there tonight. One look around was enough to sway my decision. There was always a chance it might be better in San Jose, but it sure couldn't be worse.

Around every bus station there is a collection of illegal taxis – basically men who happen to have cars who are looking to earn a few U.S. dollars. A small town like this would rarely see a customer wielding negotiable currency, so I would have my pick of the fleet. I returned to the station and spotted two likely *guajiros* standing next to a refurbished '57 Chevy. I decided that would be my chariot. We agreed on a price and were off on the three-hour ride to my rendezvous point with Fawn.

Most Cubans are surrendered to the deprivation of luxury items, but human nature is human nature, and the Dollar Shops cater to those who aren't. Of course locals must be willing and able to illegally collect U.S. dollars. If they can meet that challenge, a myriad world of goods opens up to them. Legally, the Dollar Shops are designated for tourists, but why would a tourist buy an air-conditioner? The government obviously wants dollars, and they aren't beyond getting the population to help collect them.

A few years ago, after the subsidies from the Soviet Union dried up and trade with Eastern Europe along with it, Cuba found itself without access to hard currency. Up to that point, a Cuban could go to jail if he or she were caught with U.S. Dollars, but that had to change. Fidel decided to legalize possession of American currency. Cuba established what became known as the Dollar Shop. It was the most effective way of becoming part of the flow of money from the newly established tourist business and from Cubans living abroad.

At first, the Dollar Shops sold only luxury items like one could buy at Duty Free shops in airports. But the government's need for internationally accepted currency caused them to begin to offer a broader and broader range of ordinary goods in exchange for U.S. dollars.

Over the past few years, these Dollar Shops have called more and more attention to the shortcomings of the current Cuban system of finance. Cubans with government connections have access to U.S. dollars and can buy items that ordinary Cubans cannot. Though there is a rationing system in force, it only grants minimal amounts of food each month. If an ordinary Cuban wants to supplement his diet or that of his family, or purchase other needed goods, he must find access to money from tourists. Even if he is a doctor, who in Cuba earns only a minimum in pesos, he must drive a taxi to accumulate U.S. dollars. Taxi driving is one of the more wholesome occupations that have burgeoned as Cubans' desperation has increased. Sadly, and understandably, prostitution has become a major source of dollars for some in the recent Cuban situation.

I couldn't say whether the ride was eventful or not because I slept in the back seat the whole way. I do clearly remember the smile on my chauffeurs' faces when they saw a $100 bill and heard the words, *"quédese con el cambio."* I tried to imagine the Dollar Shop acquisition to which my C-note was to be applied, but I aborted the fantasy.

The hotel they deposited me at was known as the best in San José de las Lajas and would probably rate half a star in the U.S. I had gone the fleabag route before. As long as I knew it was for a limited time, I had no problem with that. This was one step above that category so I actually felt fortunate.

In keeping with the mood of the evening, I bought three bottles of the generic Cuban beer known as Claro. I spent most of the time sitting out on the patio of my room either dozing or listening to the radio. The rest I spent staring at the piece of paper on which I had written what had been divulged on the recording device:

(1) The basic tobacco option deal
(2) The basic tobacco deal with the return of Vuelta Abajo fields
(3) The free-market entry deal
(4) Fidel's health
(5) Someone called El Jugador working with Raoul
(6) Enrique Magelinos and Eric Lynne working together

The time passed as it always has a way of doing. I was older but no wiser. I figured I had a lot of days left in my account, so wasting one was okay. Of course I was proceeding like I was right about that.

Chapter 28

The Mirador Café was as good a place to wait as any other in San José. As noon pulled up, so did a pre-rev white Chrysler Imperial convertible with a flashy continental tire on the trunk and an even flashier blond at the wheel. This was definitely the Fawn I remembered. The moment I saw her, I knew I had made a good decision. Holding sick children's hands didn't seem to fit into the photo, but if Fawn was up to it so was I.

I had always been a little jealous of Fawn Brisco. She had the body of a model, while I had the body of a hooker. She usually had her blond hair piled up on her head, but when she let it fall, a photo of her wouldn't look out of place on the cover of any fashion magazine. When her voice came out of her mouth, it was a few octaves higher than you expected. It was a little bit shocking, but mostly it affected people taking her seriously. I didn't know her well enough these days to know how it went with her being a lawyer, but I'd heard that she was successful. I certainly knew that she was smart enough to be one of the best. When we were in school together, her name always appeared somewhere above mine whenever exam results were posted – that is except for foreign languages – then and still my forte.

Two attractive women in a classy car with their hair blowing in the wind managed to attract all the machismo attention that rural Cuba had to offer that day. It was diverting and it was fun. Fawn and I talked nothing heavy: old times, fashion, movies, and of course, men. The ride seemed to erase my blackboard and that's just what I had in mind. When we got near Ciudad de los Pioneros, we stopped and checked into what I assumed to be a standard local hotel. The management insisted on giving us a lovely suite in what appeared to be an even lovelier hotel. The suite had a bedroom with two big four-poster beds and a sitting room with a couch and table. Fawn told me that her volunteer work wasn't the stimulus for the special treatment. Her father had procured some cutting-edge medical technology for the nearby clinic in the form of a visual imaging radiograph, and the hotel owner was on the board of the clinic. She had paid the price for being the daughter of an international fugitive, so I guess she had the perks coming when there were some. I was very willing to share in the wealth.

The next four or five days are hard to describe. When problems arise, they always seem to be absolute, but really they are relative. All you need to make that discovery is to find someone who has either worse ones, or more of them than you do. Well, these innocent victims of the largest nuclear incident since Hiroshima and Nagasaki had problems that were both more and worse. I had been tricked by circumstance into an activity that put my relatively ridiculous drama into perspective.

Sometime during those days, I was doing a jigsaw puzzle with a twelve-year-old girl who had developed leukemia and was undergoing chemotherapy. One of the parts of the puzzle reminded me of Eric, and I drifted into some negative inner dialogue relating to his delaying our sexual reacquaintance. I wondered if he could possibly have known about the implant, and if that was the reason for the postponement. At that moment I looked over at my charge, and the world appeared a very unfair place, but this time not toward me.

Fawn and I spent only a little time alone together over those few days. In what time we did spend, it became obvious to me that she had really changed. Sure, she was a Brisco and wasn't going to be invisible wherever she went. Not only because of her name – her face, her body, and her vibrancy would always attract attention. But she had definitely deepened. Being around her made me wonder if I had. There were so many demands on our time that our evenings were spent quietly, and early bedtimes were the obvious choice. The night before we were scheduled to leave, we planned to have dinner and spend some personal time together.

We stayed up late that night drinking beer and talking about school memories and friends. We planned to sleep in the following morning. Our plans were disrupted by construction noises coming from the floor above us. The noises must have started shortly after sunrise because I had been tossing and turning for a couple of hours before I actually noted that the racket was happening above us. We both had the same reaction of burrowing under the covers with pillows on our heads.

The light from the window made it clear that it was morning, even though it felt like it should be about three hours into sleep. I looked out from my bunker. The room looked like a New England snow scene. The entire room was coated with a quarter inch of pure white dust. Sheetrock dust had apparently come through the vent in the ceiling and had been distributed around the room by the ceiling fan. I couldn't see my face and hair, but the rest of me that was exposed before I burrowed was similarly coated. Fawn peeked out, looked at me, and burst out laughing. I saw her and had the same reaction. Half of our faces and hair were as white as they would have been had we been spray-painted. I looked around the room and what could have looked like a disaster struck me with maximum hysterics.

I stood up on my bed with my head close to the ceiling and kept repeating, "I got to get this stuff off of me!" Fawn looked over at me from her bed and decided that the best way to help me out with my dilemma would be to dust me off with her pillow. She brought her pillow over, climbed onto my bed and yes, we ended up having a girls dorm pillow fight, complete with laughing and falling down and getting up and falling down again.

It only took a few minutes of laughing while swinging pillows to get exhausted. I suggested we take photos of the scene to get some kind of compensation from the hotel. Fawn agreed and disappeared into the bathroom. She came out looking perfect, making me laugh even harder. Fawn wasn't about to have a photo of herself taken unless she looked perfect – even if the purpose of the photo was to demonstrate the mishap.

We both eventually laughed our way to the office to explain the situation. I still had white dust in my hair and on half of my face. Someone would have certainly threatened to sue them for cleaning bills and potentially ruined stuff, but we were having too much fun to feel that we had been violated. The hotel manager apologized profusely, gave us another room away from the construction, and comped our whole stay including a great breakfast later that morning. The whole episode, along with my experiences with the kids, was the best medicine that I could have had.

Sitting at breakfast, I wanted to express my appreciation for the opportunity of the past few days, but I never got around to it. They say, "Into each life some rain must fall." I can handle that. But I don't think all the Chernobyl children at the hospital could have prepared me for the downpour that Fawn was about to drop on me.

"So it's been how many years since your dad came here?" I asked.

"Ten . . . I think ten years."

"Do you think the pressure on him is easing up?"

"In some ways," she answered, "but in others it's gotten worse."

"How so?"

"I guess maybe it's because he's getting older – every once in a while he talks about going home. I don't think he means Detroit or maybe not even the U.S., but more like a place where he can be safe. You know what I mean? It must be the same for your dad. He's even older than my dad isn't he?"

I thought I hadn't heard her right, but I knew I had. What did she mean? Fawn knew that dad had died years before. I didn't want to embarrass her by reminding her, but I didn't see any other way. "I guess you forgot that my father died in a car accident in Havana six years ago."

I was looking down when I told her. I wasn't feeling melancholy or anything like that. I just didn't want to make her feel any more awkward then necessary. I looked up after I finished and she laughed. It was the most unlikely response possible to what I had said. I was so taken aback that I got a little angry. I wasn't really angry, but at the moment it was the only emotion that I could plug into the absurdity of her actions. "What is there to laugh about?" I stammered. "*Your* father's a fugitive, but at least *he's* still alive!" I said, sounding to myself like a self-righteously indignant teenager.

"I didn't remember your being such a good actress Callie," she said, having curtailed her laughing but still definitely smiling.

"And I didn't remember your being so insensitive," I retorted sharply.

"Callie . . . I *know* – dad told me *years* ago. He doesn't tell me everything, but he certainly told me that your dad's accident was faked to keep him from getting nailed by the CIA."

Chapter 29

This was not a route that Magelinos' Oldsmobile frequently traveled. So it was neither a coincidence nor was it fatigue that supplied the real impetus for his choosing this particular spot to change drivers and fill up with gas. The junction where he stopped was the turn-off to Playa Girón.

All Cubans knew about the events of April 1961, but few had actually come to visit either the sight of the ill-fated CIA invasion carried out by the Cuban-exile brigade from south Florida, or the small museum that marks its location. This was not the case for Magelinos. He had not only been a participant in the actual fighting that took place that day, but in the weeks that followed, as an officer in the DGI, he helped coordinate the rounding up and incarceration of all probable sympathizers. Those were weeks in which almost all resistance to the revolutionary government was obliterated. Cuba may have called the events of that spring "Her finest hour," but for Enrique Magelinos, arresting and torturing political prisoners certainly didn't feel to him like his finest hour, even though it represented a widely celebrated embarrassment of the colonialists to the north.

Most people blame the Kennedy administration for the whole fiasco, but actually President Eisenhower first approved the program in early 1960 with the establishment of training camps in Guatemala. A former member of Castro's government, Jose Cardona, who saw himself as the rightful president, led the anti-Castro Cuban exiles in the United States.

Kennedy eventually did authorize the Bay of Pigs invasion in February 1961. The Bay was a swamp in remote southern Cuba – a place that would be unwatched by local authorities. The plan involved air strikes, paratroopers, and more than 1,000 well-armed invaders hitting the beach at night. The eventual list of mishaps was lengthy, including the use of disguised old World War II planes that proved entirely ineffective.

After killing more than 100 invaders, the Cuban Army took the rest as prisoners. The prisoners were not released for almost two years. Eventually, after a trade of millions of dollars worth of baby food and medicine was negotiated, they were released.

As Magelinos' car sat under the canopy that covered the gas pumps, Eric awoke to see him about 100 feet away at the crest of some low hills that bordered the gas station. He was looking south toward the swamps of the Zapata Peninsula, and yes of course – to the Bay of Pigs.

They were only an hour from Cienfuegos now. At Aguada de Pasajeros they turned off the thruway and headed south toward the Caribbean. It had only been two weeks since Eric's last trip to Cienfuegos and that day of sailing with El Jugador on the magnificent bay. That day his principals and his future met a cusp that began to dictate all his actions.

It had been years since Magelinos had been to Cienfuegos, but for him too it was a bit of a homecoming. In the mid-seventies he had done a tour of duty there as an information officer. It was his responsibility to escort visiting Soviet dignitaries around the port and the adjacent Naval base. During the last few minutes of their drive, Enrique reassumed his role as guide and told Eric about the port. It was Cuba's largest for shipping sugar, with a capacity of 1,200 tons an hour. He also entertained Eric with his personal recounting of the times when Soviet ships came in for servicing – many even being missile-carrying subs. He reminisced about the Soviets building a base there for both R&R for their sailors and a facility for repairing Akula-class nuclear-powered ballistic missile submarines. Pride didn't let him add that Moscow had abandoned the project after strong objections from the U.S.

Their destination was the small village of Perche. It was a ferry ride across Cienfuegos Bay, where the villa of El Jugador lay in the shadows of Jagua Castle. There were few Cubans who lived as well as El Jugador. He was a guest of the state. The arrangement he was afforded was far different from that which was allowed to Roger Brisco. Brisco's was one of expedience. El Jugador's was one of appreciation and honor.

Eric spent the ferry ride standing at the rail trying to use his body as an airfoil to catch the coolness of the wind as an escape from the heat and humidity. It was much as his newly-found mentor had done on the ferry ride *he* had taken that night 35 years before. But there would be no flotilla appearing this day, only thoughts of Callie.

The ferry deposited its charges and their car on the dock which led to the only road past the castle and through the village to Carolina del Sud, El Jugador's residence. They turned into the hedged circular driveway and were met by a smiling El Jugador. With him were an even older man with thinning red hair, and a young woman whose hair was in the full bloom of color that the old man's probably was at one time.

"Eric, good to see you so soon after our last visit. Is Enrique Magelinos of the DSE also to be my guest?" Eric knew that he was expected to be arriving alone. He contributed his assurance that he would explain the presence of his companion. El Jugador's arm around his shoulder accompanied by his hardy laugh served to postpone the subject as well as any verbal encapsulation might have done.

El Jugador introduced the two with him. "They are my relatives and my comrades, not my employees. I wanted them to be out here to greet you. It was meant as a gesture of my hospitality, not an expression of my affluence. Here we all carry our own luggage."

While on the way to their bedrooms, they were led on a brief tour of his home. The young woman and her grandfather lived in a small cottage next to the house and had known El Jugador since the woman was a child. Eventually Eric was left alone. It was not to be a comfortable solitude.

There were three things he knew had to be discussed. The first was the disappearance of Callie Barton. The second was the inclusion of Enrique Magelinos in the plan. The third was the handling of Wyndam Otnabe, always a potential problem, and now even more so since Callie had gone missing.

The travelers found the comfort of the villa to be a pleasant change from the austerity of the caves and the camping out in the halls of the deserted embassy before that.

El Jugador's comrades attended to both the household responsibilities and making Eric and Magelinos feel like they were honored guests. It wasn't until evening that the three met again. Each of them knew that the delicious dinner of paella was not the common denominator that brought them together. They played that game graciously until Eric could no longer repress the questions that had never been very far from his consciousness.

"There are some things we must talk about Señor Jugador," Eric said with a sense of urgency.

"I agree. And are there to be three of us now discussing these matters, or are there to be even more?" El Jugador said, implying that anything Magelinos heard might shortly be available to his superiors at the DSE and who knows who else. "After all, our friend Enrique here was only assigned to keep watch over you and make sure you stayed out of sight."

"Please allow me to explain my position señor," Magelinos interjected with his customary humble dignity. He went on to candidly describe his growing doubts about current political policy and what he concluded when he became aware of El Comandante's illness. He left it to Eric to bring up the subject of the implant, but he did allude to his suspicion that a U.S. government agency might be involved with Otnabe. Everything Magelinos had learned had come by way of the implanted device. Eric had never either confirmed or denied any of it. That was for El Jugador to do. That was why Magelinos was there.

"This is all very interesting Enrique, but where is the young lady, Miss Barton? Why has she not come with you?" El Jugador said, seemingly preoccupied with the subject of

Callie to the point that even his attention for Magelinos' explanation wavered.

"That's something else we have to talk about," Eric interjected. "Miss Barton, Callie – is gone." Eric went on to explain about the implant and Callie's probable psychological state. "That's how Enrique found out about Fidel and the plan – it was monitored by General Gomez when I described everything I knew to Callie. Enrique didn't have to tell me he knew – but he did tell me. He wants to put in with us, and I brought him here so that you could make that decision."

"It seems to me," El Jugador countered, "that even before we talk about Señor Magelinos and his allegiances, we should discuss how to keep you alive long enough to act as our negotiator. After all, Mr. Otnabe now knows that your fidelity to the Roca Group is definitely in serious question. Maybe you should tell us exactly what you said to Miss Barton so Enrique and I can assess just what level of danger you're in."

To the best of his ability, Eric recounted his conversation with Callie at the cave. When it came to divulging that he wanted this to be his last deal, he balked. It was not the image he wanted to portray to this man whom he respected. It was more a decision of pride rather than one of manipulation, and he let it govern the moment.

These three were playing a very dangerous game and each knew it all too well. The tension in the room increased in stages – first with Magelinos' explanation, and then with Eric's. It was clearly time for El Jugador to voice his views on what had been said, but instead he called Deborah, his niece, and she brought out dessert – vanilla ice cream with fresh fruit topping. After she served the three men, she served herself some and sat down at the table with them. Deborah appeared to be in her early twenties, quite striking in appearance, and along with her red hair had the facial contours and the blue eyes of many of the Cubans that had come from northern European countries.

It was obvious that El Jugador had prearranged this interlude, but it still played as well as if it had been spontaneous. The conversation went to matters of literature, art, and most of all, sports. The young lady was an ardent fan of baseball, as are many Cubans. At one point she even rushed out of the room and returned with a picture that she had framed of a young El Comandante, the pitcher, wearing a baseball uniform in a Latin American stadium. According to her, he had quite a curveball. Eric noticed that when Deborah talked she addressed everyone present, but her look was toward him. She was flirting, and he was not immune.

The mood lightened to such a degree that everyone present managed to have seconds in dessert and the weighty subjects that certainly would eventually return were obfuscated for a time. Eric watched, fascinated with the artistry of El Jugador. He began to see how this man had managed to stake out such a privileged position in the hierarchy of the communist government of a country of which he was not even a national. After a while, the magnet in the smiling eyes of the woman and the enthusiasm of all concerned relaxed Eric. He soon became energetically involved in both the comparison between U.S. and Cuban baseball and the exchange of flirtatious glances.

It was in the spirit of this lightened mood that, during a pause in the four-way conversation, Eric said to El Jugador, "On my last visit, most of our time was spent on your sailboat. I never got around to asking something that I'm curious about. Perhaps it was because our discussions were more formal and certainly more political. At any rate, why did you name your villa Carolina del Sud? I thought from your accent that you were from New York?"

"Does it still show after all these years?" El Jugador began with a chuckle. "Yes, a difficult accent to lose after having been a product of the New York City school system. If you allow me to digress a bit, I promise I will answer your question," El Jugador went on as Eric nodded his approval.

"The education style of the Cold War decade that I grew up in was a heavy serving of science and math with a side order of graduate young. The aim was to become an astrophysicist so that you could help develop the next generation nuclear weapon. Skipping grades was the fashion if a youngster had the IQ, and at 140, mine weighed more than I did."

After a slight pause for a sip of water, he continued. "My family had a country house on a lake in Putnam County, New York. We spent summers there and I caught my infection for sun and water during those times. My gifts leaned more toward words than numbers, so I eventually became a lawyer. I worked for various lobbying groups until I found a lucrative position as attorney for the HGIA, the Hotel and Gaming Industry Association.

"My affinity for swimming and boats went unsatisfied during my years as a city dweller, until my opportunity to live in Miami and then Cuba brought it back to the surface. From then on I swam almost every day of my life. Whether it was in a pool, a lake, a gulf, or an ocean, I swam, and I made sure my daughters learned to swim as well. When my youngest daughter was three, I made her promise to swim in all the oceans of the world. Later I'm sure she realized that the polar oceans were exempt from the promise. Well, she made that promise, and she kept it.

"So my friend, your question about the naming of my house has a very simple answer. It is an answer that has now become time for you to hear directly from me, before you discover it elsewhere." El Jugador looked squarely at Eric, and with a smile remotely recognizable at the corners of his mouth he continued, "The villa is named for my daughter Caroline – I believe that you call her Callie."

With the surprise still etched on Eric's face, Harris Barton began to recount the story of his friendship with Fidel, the necessity for his emigration to Cuba, and the greater necessity of keeping his existence unknown to Callie for her personal safety. In addition to his impersonal hopes for his adopted homeland, he revealed his personal longing to be reunited with his daughter.

As a key word in a crossword puzzle can break the logjam that its absence created, this astounding piece of information sewed together, for Eric, some of the unknown parts of the drama in which he had become a principal player.

The rest of the evening was spent on the covered patio sipping the evening air that blew in over the bay. Hours passed listening to Harris Barton and Enrique Magelinos recount each of their personal versions of the recent history of Cuba. They each had come to the eventual conclusion that it was time for what, at one time, would have been considered unthinkable – to embrace the rest of the world's economic system and adopt it for Cuba.

"You might be surprised to hear that I traveled to New York City in 1955," commented Enrique. "Something happened while I was there that affected my view of my country for many years. It also raised my hopes that sometime, somehow, a person would come along and set things right. I was in a restaurant on the upper west side of Manhattan and an older man came up to me and said that I looked familiar to him. He asked me where I was from. I hesitated for a moment, and said I was from Medellín, Colombia. You see, my view of my image as a Cuban was that of a bartender in a gambling casino for wealthy Americans. I have not been back to the U.S. since, but I have traveled in other countries. Since January 1, 1959 I have never again denied that I am a Cuban."

"My friend," Barton said warmly, "you certainly were in a position to know that although, as you say, the revolution brought back pride to the people, there was little tolerance for those who disagreed. Some of those who became part of the one million that fled to Miami were my friends. You can't forget that had they stayed, many would have been either shot or sentenced to long prison terms."

"Yes, Señor Barton, in this you are correct," Magelinos acknowledged. "I'm sure you've heard the argument that after your war of 1776, numbers of Americans who were friends of the British opted to set up lives in Canada, rather than stay with the newly-formed government where they may have been in danger. But even that comparison to the Cuban exodus has never made me feel comfortable. I have also never been comfortable with the concept that one person has the right to take another's life for having an opposing political view of how their country

192

should be run. Removing illiteracy and providing free medical care is one thing; murder is quite another."

As the discussion continued, Eric observed that the position usually attributed to the displaced North American and liberated Cuban reversed. It was fascinating for him to listen to Barton defending the revolution to Magelinos' criticism. By the end of the evening, a new bond had been developed between these two men. Eric was right. All he had to do was bring them together. People of depth and quality have a way of recognizing each other.

Eric felt relief in being able to lose himself in this less personal political ideology – at least less personal for him. Thoughts of Callie were always on the periphery of his mind, but since no pleasure could be taken in them, better to take refuge in a view of the world more encompassing than his personal drama. If not that, perhaps fate was supplying him with a stand-in for his romantic fixation. He would not be above that kind of diversion this night.

In the minutes before sleep furrowed his fantasies into dreams, he wandered between thoughts of taking a casual walk to the cottage behind the house and wondering if a soft knock would come to his door. His fatigue wouldn't wait for a resolution, but the young red-haired woman had a stronger resolve. The knock came just before dawn.

In the moments after Eric awoke the next morning, he knew that it was time to call Otnabe. The charade of his disappearance had gone far enough. The purpose of going MIA was to bring Callie down to Cuba, but that was only the first step in a process. Now that she was here, it was time to proceed with the assignment of bringing Cuba into the free-market world and eventually into the family of democratic nations. "Yes," Eric thought, "Otnabe had to be convinced to back off and allow the transition to take place without interference." Eric knew it would not be an easy sell, but he had to try. El Jugador would know the best way to make contact.

It was a large sprawling house and Eric was unfamiliar with El Jugador's morning ritual. After wandering around both upstairs and downstairs, Eric's search for El Jugador ended on the small open-air patio that overlooked an overgrown vegetable garden. Barton was sitting in a patio chair with his feet up on the railing that faced the garden. He was flipping through some papers and laid them aside when he saw Eric approaching.

"Good morning Mr. Barton, or should I say Señor Jugador," Eric said quietly. "I hope I'm not disturbing you, but I need to contact Wyndam Otnabe from a secure and untraceable link-up. Can you help me with that?"

Barton looked past the top of his reading glasses at the man standing over him. He pointed to the chair opposite him and with a smile gestured for Eric to sit. "Yes, I can help you," Barton said after taking a long deep breath. "But before you make that call I would like to give you some advice on a subject that may be more in my field of expertise than yours. But even before that I would like to ask *your* advice on a matter that is more in the field of your expertise than mine.

"I recognize that it is almost time to invoke the assistance of *Big Brother*," Barton began. "The stage is all but set. Even though they are unaware, the decades-old aspirations of both the Miami Cubans and the U.S. Government are near to becoming a reality. Once it is underway, U.S. support for the transition could only be an asset for all concerned. If the U.S. would lend its support without getting greedy about the participation of American industrial interests, the process will go smoothly. I'm sure that you would agree that this is no time for partisan rankling. There are few if any world politicians who are unaware of the partisan nature of U.S. politics, and Raoul Castro is certainly not one of them.

"He wants U.S. support, but knows that for the success of our plan, U.S. entry into the process will have to be delayed until the 11th hour. Yes, before that there could be some back channel contacts, but they would have to be very secure and confidential. Raoul and I would like your suggestion of someone who would have high level connections in the U.S. intelligence community. Those connections would have to be able to act discretely and lend assistance only when asked. They would also be acting with incomplete information. To play that part would require a high level of autonomy, and we would have to have a great deal of confidence in whoever you might recommend."

Lynne suggested an ex-naval intelligence officer he knew and trusted completely to serve as contact person – one who had maintained just such connections – his father, Lt. Commander Malcolm Lynne, U.S. Navy, retired.

Barton agreed to have Eric approach his father with the idea. If the Commander agreed and actually knew of such individuals, he would be given the go-ahead to make contact. Eric was instructed on exactly what it was okay to divulge to his father, as well as what the Commander was to ask for in terms of assistance.

After a short pause in which Eric almost forgot his prior compulsion, Barton reminded him, "And what do you expect to accomplish by calling Otnabe? Now that he clearly sees you as an obstacle, he knows what he has to do. Your life may be in danger."

"I've known Wyndam for a long time. I've got to try to talk to him," Eric reasoned.

"Very well then. My cousin Jacob will help you. He repairs radio equipment and has access to one of the few private communications up-links left on the island."

The garage behind the cottage was where Cousin Jacob spent most of his time. From the outside it looked as does much of Cuba, surrounded by overgrown foliage and badly in need of a coat of paint. But inside it was a mass of diodes, transponders, digital readout displays, and other state of the art communications technology. Jacob obviously did a little more than repair radios.

"Career Management, good morning."

"Wyndam Otnabe please."

"Company name please."

"This is the Postman."

The call was somewhat of a surprise to Wyndam Otnabe, but at the stage of an operation when the number of variables began to exceed one's ability to correlate them, one had to expect anomalous events.

"Eric, I'm honored that you finally see fit to include me in your loop. Where are you?"

"Let's leave my location out of it for a while. Who's really your client Wyndam? Is there some U.S. government shit going on here?"

"I'm not at liberty to tell you that Eric," Otnabe said, knowing that the only client Eric didn't know about was Otnabe himself. "But I can assure you that if you had carried out your part of this operation, you would have been a candidate for a huge bonus. It still might not be too late," he said, knowing it probably was.

"What were you thinking when you bugged Jelinda?" Eric countered.

"This operation is very complicated, Eric. I have an important client," he said glibly. "I have to represent the Roca Group to that client, and that requires me to know what's going on. You certainly weren't telling me, so I had to go dirty. You know the game. Why were you incommunicado for a month"?

"Okay Wyndam, what do you want?"

"What do *I* want?" Otnabe responded, trying to act incredulous. "That's a curious question from someone who has gone solo. I want what I've always wanted – what's best for the Roca Group and all of its people. You used to be one of them you know."

"Let's cut the crap, Wyndam. What is it you want? If two-and-a-half million isn't enough, how much is?"

"You know as well as anyone Eric, that it's only enough if I can't get more. Can I get more?"

"Listen Wyndam, I think there's something going on here that we have to take into account. This country is finally going to have a chance to get out from under. I think we can get our money and not ruin it for them."

This was clearly not the voice or thinking process of a Roca Group operative. Becoming personally involved with internal affairs of any country for other reasons than the success of the operation was against basic Roca Group policy. Any moralizing would be an inhibiting factor, and there was too much at stake here.

"We've known each other for a long time, Eric. What would you suggest I do?" Otnabe said, hoping he could get Eric to divulge his location.

"If I can find Jelinda, I think we can swing this deal. If I get you three mil instead of two-and-a-half Wyndam, will you stay out of it? I want this to go through."

Now Otnabe had confirmed for certain that he no longer had an agent on the scene. If the Postman's statements on the tape weren't evidence enough, then these last ones were. It was clear that he either had to send Miranda to Cuba to supervise the operation, or go himself. Violence was rarely a necessary recourse of Roca Group operations, but in this case the Postman would have to be eliminated. There was no avoiding that unpleasantness. Otnabe knew that if he was in Cuba when it happened, there might be a connection made. Better send Miranda and Manny and stay a safe distance from anything wet.

Otnabe didn't waste any time in making his next move. It would not be prudent to involve any new personnel. Roger Brisco was already involved and fully incentivized. The word was that when Brisco first arrived in Cuba, his stolen funds arrived with him, at least those that were not deposited in the Swiss bank accounts that Roca arranged for him. In an effort to establish himself and make the kind of friends that would grease the wheels of whatever he was up to, Brisco began by sprinkling cash about the island. His sprinkling turned to showering and eventually to pouring. By the end of his first year in Cuba, his ability to get favors was almost unlimited.

This would work perfectly for Otnabe. He would confirm his efforts to not only get Brisco asylum in France, but to get him full citizenship. Brisco certainly knew the kind of person that would do the deed for the right price, and Otnabe was feeling very generous about now.

Yes, Otnabe thought. *Brisco would be the best person to arrange for the retirement of the Postman. He had enough at stake in this operation that there would be no leaks and no trail. Something unexpected might arise, so better have Brisco keep General Gomez handy also. Miranda could handle the liaison. She was ice when it came to nationalistic sentiment. She could take care of the operation, and Manny would handle Brisco and Gomez.*

"Let's meet and talk Eric. Maybe we can work something out. Where are you? I can be in 90M by tomorrow."

"I have to sit with this one Wyndam. Jelinda has split and I don't know how to read that. If I want to set up a meeting, I'll make contact this afternoon."

"I'll look forward to your call, Eric. I'm sure we can work something out that's mutually beneficial." The receiver of Otnabe's telephone never hit its receptacle. Within a few minutes he was connected with another telephone in Havana. This one was attached to the wall behind a booth at La Flora artisan's workshop in Miramar. He knew it might be a day or so before he received a response from Roger Brisco.

Chapter 30

It didn't take long for Fawn Brisco to realize that she had dropped a bomb on me. Having been an intelligence operative for eight years didn't even begin to imbue me with the capacity that I would have needed to calmly absorb the news that my father was alive. With her last words still resounding in my ears, I almost ran out of the hotel's breakfast room and closed myself in the bedroom of our suite. After an hour or so, the shock lessened, and I came out of the bedroom ready to receive any other details that Fawn could fill in. She was sitting on the arm of the couch that faced the window.

"Where is he, do you know?" I asked, speaking to her back.

"I don't know Callie, maybe my dad knows. We could call him," Fawn answered helpfully as she turned around slowly to face me.

Fawn must have noticed that after hearing her answer I was staring blankly at the wall. She came over, took my hand, and led me back to the couch. She proceeded to fill in the few details that she had omitted – the only ones she knew. The story still remained mostly sketchy – CIA, faked accident, rumors of collusion . . . nothing much to go on.

"I have to think about all this first. Why didn't he want me to know?" I asked rhetorically with a mixture of self-pity and anger.

"He probably wanted to protect you," Fawn guessed. "Listen Callie, let's go back to Havana together. Dad knows everything that goes on. He'll help you find him if that's what you want."

"I thought I couldn't go to Havana, but right now I can't remember why," I said, confused. "Okay, I guess we should go. Should we call Roger first?"

"No, let's just go."

Fawn had no more information to add. Since Callie couldn't forget about the subject, she did the next best thing. She reminisced about her father by telling stories of their time together almost all the way back to the Hemingway Marina.

"Tell the story about the fishing boat," Fawn chirped in her high-pitched voice as though she were excited to hear it. If Fawn was sensitive enough to care as much as she did for Chernobyl children, she certainly understood what Callie needed about now.

Everyone Callie had ever known, Fawn included, had heard her tell the story of fishing with her father on the "party boat." But she loved to tell it anyway. Party boats were popular during the Batista times, when gamblers from the U.S. were plentiful in Cuba. Large fishing boats would take 50 or 60 tourists out past the bay into the open waters for a day of fishing. The boats would supply all the tackle, bait, food, and of course beer, so the trip was not relegated to ardent fishermen. Plenty of men who wanted either to get away from their wives for a day or were bored of sitting on the beach would go along.

"One of the parts I remember the best," Callie began, "was the ride out to open waters. Everyone going would meet on the pier at 5:00 a.m. It was dark and really mysterious to me. The ride would sometimes get rough and some guys that were either drunk the night before or just unused to the motion of a boat would end up at the rail. I was 11 years old but I never had that problem. Actually, I still don't. Anyway, dad was really proud of me for being what he called 'a match for the sea.'

"Some gamblers love to gamble on anything, and the boat had a set-up for them to make the trip more fun and make some extra money for the captain. It was called the ship's pool. Everyone on board who wanted to get in on it contributed ten dollars. After the captain took his fee off the top, there was around $500 left for whoever caught the biggest fish.

"One of the things I liked the best was that I was the only kid on board, and the only girl. Dad put both of us into the pool and that made me feel like I was one of the guys. There was a lot of joking and horsing around that went on and even a little fishing. I didn't catch anything until about halfway through the trip when I caught a whopper. Dad let me pull it in by myself. It took me about 15 minutes to get it in. When it was finally on board, the deck hand that was in charge of the pool weighed my fish. A big group had gathered around because it looked like I might be a pool winner. He announced the weight, and it was twice as much as any other fish caught that day.

"I was so tired and having so much fun that I didn't really care that I probably would win. I was 11 years old. What did the pool mean to me? After a few minutes someone shouted out that the fish was a lingbelly, kind of an ocean catfish. That started a big argument.

"One of the rules of the pool was that lingbellies didn't qualify for biggest fish because they were bottom feeders. The argument lasted for ten minutes mainly because a lot of the guys were a little tipsy. Some of those guys really wanted me to win and some didn't think it really was a lingbelly.

"There was so much noise that the captain finally came down from the bridge and settled the matter. He ruled that it wasn't a qualifying fish and eventually someone else went on to win the pool. I had one of the best times of my life. I loved pulling in the big non-fish, and I loved all the hubbub and the attention. I didn't care about the pool, but I did care about having such a great day with my dad."

When we got to the Marina, Fawn had come home, but I had no classification for my whereabouts. It felt like I was floating, avoiding running into one part of my past, and considering a rendezvous with another. At least I had some momentum now. I would ask Roger Brisco for a lead as to where my father might be. Fawn went into her father's study and explained the situation in private. When they came out, he told me that he would be glad to talk with me.

"I'm shocked that you didn't know, Callie. I hope you don't blame Fawn for her slip of the tongue. She couldn't possibly have suspected," Brisco said sympathetically.

"Do you know where he is, Roger?" I asked, ignoring politeness.

"You know I only met your father once, and that was during that unfortunate episode with the nuclear power plant, the one that Fidelito, Castro's son, was trying to coordinate. Raoul introduced me to your father as someone who might have information about contacts for the missing electronic components. Wasn't your friend Lynne involved in that project too?" Brisco fabricated. "How is he anyway?"

"He's somewhere on the island," I answered absentmindedly. "Have you ever heard anything about where my dad might live?"

"Now that I think about it, perhaps your friend Eric might know. From what I remember, they maintained contact for some reason or other. Maybe we can locate Eric and ask him. I'd be glad to help you with that, but you probably know how to get in touch with him already."

"I'd rather not," I said hesitantly, "but I guess if I had to I could. He's traveling with an ex-DSE man that I could probably trace."

After we talked for a while, it was clear that he had no specific information to add about the man he knew as Harris Barton. What I didn't realize at the time was that it was not really about my father that Brisco wished to converse.

"Feel free to use my private telephone. It doesn't go through the switchboard. We'll start from there and see where it leads us," Brisco added cheerily, his helpful demeanor not having raised any suspicion whatsoever with my otherwise preoccupied thinking process.

I told Brisco that I would call later but that I would like to spend some quiet time in his study. When I emerged, Fawn and he were drinking coffee by the broad window that overlooked the magnificent vista of the Gulf of Mexico. As I approached the table, the unavoidable glint of the sun on the crests of the waves caused me to walk past the table and stand with my face next to the glass. In those few sea-calmed minutes, the tears that had been collecting in my sadness found their way to my eyes, and for the first time since I had heard the news, I wept.

Fawn's personal experience with her own father allowed a deeply sympathetic reaction to my release of emotion. She came up behind me and with her hands on my shoulders, contributed some words that she thought might act to soothe.

I was unaware that Roger Brisco, harboring a very different sentiment, was looking incredulously at the scene, wondering what stroke of good fortune brought Lynne's location to his doorstep. He knew that patience, and not that much of it, was all the effort he would have to make to locate his quarry. Only hours before, Brisco had talked to Wyndam Otnabe about their amended agreement, now involving not only asylum, but actual French citizenship. When Fawn and I arrived, he had just gotten off the phone with General Gomez. Brisco offered, and Gomez accepted, a significantly increased cash incentive for his services over the next few days. What Brisco didn't know, and Arturo Gomez was certainly not about to tell him, was that whatever he agreed to do, it would be altered to meet new criteria. It would also be immediately reported to Raoul Castro.

"Eric might be in Cienfuegos at the residence of one of Fidel's friends. The one he calls El Jugador. Do you know him Roger?" I asked.

"I've heard of him, but we've never met," Brisco answered. "Do you know his real name?"

"No, but I can find out where his villa is located. I have a good contact in Cienfuegos." Out of habit, I declined calling Red-Jack from Brisco's condo. I still suspected nothing, but my years of undercover service denied me the casual attitude that would have allowed such a breach of my security network. I assured Brisco that I would return before evening. I would again utilize the condo originally made available to me at the Marina.

As it turned out, Roger Brisco would need no additional information. He had contacts in Cienfuegos himself. He had heard of this El Jugador. He could supply enough information so that whoever he used for the job could locate Eric Lynne. Someone who could recognize Lynne would be best, and he knew who that someone might be. The effort would be a small price to pay for Otnabe's irreversible commitment to their arrangement. The French Riviera had always been one of Roger's favorite vacation spots.

It seemed like it had been more than a week since I had left the white-clad condo. I knew that showing up here was a risk, but somehow I didn't care. As far as I was concerned, most of the worst things that could have happened had already happened. It was an indulgent attitude, but I didn't care about that either. I knew I should have been glad that Dad was alive, but the sequence of events that preceded the discovery had painted my vision black.

As I lay down on the bed, emotional exhaustion began to overtake me. I hadn't cried myself to sleep since the day six years ago that I heard about dad's accident – or at least what I had been told was his accident. Here I was, Dad back in my life, and I was crying myself to sleep all over again.

The digital clock read 4:02 p.m. I had slept for only 45 minutes, and I knew as I awoke that sanity was reentering my body. I called Red-Jack, and a woman's voice gave the acceptance code and took the information for a call back. Nothing unusual – just had to wait. At 4:11 p.m., the phone rang and Red-Jack and I were phone-to-phone again.

"I need some information. Do you know a man known as El Jugador?"

"What is your interest in this man?" Red-Jack responded formally.

"I need to find the Postman, and I believe he is with that man." In all the years I had used his services, whether for communication or information, the procedure was always the same. I would make my request and Red-Jack would reply that he would work on it or that he wouldn't. He may have asked clarifying questions, but I could never remember a time that he would inquire as to my motives or my purpose for either the requested communication link or information. Without realizing it at first, I sensed that this phone call was different.

"If I can get that information for you, will there be anyone else made privy to it?" Red-Jack asked.

His inquiry alerted me to nothing short of extreme danger. If my brain couldn't assimilate it, the sharp, heated pain in my middle left no room for doubt. "What the hell is going on Red-Jack?"

"It's important that you answer my last question precisely," he responded coldly.

I didn't know why he needed to know, but I had no reason not to tell him. After I said that I was working on something with Roger Brisco and his daughter, he told me to stand by and he would call back in less than ten minutes. I tried to find out what was going on, but he had already hung up. I had never considered Red-Jack a player, but merely a source of technical and informational assistance. The piecework wages I paid him couldn't possibly be those of an operative. I had no idea what was going on, but at least I was out of my stupor and trying to figure it out.

While I waited, I shuffled nervously through my pockets to pass the time. I felt the piece of paper on which I had written my list. As I looked at it for the umpteenth time, I was staggered by what I had omitted.

(1) The basic tobacco option deal
(2) The basic tobacco deal with the return of Vuelta Abajo fields
(3) The free-market entry deal
(4) Fidel's health
(5) Someone called El Jugador working with Raoul
(6) Enrique Magelinos and Eric Lynne working together

Raoul would have to use Otnabe if Eric declined to sign on. That should have been (7)! That's what Eric told me at the cave. That was on the tape! Otnabe knows that now! He knows that! If he wanted in on the whole deal, all he would have to do is get rid of Eric. For the first time it was clear to me: Eric had nothing to do with the implant. He was the one in danger. My self-indulgence had clouded my vision. Eric was at risk, and I had been oblivious to everything except myself.

The phone rang again at exactly 4:30 p.m. and I instantly recognized the voice. It was a total non-sequitur to be speaking to Enrique Magelinos when I was expecting a call back from Red-Jack. He started talking before I could let the confusion begin to spiral.

"Miss Barton, the Postman is in grave danger. Do not give anyone information about him or his whereabouts. It is extremely possible that Roger Brisco is involved – consider him dangerous. Do you understand me Miss Barton?" Magelinos said in a voice that revealed that he was very strained.

"It's too late! Brisco knows! I just realized what I did. What's happening Enrique? Is he safe? Can I help?"

"Yes, Miss Barton, you can. Meet me on the steps where I picked you up last week.

"At what time, Enrique?"

"Go there right now and don't stop to talk to anyone else, not anyone. Stay in a hotel nearby, and we can meet at 9:00 a.m. tomorrow."

There wouldn't have been anyone to tell anyway. By the time I was off the phone, Brisco had left his apartment and had taken his daughter with him.

Just as Magelinos hung up the phone, he remembered something that he had to tell Callie. They had an ally that she didn't know about, General Gomez of the DSE. *No matter*, he thought. *I'll tell her in the morning.*

Chapter 31

Several hours after Otnabe's call, Carmen Miranda and Manny were on their way to 90M to supervise the elimination of the Postman. It was not difficult to hire a comfortable motor yacht to sail south from Miami, as long as it was clear that entering the twelve mile limit around Cuba was not being required. Miranda and Manny were the only passengers on board, and the three-and-a-half-hour trip went smoothly. They were transferred to a Cuban navy patrol boat sent by General Gomez of the DSE. It was necessary for the General to continue to cooperate, so as to remain a conduit for useful information. They were deposited at a discrete landing spot near Santa Cruz on the north coast. The entire trip from Miami to the island took four hours. They were in Havana at the General's office at DSE headquarters by evening.

When most Roca operatives negotiated their comings and goings from Miami to Cuba, they could use the charter flight from Miami. But for Miranda and Manny, a clandestine arrival was a necessity, especially under the circumstances. Even under normal conditions, four Roca operatives on the island at one time would surely present too obtrusive a presence.

I arrived at the museum at exactly 9:00 a.m. for my meeting with Enrique. The hotel I found the night before was adequate, but I don't think even the Nacional could have granted me a night's sleep. I was too tired to stand and wait, so I sat on the steps and lost awareness of the passage of time. If I had remained alert, perhaps I would have changed my location suspecting that something had gone wrong. When I realized that Magelinos was very late, it was almost ten o'clock. The Oldsmobile finally pulled up, and I was so relieved that I made the stupid mistake of rushing toward it. There was no time to change direction and correct my blunder. Two men jumped out of the car, one from the back seat and one from the shotgun seat. I was wrapped up and in-between them in the rear of the Oldsmobile before I could even struggle. My first reaction was to think that Magelinos had sold me out, but when I saw Gomez in the driver's seat I didn't know what to think. Did Enrique have a similar reception?

When I was brought in to DSE headquarters, I was told that Miranda and Manny had already arrived. I was ushered into the General's office on the third floor, far from the basement in which, unknown to me, Enrique was meeting with a very different reception.

I certainly was familiar with what the inside of institutional buildings in poor countries looked like. I had been in enough of them, rarely as an apprehendee though – usually in an attempt to get some favor or other. The amount of light-green paint sold to cover all the walls of all those buildings must have made someone a very rich man. Chairs have a way of wearing out or breaking after years of use and replacing them is rarely on the budget, so there are usually not more than one or two in any office. When there are women around, the men have to stand, creating an interesting dynamic.

Facing Manny and Miranda, whether standing or sitting, would be an awkward encounter. It was actually more like a confrontation, but I was finally in full professional mode and ready for combat. If the realization that in a non-professional state of confusion I had divulged information that could put Eric in harm's way didn't bring me to sobriety, the recent incident on the steps of the museum did.

"The situation here has gotten out of hand Callie. Wyndam is very concerned," Miranda said with an official tone.

"What are the two of you doing here, Miranda? And where is Major Magelinos?" I insisted.

"The Major is in the basement, in very different circumstances than these," General Gomez contributed from his place behind the desk in the far end of the room. His job had become more complex in the past few months. As assistant director of operations at DSE, his regular duties carried considerable responsibility, ranging from internal security matters to the supervision of the country's borders. Gomez had never been an operative in the field and certainly never a double agent. The age of 63 was a curious time in life to start.

Enrique Magelinos had an intimate familiarity with the basement of that very same office building, but he had never before been confined in one of its cells. His point of view, now having been reversed, allowed him a perspective about which he had long been curious. The situation would have been simpler had he been left alone with Gomez.

Standard protocol in the interrogation rooms was that there were two officers present with a detainee, so Gomez had to play the scene like it was real. Magelinos certainly had not been badly treated in the initial interview with the General. But he knew it was only a matter of time before the pressure on Gomez to produce the location of Eric Lynne could translate into a difficult situation for both of them.

Magelinos had arrived early for the scheduled rendezvous with Callie in downtown Havana. Just as he pulled up he was apprehended by two DSE officers and Arturo Gomez. The General put on a show of asking both the location of the meeting place with Ms. Barton and the whereabouts of Eric Lynne. Magelinos held back the information about Callie until hopefully she was no longer there. He then divulged it in order to keep the more critical data, Lynne's location, secret.

Enrique had been left alone for several hours in which reflection became his main source of perspective. However unpleasant it was to do so, he allowed his conscience to take him on an odyssey of remembrance back to the times in the early '60s. As an interrogator for Cuban Intelligence, he had ordered severe measures to extract information from those who were suspected of opposing the revolution. Those episodes were difficult for Magelinos to reconcile, but they also could be looked upon as ancient history. The drug and corruption purges and trials of 1989 could not.

These were the times when Magelinos first began to question the severity of military justice *for the good of the revolution.* But he had participated in it nonetheless. If it weren't for his friend Arturo, perhaps now he himself would be the recipient of that type of treatment. It would have been the same type that one who questioned El Comandante was known to have received. Magalinos was not a particularly literate man, but he was not unaware of the concept of Karma. Sitting in a jail cell could cause a person to take stock of his life even if he were in no real danger. Magelinos allowed himself to feel the situation as though he were. *Though pain might be the instrument of payment for my debt,* he thought as he sat on a wooden bench in the far corner of his solitary cell, *freedom from the burden of the guilt that I carry might be my reward.*

In the presence of several DSE officers, Magelinos had pretended to reticently divulge the place of his arranged meeting with Callie Barton. He knew that she would not be in any danger with Gomez there. She didn't know Lynne's whereabouts, so the worst Brisco could get Gomez to do was urge her to leave the country. And although she wouldn't know it, he would only be pretending to do that. After all, she had friends in high places, and jeopardizing her personal safety while in Cuba would not be prudent for anyone concerned, Brisco included.

Lynne was another case. He was a personal liability to Otnabe. Otnabe smelled a massive payday, and Lynne was the only obstruction. Neither the tobacco consortium nor the soon-to-be Raoul Castro government would have a problem with Lynne's newly-found conscience. Curiously enough, they were rivals on the same side. It was only Otnabe's grandiose aspirations with his accompanying greed that created the necessity for Lynne's removal.

"So what's the game now, get the Postman?" I wisecracked to Manny and Miranda.

"You know as well as I do that Eric has become a loose cannon. He's off on his own, and Wyndam can't allow that," Miranda stated factually.

"Well, that's going to be your problem, Miranda, because as far as I'm concerned I'm finished with all of you . . . again." I added the little extra *again*. I thought it was a nice touch. I knew what their next *suggestion* was going to be, and I knew I would have to pretend to go along. There was no way I was going to leave Cuba while Eric's life was in danger. I had a fleeting thought about the search for my father, but Eric's dilemma seemed so immediate that it left my mind almost as soon as it entered.

I sympathized with Magelinos' situation, but I was glad that I hadn't misjudged him. He probably knew where Eric was. Whether he told them or not, he was in trouble for sure. I had a gut feeling that he wouldn't give Eric up, and I winced to think of the implications of his loyalty. I knew I couldn't dwell on Enrique. There was nothing I could do to help him. I had to concentrate on getting to Eric before they did. I knew that neither of these Roca Group compatriots would be the perpetrator of Otnabe's proposed crime, but I also knew that if Roger Brisco was involved, probably some anonymous professional would be called in.

"Wyndam wants you to leave Cuba for a few days. He wants you to leave as soon as possible. It's his view that your presence here is complicating our solidifying this deal. When we have all the details confirmed, you can come back as the primary operative. I secured passage for you on the night charter. The General will arrange to have you driven to the airport," Miranda said matter-of-factly as she presented me with an envelope.

"Fuck Wyndam, Miranda!" I spat out as I grabbed the ticket she held out to me. "I'm leaving because I want to, not because your prick boss wants me out of here." I knew that my act wouldn't hold any credibility if I didn't bring up the money, so the last words I said before I stomped out of the office were an ultimatum. "If this deal works out I'm expecting to be paid what we agreed on in full, and if it doesn't, I at least want the money that fatso there took from my box. Don't fuck with me on this one." I looked over at Manny sitting on the couch. He was smiling. I had a momentary doubt about being believed and then I was in the hallway.

The police car was waiting for me outside the front door, and the driver started the motor when he saw me. He obviously knew that he was supposed to drive me to José Martí Airport because when I got in he just took off without saying a word. I knew that once I got to the international terminal, there would be someone watching to make sure I got on the plane, so I had to make my move en route. I had travelled to and from the airport many times, so I reviewed the route in my head. From where we were, he would probably drive south on Calzada del Cerro and at the roundabout take Avenida de la Independencia all the way to Terminal 2 at José Martí. It was about twelve miles, and with average traffic it would take about thirty minutes.

In an effort to make it all seem casual, I made some small talk with the uniformed sergeant who was driving. I had no idea what he had been told, but I had to proceed like he would cut me a little slack if I put forth the right situation. Women and bathrooms are usually a good percentage option, so I tried it at about the halfway point. He balked and confessed that he was told not to stop for any reason but to take me directly to the airport. I made a few attempts to persuade him, but nothing short of a gun was going to get him to pull over.

We were about five minutes from the airport when his car radio squawked a few times. I could make out the words he said when he answered, but when the voice came through the line, the response was unintelligible to me. It must have been audible to the sergeant because he said a whole bunch of "I understands" and "Yes sirs," and then he signed off. I couldn't tell if the call had something to do with me, but even if it did, I knew what I had to do.

We were approaching the exit for the airport. This would be the first place that he would have to slow down. I knew what was next and I prepared myself mentally for it. I put my satchel next to the door so that I could push it out ahead of me and hopefully fall on it as I exited the car. I had never jumped from a moving vehicle before, but I had seen it done in the movies. I figured I might get a little scratched up, but I had no choice. Enrique was sure to be paying a much dearer price than that.

I was prepared to go. When the light at the intersection we were approaching changed to red, I saw it as an opportunity to be saved from having to jump while the car was in motion. Unfortunately, by the time we slowed down, the light had already turned back to green. Instead of speeding up, the driver slowed down and came to a full stop right at the intersection. He glanced back at me, and without hesitating I was out the door. I chose to run across the opposite side of the highway so that the sergeant couldn't follow me with the car. He would have had to get out and run after me himself. As I looked back over my shoulder, I saw him on his radio phone. He was waving at me and smiling – smiling! I reached the cover of the buildings on the other side and stopped for a breath. I couldn't figure that one out, and I didn't want to take the time to try. I had somewhere I had to go.

Chapter 32

My experience told me that I had to get as close to the top of the pyramid as possible. The higher up you go, the safer it gets, and the more you can accomplish with the least interference. I had met Fidel several times, and on a few of those occasions thought that he even liked something about me. I had to dismiss the idea of trying to see him though. Not only was he very ill, but for practical purposes he was probably substantially out of the loop. Raoul was next in line, and approachable too. I had talked to him many times. Anyway, this plan was his baby, his and Eric's friend El Jugador's. I had to get to Raoul.

Miranda and Manny might already know I was on the loose in Havana, but could never guess that I would try to see Raoul. Raoul lived in the western suburb of Cubanacan near the International Conference Center. I had been to a reception at his house several years before. If I remembered correctly, it was a non-ostentatious suburban house only distinguishable from the others around it by a cyclone fence and a manned security gate.

Cabs are always easy to find in Havana. Their drivers are usually part of the police information network affiliated with the CDR. The Comités de Defensa de la Revolución is a system of neighborhood surveillance committees that report any questionable behavior to the authorities. It was probably the most effective crime prevention mechanism in Latin America and possibly the entire hemisphere. Opting to play it on the cautious side, I went into a corner market and offered a young man with a car some pesos to drive me to Cubanacan.

Raoul's suburban house had become more of an estate, spreading out to encompass the tracts on either side plus the houses that set on them. It was night by the time we arrived but the roadway was still fairly well lit. I asked my ride to drop me off across the street and down a ways from the booth that housed a security guard. As he drove off, I stood there alone in the near dark across from that booth. Unless the sergeant's smile was intended to indicate something else, I was a fugitive with questionable resources, but for some reason I felt confident and strong. My mission was clear and I was probably Eric's best shot at staying alive. That type of motivation always helps.

Raoul had been there from the beginning with Fidel and Che. Of the 82 men who made the perilous sea journey from Mexico to Cuba in November of 1956 aboard the Granma, these three were among the only 12 who survived the landing, betrayal, and ambush, and were eventually able to set up camp in the Sierra Maestra Mountains.

I had once heard him talk about his aversion to public exposure. He preferred to act behind the scenes and did his job as the commander of Cuba's armed forces in the shadow of his brother.

As I walked up to the security cubicle, I noticed that there were quite a few people behind the hedge in front of the house, maybe ten or twelve. It didn't look like a reception of any kind, more like the milling around in the aftermath of a meeting. I had no other alternative, so I walked directly up to the booth and told the corporal that I wanted to see Raoul. He seemed less obstructive than I would have expected, because he simply asked my name and got on his phone. I stood there for two or three minutes planning my next move after the refusal that I expected would be forthcoming. To my surprise, a middle-aged woman emerged from the gathering in front of the house, walked toward the gate, opened it from the inside, and ushered me in. As I looked back at the corporal in disbelief, he saluted me – me, a fugitive coming to see the commander of the Fuerzas Armadas Revolucionarias. The group of men and women were now getting into their cars and I was politely led past them and deposited in a waiting room on the first floor.

"Would you like some Cuban coffee? We are very proud of our local brew you know."

"Yes, that would be very nice," I said, trying to be gracious, all the while my mind scrolling potential reasons to which I could attribute this more than cordial reception.

As she poured coffee from an urn on a serving table in the corner of the room she said, "Señor Raoul has just finished meeting with the ministers, so it will be several minutes before he will be able to speak with you. If you are hungry I can bring some other refreshments. Would you like that?"

"No, this will be fine. Thank you for your kindness," I answered. As she left the room, I sat down with both my coffee and my confusion.

I was hardly halfway through the cup, when the same woman returned with the announcement that Señor Raoul would see me now. She ushered me out of the waiting room and up the steps to a book-lined study on the second floor. I brought my coffee along, feeling more comfortable holding onto something that was at least momentarily familiar. The room was empty, but the woman said that Raoul was next door and would be there shortly. She suggested that I make myself comfortable. I had spoken to heads of state before, so speaking to the brother of one was not about to make me nervous. I attributed the intensity I felt to the urgency of Eric's situation.

It had been two or three years since I had actually seen Raoul but I recognized him instantly. I could tell from his expression that it was likewise. We had a very few moments of small-talk before he invited me to sit closer to him as he had some pictures he wanted to show me. They were photographs of me, obviously taken by telephoto surveillance. I was playing with the Chernobyl children in the hospital at Ciudad de los Pioneros.

"I have always been impressed with your work, but it was not until I saw these pictures that I realized what a remarkable woman you are."

"That's very flattering Señor Minister. I compliment you on your surveillance but I have some urgent business that I must talk to you about."

"You underestimate me, Señorita Barton. Since you are aware of the plan for which you were brought to Cuba, you must also realize that, as one of its architects, it is for me to keep abreast of all the surrounding circumstances."

"Are you aware of Mr. Lynne's predicament? That is primarily why I'm here tonight," I said soberly.

"Certainly I understand. Both a personal and professional relationship make for a very close bond. As you know, my experience in this area has not been unlike your own, only perhaps a bit more public."

He smiled at his own joke, and we laughed together. It was a nice moment and one in which some of the barriers of formality were invited to droop, if not drop altogether. He continued. "Roger Brisco is a force to be reckoned with here in Cuba. His business connections have brought about much progress that would have otherwise been impossible. If he has put out an order for the removal of our friend Mr. Lynne, it will be a difficult one to intercept."

"I want you to understand, Señor Minister, I intend to do whatever is necessary to neutralize any such order, and that includes eliminating Mr. Brisco if necessary," I said.

"Perhaps before we get into deliberating such drastic measures, we should discuss a preliminary issue. As you know, I have had an ally in these last months, one whose council and friendship I have grown to value and respect. I would like you to meet him. I think he might have some input concerning preserving the well-being of your Postman."

Raoul didn't only want me to know that he knew Eric's code name. He wanted me to know that he was in charge, and that one who is in charge is privy to all the information needed to maintain that responsibility. I was pretty sure he was referring to El Jugador, but whoever he was talking about, I was anxious to hear any suggestions for how to help Eric.

"I would be delighted to meet your comrade," I said, and added, "I understand that he is from the U.S., so we probably have much in common."

"Yes," he said smiling, "I think you will find that to be an extremely accurate statement. If you wouldn't mind waiting a few minutes, I'll go and get him. He is in my office talking with some of my financial advisors."

I took the few minutes to finish my coffee and gather my wits. Overlaying my concern for Eric was a curiosity about what kind of man could have made such an impression on him. I had a few minutes to think about that, and even conjured a picture of El Jugador.

Sure I believe in intuition, but as for premonition I tend more toward the practical. But just as the handle of the door turned, and the door itself had not yet opened, I saw a face in my mind's eye that slightly alleviated the shock that I was to feel when, in the next moment, Harris Barton, my father, walked into the room.

Chapter 33

Cuba was the first country in the Caribbean selected by Canada in 1945 for a diplomatic mission. They have maintained uninterrupted diplomatic relations with Cuba to the present. Canadian Prime Minister Pierre Trudeau spent time in Cuba, and he and Fidel developed a close friendship. In the 1990s, the two countries cooperated on mining and metal refining ventures as a beginning to their commercial association. Canada also expressed displeasure with the presence of U.S. customs agents in Canadian airports looking for Americans traveling illegally to Cuba. It has been critical of the U.S. trade embargo against Cuba, calling it "the wrong approach." Last year tourism became Cuba's largest industry even surpassing that of sugar. Canadians were mostly responsible for that increase.

Their passports read Arlen and Edwina Medavoy from Toronto. In the short run, the cover of a Canadian tourist couple on a Caribbean vacation would play in any number of resort venues around the island. As pleasant as a temporary liaison with Harris Barton's red-headed niece would be, Eric still was hoping for a very short run in hiding. At first, Eric was reticent to acknowledge any personal threat that Otnabe could represent. When the word came from Callie by way of Red-Jack that Brisco was involved, it became clear that he had to go under for a while. Finally convinced of the danger, the only thing left to decide was where he should go until his well-being was no longer at risk. Harris' niece supplied the inspiration for the Canadian tourist presentation, and it took little coaxing for her to volunteer to play his counterpart. Harris insisted that any place west of Cienfuegos would be a mistake. They agreed on Playa Siboney, a beach resort area near Cuba's second largest city, Santiago. More importantly, it was only 45 minutes away from the U.S. marine base at Guantánamo – a place that Brisco would avoid like the plague.

Flights to Santiago on Cubana de Aviación are frequent, and the couple found themselves on the beach at Playa Siboney before the sun sank over the horizon that it faced. Eric's newly adopted mustache, glasses, and flowery shirt, combined with the attractive young woman on his arm, created the appropriate image. It was an image that the tourist population would not question, and a magnet that brought other like-minded vacationers forth with invitations to join them. As part of a group of Canadians, Eric would be virtually invisible, and in being so was insulated, at least temporarily, from any inquisition that Brisco or his confederates could mount.

Playing the part of a vacationer was a curious role for someone whose life was in danger, but Eric had been under enough pressure since this operation began that he had a strong intention to play it to the hilt. His traveling companion was both affable and beautiful, which increased the possibility of immersing himself in his cover – so to speak. Of course, there was a danger intrinsic in such frivolity. Being constantly on guard was the method he had historically chosen to maintain his safety when it was in potential danger. Considering this to be his last operation, instead of sharpening his edge, was having the opposite effect. He was relieving himself of the role of operative little by little, and in doing so was increasing his vulnerability without knowing it.

His companion was somewhat familiar with the skills necessary to maintain their cover. Although her experience was limited in comparison to Lynne's, she was willing to do whatever was necessary. Ultimately, she would follow his lead. If he was going to let down his guard a little, she would also.

The beach was the perfect place to spend the days. The sun was powerful, but umbrellas dotted the sand and the water was always close enough that a few minutes immersion would adjust one's body temperature. The vacationers found a spot well down the beach from the hotel and spent their time commuting from the sand to the water. It was in the evening that people congregated. The density of hotel lobbies and dining rooms beckoned the couple to innocent socializing. It may have been innocent for the Canadians, but for Lynne and his companion it was more of a risk than he should have been taking. Somewhere in him, he knew it.

It was on their third evening that they sat at the cocktail bar with five other tourists, three of whom they had met before. The rum was copiously flowing from the bottles into the glasses and the mood it precipitated was festive. One of the tourists was flirting with Deborah when she temporarily lost her temper and said a few caustic words in Spanish. The Cuban bartender, who was standing very nearby, laughed at the remark and looked over to see that those words had come from the mouth of a Canadian tourist.

It could barely have been categorized as an incident. The flirtatious tourist disappeared when he found out that the redhead was escorted, and everything seemed to be back to normal. Unfortunately, what ensued amongst Eric's fellow tourists was an exchange of information as to home town, job, etc. Having had assignments in Canada, this was no problem for Eric, but when Deborah was brought into the conversation, the situation got a little sticky, and Eric had to bail her out. By this time, the bartender was auditing the conversation. As bartenders in Cuba sell as much information as Bacardi, Eric, had he been more alert, could have been aware that there was potential trouble.

Chapter 34

The trauma of Dad's reappearance in my life had begun to normalize. It was incredible to me that after just 24 hours I could look at him and not feel completely disoriented. I didn't make it easy for him in the first few hours. Sustaining a position of self-righteous indignation was what I seemed to need to maintain my composure. After a while his explanation became more understandable and his view of protecting me was also.

It was surprising that even having been on the island numerous times since his "death," I was completely oblivious to his presence. What was equally remarkable was that I had no suspicion whatsoever that what I called my Red-Jack communication set-up was really through his red-headed cousin Jacob. It was Dad's way of keeping in contact with me, even though I couldn't know that the contact was with him. It was not I who, in my early days as an operative in Cuba, discovered a secure communication link called Red-Jack. It was Red-Jack who found me. I realized how difficult it must have been for Dad to know about my whereabouts through Jacob, but for my security, not be able to communicate with me.

As our normalization proceeded, the necessities of the moment began to re-present themselves. Eric was still in danger, and Dad's plan with Raoul was in process.

The news that everyone in our camp but me already knew was that General Gomez was no longer helping Brisco and Otnabe. He was helping us. Dad told me the whole story as Magelinos had told him about the General's having changed sides. I reviewed my time at the DSE office, and it all made sense. I must have been dull not to pick up the signs. What made even more sense was the sergeant's smile. It took me a few minutes to process the reversal to the point that I realized that Enrique wasn't in danger. I breathed out a phrase that I couldn't remember the last time I'd used – "Thank God." I guess I cared about Enrique more than I realized.

Dad and Enrique were the only ones who knew Eric's whereabouts. I had every intention of getting to wherever he was ASAP and setting up some kind of security for him. He might be incommunicado now, but with Manny and Miranda looking for him with the help of Roger Brisco and his goons, that wouldn't last long. Brisco's information network on the island was probably well-primed with favors – the kind that he was uniquely qualified to dispense.

"There's nobody better at becoming invisible than Eric, especially here in Cuba, but sooner or later someone's going to make him," I said authoritatively. "A solo gringo is going to get spotted if he . . . "

"He's not alone Caroline," dad interrupted. "He's traveling with my young cousin Deborah, Jacob's granddaughter. They're posing as a couple."

Dad explained that his cousin, who I guess was my cousin too, went along for cover, but that didn't sound like much security. When I heard the word *couple* I managed to avoid asking any questions pursuant to what it *did* sound like, because this clearly wasn't the time for emotions of that variety to surface. My sense of humor came to the rescue with the thought, *it's all in the family anyway*.

Dad tried to dissuade me from going in person to help Eric, but finally backed off when my response to his input reminded him of how tenacious I was. And I was tenacious.

"So what's the story with Enrique? Is Gomez keeping him locked up for show?" I said.

"Caroline, I think you may have to forget about Magelinos for now."

"I forgot about him *till* now, but now I need to start remembering him again. I need his help," I said, dealing with my father more as a resource than as a parent. "I don't want to blow Gomez' cover, but I really want to take Enrique with me to help Eric," I said, already knowing that getting to him soon enough for us to travel together was unlikely. I had to be prepared to go alone – and I was. I would wait until morning and then fly to Santiago de Cuba where Dad told me Eric had gone under.

Chapter 35

Fidel's youngest brother Ramon had never taken a government position but was always at Fidel's side as his personal assistant. Now in what could be his last days, Ramon acted as Fidel's communication link to the outside.

It was a relationship that had only once been tarnished by dissent. It was a disagreement that was brought about by Ramon's fervent communist ideals. He was the most radically thinking socialist in the Castro family – even more so than Fidel. It was during the missile crisis of 1962 that Ramon staunchly supported Khrushchev's keeping the missiles in Cuba and not backing down to the U.S. It was his view that even if Cuba was to be sacrificed in a nuclear holocaust, it would still be better than allowing the U.S. to prevail. That would not have been acceptable to Fidel, and though he urged Khrushchev to maintain the Soviet position longer, he later acknowledged the wisdom of avoiding military confrontation.

Ramon also hated Kennedy, as opposed to Fidel, who was curious about him. When Khrushchev agreed to withdraw the missiles, Kennedy agreed to a no-invasion pledge. Fidel was pleased with Kennedy's commitment, but many of his enemies were not. The exiled Cuban community in Miami was deeply disappointed. Organized crime families from both Miami and Chicago saw themselves as victims of Kennedy's promise, because now any hope of regaining their lost hotel and gambling assets were gone.

Some months later, a French journalist acting as intermediary between Castro and Kennedy alluded to the possibility of concessions on both sides and the potential of détente. Both organized crime and the Cuban exile community fervently opposed any such conciliatory actions. The next week Kennedy was dead in Dallas.

There were those who said that the secret communication between these two heads of state came to the awareness of those two hostile groups by the actions of a close associate of Fidel Castro – and without his knowledge. It was not only a rumor, because the only two individuals publicly known to have been involved before and after the assassination had previously been seen in Cuba.

More than 30 years had passed since those tumultuous times. Ramon had tempered his youthful fervency to enable himself to assume a position of confidence and intimacy with El Comandante. In these last few weeks, he was to keep much that could be upsetting from his ailing brother. The reports from Raoul remained consistent. He would read those reports or listen to them in his conversations with Raoul and decide what to pass on to Fidel.

When it was time for Harris Barton to make what might be a final call on his ailing friend, it became Ramon's responsibility to update his brother on the details of El Jugador's recent activities, in addition to the activities of his daughter.

Ramon had an apartment at the foot of the stairs that led to Fidel's bedroom. If anyone had the credentials to enter the house, Ramon would be notified by the security men on duty and would come out to screen the visitor. In recent days, many came to the point of screening but very few went past. El Jugador was not to be screened by Ramon this day. Fidel had asked for his friend several times, and Ramon was relieved to see him arrive. El Jugador followed Ramon up the stairs while Ramon gave him the most recent update on El Comandante's condition. Ramon gave a subdued knock on the door and proceeded to sit on a couch in the hallway as Harris Barton opened it. The lights were dim, but Fidel had no trouble recognizing the man who entered his room.

"So my friend, we meet as we did the first time, at the door to another one of my grandiose adventures." Fidel attempted a laugh, but it pained him, and he suppressed it.

"It's good to be with you Comandante, even in these circumstances."

"I have always preferred you to call me Fidel, my friend. After all, I have been your comrade, but though I may have tried, I was never your Comandante."

"And I Fidel, what have I been to you?" Barton asked in the spirit of candor that marked their relationship as unique.

"You have been my Jugador, my game player, my gambler – the conscience of 'a taker of chances' that I have so valued and still value at this very moment."

Barton was deeply touched by Fidel's response. He looked down with eyes beginning to fill. There were a few moments of silence between them before Fidel continued.

"How would you rate my odds, señor gambler?"

El Jugador tried to assess the appropriate answer to a question of such consequence. "You are very ill my friend. I'm sure you know that it doesn't look good."

This time Fidel did laugh. Though the wince of pain showed in his bearded face, the pleasure of the irony showed as well. "No, no, no, I don't mean my personal odds. They are of only relative importance. I mean the odds for the dream that we shared – the dream of a classless society."

"It has always been up to the people, Fidel. If they want it enough, they will get it."

"And do they want it enough?"

"I am less sure about that than I once was," El Jugador replied sadly.

"You must be even less sure of it than that, to be playing your most recent game señor gambler. You must know I have grave misgivings about it."

The level of integrity on which their relationship was based didn't allow Harris Barton the flexibility or the desire to try to maintain the deception. "I wasn't aware that you were informed about what you call, 'my most recent game.'"

"The inning is very late for me, and I know whether I live or die I cannot stop you and Raoul. But I can ask you to consider an adjustment to your plan. Will you listen to my suggestion?" Fidel said, his voice clearly weakened from the output of energy necessitated by their conversation.

Barton of course agreed, and Fidel went on to propose a compromise. He called in his brother Ramon, who presented Barton with a folder of papers on which was delineated his proposal for a free-market Cuba with certain constraints. These constraints focused on maintaining Cuban autonomy by keeping the multinational corporations and what he called the "octopus nations" from wresting control of the Cuban economy from the Cubans.

As Barton sat by Fidel's bedside, he read through the proposal. After an hour or so he was prepared to discuss some of the points with this man who had not *had* to discuss anything with anybody for 35 years. The discussion would have to wait. Fidel was asleep. As his doctor entered, they passed each other at the doorway. A light touch on the shoulder of each man for the other expressed all the sentiments that needed expressing.

Ramon was sitting where he had left him in the hallway when Barton emerged from the room. Ramon caught Barton's eye and patted the seat next to him for Barton to come and sit down. From time to time, Ramon had bouts of jealousy toward those who were taken into his brother's confidence, but this was not a time for petty emotions.

"Señor Jugador, may I call you that?"

"If you mean that it's time we got to know each other, I agree," Barton answered, the gravity of the scene he had just left still weighing on him.

"Do you remember the incident with Fidelito and the nuclear power project?" Ramon asked. "It was a difficult time for me. Fidel wanted me to protect his son's reputation, and I tried. It wasn't easy. Fidel was very troubled about Fidelito's future. Our children are very important to us, are they not?"

There was no need for Barton to respond. As they faced each other, Ramon continued, "Your daughter has enemies who might cause her harm. Knowing who her father is might keep her safe here in Cuba, but elsewhere . . . who can say? El Comandante knows of her involvement, and he asked that I inform you of her situation. This man Wyndam

Otnabe is no friend of Cuba, nor is he a friend of anyone other than himself. Please watch out for him. He may take action against your daughter and possibly even yourself."

Barton, appreciating the sincerity of the warning, replied, "I know you have children Ramon. Since we are close to the same age, probably our children are too. Tell me, can you tell them what to do – and if you can, what is your secret?" Both men laughed, and the friendship that had been postponed because of the circumstances of the past saw its opening in the intimate sadness of the present.

"Ah my friend, in some ways you have become a Cuban, but in many ways you are still a complex Norte Americano."

Holding up the proposal that Fidel had given him, Barton said, "I'll see what I can do about these. I promise that I will do my best."

Chapter 36

Dad and I both spent the night at the estate of Raoul Castro. I couldn't chance the exposure of making a reservation for the morning plane to Santiago, so I figured I'd take a cab to the airport and catch the first available flight out. When Dad returned, he told me about his visit with Fidel. He was very emotional about it. For the first time, I could appreciate the depth of the relationship they had formed. As he recounted the whole story, starting with the ferry ride in 1958, I had some twinges of jealousy for the intimacy he shared with someone other than me. I managed to let it pass.

I had been sleeping a little more than an hour when there was a knock on my door. The aide who had originally served me coffee said there was a phone call for me downstairs. At first I thought that it might be Eric, but I knew that he couldn't possibly take the chance to call. I didn't have a second guess, so I just hurried downstairs and picked up the phone. It was the same voice that had surprised me two days before, and I was even more startled this time.

"Enrique, when did you get out, and how? Are you okay?" I stammered excitedly.

"I am fine, señorita. I am at a pay phone about half a mile from the DSE office where I was being held,"

Magelinos explained. "Arturo . . . General Gomez came in to check on me while I was sleeping. When he went out, he made sure I noticed that he was deliberately leaving the door to my cell open. I knew the code to the rear private security entrance so I just walked out of the building."

"Can you meet me?" I asked. "I'm going to the post office. I have some urgent mail to deliver. I'll be sending it air-mail because it is quite a distance away. Can you meet me? Can we go to the post office together?"

"I would be delighted to accompany you señorita, but as you can imagine, I am not very presentable at the moment. If we can meet in a few hours, it would give me time to go to the home of a friend and clean up. Will that do?"

"I'll meet you at noon at the airport Enrique."

I had to get both of us on a plane to Santiago. I was optimistic for the first time since I had realized that it was up to me to bail out Eric. Up to this point, I had been cruising on pure bravado. Now I had an ally, and Magelinos was a good one. Without Gomez, Otnabe had no police power, so the airport would only be a problem if we were spotted by one of Brisco's people. They might be watching for either of us, hoping we would lead them to Eric.

Enrique spotted me getting out of a taxi in front of the airport and quickly led me to a private departure lounge. As he promised, his son, the director of airport security, brought us our tickets, so we didn't have to go upstairs and take the chance of being spotted. We were ticketed as Señor Enrique Balesteros and his daughter Valentina. The chairs in the lounge were new and comfortable just as Enrique said they were. I followed his advice and rested my head back and closed my eyes. By the time we were called for our flight to

Santiago, I had systematically recollected as many moments of the past weeks as I could remember. I didn't even need my computer to write anything down. My memory and proficiency at daydreaming were sufficient. The process helped me feel clearer than I had been for a while. I knew what I had to do. I was confident that the blundering mistakes I had made that put Eric's life at risk were a thing of the past. With the one hour flying time, we would be in Santiago by mid-afternoon. That would be plenty of time to find our way to the same hotel where the happy couple was vacationing.

It was not that Carmen Miranda had a conscience, or that eliminating one of her agents conflicted with some ethical code to which she subscribed. It was more that she was beginning to sense that Otnabe was making the Postman into more of a problem than he actually presented. It was Miranda's view that Lynne could be bought. So why not buy him? If he wanted out, let him out. There was plenty in this one to go around, and violence rarely supplied anything other than a temporary solution.

She tried to communicate her assessment of the situation to Otnabe, but the telephone just didn't seem to be the proper vehicle for conveying her opinions. The more she expressed her views, the more furious Otnabe became. Finally, he threatened to come to Cuba himself if Lynne wasn't eliminated by the end of the week and then he hung up the phone.

Miranda went from vacillation to decision when Manny came up from the DSE basement interrogation area with the news that Magelinos was gone. She knew for that to happen there had to be some powerful interest groups opposing Otnabe – interest groups that had a lot more influence on the island than she could muster. If it were discovered that she was involved in felonious activities, i.e. murder, those interest groups would not be easy to deal with. After all, Fidel Castro still ran this government, and at last word he was still alive.

After confiding her misgivings to Manny, they both decided that it would be prudent to try to countermand Otnabe's orders by intercepting Brisco and whoever he had contracted to do the job. Nobody would know that it was actually a countermand. Miranda and Manny would simply claim to have found some extenuating circumstances that would make eliminating the Postman a counter-indicated scenario.

Intercepting Brisco would require some foreknowledge of Lynne's location. Unfortunately, any hope of that was lost along with the escape from jail of Enrique Magelinos. Miranda did have one more option. It was the prearranged communication link she had established with Callie in Miami. It had only been used a few times, but each time it eventually got them voice to voice. It was worth a try. Miranda knew that Callie couldn't afford to trust her. Then again, they did have history. Miranda thought it might be possible to convince Callie that they both were on the same side – at least on this one. They both wanted to avert any harm to Lynne, so just maybe . . . Miranda knew that Callie would never respond to a request to contact her, but she did have one idea that could put them in touch with each other.

"What was that like back there at DSE when they were questioning you?" I asked Enrique, once we were soaring over some of the blue-greenest water a person could imagine.

"General Gomez and I have known each other for a long time, señorita. I think the situation was as difficult for him as it was for me. Of course if we had been alone, there would have been no problem at all. Breaking his own rule that there must be at least two interrogators to one detainee would certainly have aroused suspicion. Actually, there were three of them with me most of the time. It was really not a problem because Arturo knew that I would tell them only what I saw fit to tell them and that I wouldn't go any further. The General knows me well enough to know that."

"What happened to your cheek?" I asked, pointing to a bruise under Enrique's left eye.

"Only the enthusiasm of a young sergeant who has never liked me," Magelinos explained casually. "Arturo made the mistake of leaving me with him and another soldier that I barely knew. He took the opportunity to express some of his displeasure. One has to expect that type of behavior from a certain kind of person. Fortunately, my reputation at DSE and DGI before that is good, and I have made very few enemies over the years."

By the time I had consumed his story along with the less interesting snacks to which not only I, but all the passengers were subjected, we were circling El Morro Castle on the way into the Santiago airport. First thing I would have to do was call Red-Jack. That was the only way I had of keeping in close touch with Dad. If I needed any clout, Harris Barton would be my best shot. He was in deep with Fidel and Raoul; I was just in deep.

"This is Jelinda. Do you have anything for me?"

"You have a message from the Commander. He will call back at 5:00 p.m. our time and I can patch him through to you if you call me at 5:02."

"The Commander? Are you sure that's current?" I asked.

"That's an affirmative. The Commander at 3:12 p.m., 20 minutes ago. It was international. Do you want to go for it?"

I knew there was something fishy, but the chance that it was Eric made it impossible for me to refuse. There would be no way that a patch could disclose my location, so I knew I would have to take the chance. "Go for it Red-Jack. But don't under any circumstances reveal my location. Let's not put your little girl in any more jeopardy than she's already in, okay?" I knew I was being sarcastic with the *little girl* stuff, but Red-Jack probably didn't – or at least I hoped he didn't.

"That's affirmative, Jelinda. The security of your location is top priority. I'm expecting your call on #22-944-6622 at 5:02 p.m. Got that number?"

"Got it, speak to you then," I said as I hung up. I had a pad full of updated numbers from calling Red-Jack over the past week. He had a digital circumscribing system that allowed him to change receiving numbers as often as he wanted to. This was great for security, but it was impossible for remembering, because there was never the same number twice. I threw all the old sheets into the ash tray under the phone and kept the new one for my 5:00 p.m. call to someone who may have been international, but probably wasn't the Commander from Fort Lauderdale.

"This is Jelinda. You have somebody there for me?"

"Jelinda, before I patch you through, you should know that the first call was foreign, but this one is domestic. Also, it's a female voice and the first one was male. Do you still want the patch? Your location is 100% secure. By the way, any word from the vacationers?"

I knew the last words were those of an anxious grandfather. As petty as the feelings were that arose in me whenever Eric's name was linked up in that way, I knew that Jacob was not only her grandfather, but that he had bailed me out of numerous tight spots in the past with both information and communications. I owed him more than my jealousy. "No word yet, but I'm on top of it and I've got Magelinos with me. We'll keep her safe," I said, knowing what he must be going through. "Patch me through."

"To whom am I talking?" I opened the conversation with what I considered the most important question. Once I heard the word "female," I pretty much knew who was on the other end of the line.

"Pepper! Please don't hang up!"

"I didn't know you had a female voice in your trick bag Manny."

"She's standing right next to me Pepper, but I wanted to talk first. Listen, she's going to double on Wyndam, not for the whole deal but just for the Postman part of it. I'm not bullshitting you. We both agreed that Wyndam has gone over the edge on this one. He's coming down and there's no stopping him. Listen kid, talk to Miranda. Can I put her on?"

"Why not Manny, she isn't any more full of shit than you are," I snorted.

"Jelinda?" Miranda asked, hearing my prolonged silence.

"I'm here Miranda. And I haven't forgotten the implant. I owe you something. I'm not sure what, but it'll be something."

"Jelinda, I'm truly sorry about that. I mean it. It was disgusting. I tried to call it off, but he's the boss. This deal with the Postman is the first time I've ever decided to go up against him. I know you and Eric have, but for me this is the first time. So will you help me?"

"Help *you?* Eric's the one under the gun," I said, taking every opportunity I could get to make her feel guilty.

"You know that's what I mean Jelinda. There's no reason for Eric to get hurt if we work together. I don't want it, and you don't want it. And Manny . . . he's with us on this."

"Listen, Miranda. I'm not with you on this, and I'm not with Manny either. I'm going to keep Eric from getting killed and that's all. If I think I need to tell you my location to get that done, I'll do that. And if not, I won't. So tell me just what it is that you can do that I can't?"

"I can call Brisco off," Miranda said succinctly.

The minute she said it, I knew it was true. I could make a security net for Eric and his companion, but I couldn't cancel the contract. She could. The problem was, if I led her to Eric and things got screwed up, I knew I'd never forgive myself. If Miranda knew where to look for Eric, she'd also find Brisco there sooner or later. Unfortunately, Otnabe would also eventually show up and counter Miranda's cancellation, and the hit would be back on. Adding it all up, I could see that even if it happened that way, it would still be worth trying. Even if the hit was only called off temporarily, that would still give me time to throw a little party that this conversation with Miranda was beginning to inspire in me.

"Miranda, find the Hotel Balneario del Sol. It's on Playa Siboney right near the Santiago de Cuba airport. I'll meet you there tomorrow at 5:00 p.m." I saw an opportunity for a dig and added, "I'll be at the beach bar, like the one we met at in the Fontainebleau in Miami. I'm sure you remember that meeting Miranda."

"Where is the Postman Jelinda? Is he there?" Miranda asked, ignoring my comment and feeling unsatisfied with an arrangement that left me calling the shots.

"That's as much as you're going to get Miranda. It'll put you a lot closer than you are now," I said, as I hung up without waiting for an answer. It was a little risky divulging Eric's location, but I would make sure that he was long gone from there before anyone got close to Santiago. Anyway, if Miranda would be sure of anything, it would be that the place I arranged to meet her was the last place in Cuba that Eric Lynne would be.

Chapter 37

Roger Brisco knew that a French retirement, his agreed-upon compensation from Wyndam Otnabe, was much too valuable to trust to any underling operatives – even if one of them was on the executive board of the Roca Group. At first he was willing to follow Carmen Miranda's lead, because that's how Otnabe wanted it. When he got word that Enrique Magelinos had been released under questionable circumstances, he knew that it was time to take charge of the operation himself.

Brisco was not a man to take orders well. For years it had been the same. His metamorphosis from a legitimate business man to a mega swindler was partially the product of attitude. He always had a better way. When Otnabe solicited his participation in the removal of Eric Lynne from the equation, Brisco scanned his wealth of experience for the best way to accomplish the assignment. At first he pictured Carmine Trocadero, a Havana pimp and hustler known to be available to do anything for a healthy payday.

A bit too crude for my taste, Brisco thought to himself. His self-image had always been that of an erudite white-collar promoter, not a criminal at all. Yes, he would draft Barnes Connert for the job. He would keep Connert in the dark as to what was really happening till the last minute.

Then he would play on Connert's desire to be his partner and his hunger to be a big-time player. Obviously there would have to be some cash incentive, but this was no problem. If Otnabe had a limit on what he would pay for the job, Brisco had no such limitation. He had enough money stashed to live at the highest possible standard for ten lifetimes, and still have plenty left to make his kids rich when it was all over. The French Riviera was beckoning, and there would be no better time to seize the opportunity.

It would be simple. All he had to do was add keeping watch on Miranda and Manny to his already active information gathering system. If he got a break, then they would lead him to Lynne. Within hours of Magelinos' release, Brisco's information network came through for him again. It would not be Miranda who would lead him to Lynne, but a bartender on the eastern end of the island. There would be no need to notify the Roca personnel of his discovery. They would find out soon enough – when the job was done.

Brisco knew it was a necessity to avoid public air transportation. The briefcase his companion would be carrying would never make it through the metal detectors at the Jose Marti Airport security check. He arranged for a private flight for two. It would take off from a small airfield in Miramar just outside of Havana and deposit them in Santiago de Cuba.

That afternoon, neither the planes that shared the airways nor their passengers could know the parallel courses that were being traversed. Carmen Miranda, Manny, Roger Brisco, and his associate Barnes Connert all landed at the Santiago de Cuba airport within fifteen minutes of each other.

They never crossed paths. Miranda and Manny headed through the terminal to a taxi that would take them to Playa Siboney, while the other two got into a private car waiting for them on the tarmac at the far end of the runway and headed to a meeting with a bartender at the Hotel Balneario del Sol on the very same beach.

I needed to talk to Miranda first to see if it was going to be possible for her to call off the hunt. If that could be done, we could dispense with the theatrics that I was planning to arrange, at least temporarily. Part of me actually looked forward to those theatrics. That is, I would have, if the fireworks I planned weren't going to be as dangerous as I knew they might be. I knew Miranda would have to make face-to-face contact with Brisco to bring about a cancellation of the contract on Eric. That would probably require them meeting at Eric's hotel when Brisco eventually discovered his location.

I also had to take into account the possibility that Enrique and I were followed and the probability that Miranda and Manny were as well. Caution dictated that we couldn't afford the risk of driving our rental car to the Balneario del Sol Hotel to speak to Eric in person. My meeting with Miranda should be somewhere in the opposite direction, so as not to draw anyone to Eric's secure location.

After discussing our options, Enrique and I decided on an alternative course. While I made arrangements for my contingency plan, Enrique would go to Eric's hotel and get him and his friend out of there quickly. In order to continue to draw Brisco there, which was a necessity if we were going to get Miranda and Brisco together, Eric would have to keep his room in the hotel and rental car in the parking lot. Enrique would drive Eric and Deborah up into Grand Piedras national park about halfway between Santiago and Guantanamo. Rustic cabins were the accommodations in the park and that would be perfect. They would be able to stay in anonymity for as long as it would take to get the players in this drama together, either to call it off, or become guests at the fiesta I was in the process of arranging.

The first stage of my plan was to get Eric out of the Playa Siboney area without anyone who might be onto him knowing about his departure. Whenever Brisco got there, Miranda could talk to him without Eric being in harm's way. Then, after some creative arranging, my next step would be to go back to Eric's hotel to meet Miranda. I knew that even if Brisco and friends showed up while I was there, I wouldn't be in any jeopardy. He was after Eric, not me. But first I had that creative arranging to take care of about 40 miles away. Even if Enrique wasn't going to the hotel to transport Eric, he couldn't go with me on this one.

Chapter 38

I was heading for American soil, but no water had to be crossed to get there. The U.S. military presence had existed in Guantanamo since an agreement at the turn of the century. During World War II, it was considered the finest U.S. Naval base outside of the 48 states, and one of its most strategic because of proximity to the Panama Canal. Even though Castro asserted that the land was being occupied illegally because his revolutionary government was not a party to the agreement, little has ever been attempted to alter the situation. A few years ago, the drinking water to the base was turned off, and the Navy had to compensate by putting in a desalinization plant. Except for that incident and an occasional demonstration, life goes on as usual for the military in the 45-square-mile outpost.

As an American citizen on Cuban soil, I had often visited the base. Not that I was expressing my patriotic curiosity, but more that I wanted to maintain good relations with a well-equipped rescue squad, if it ever came to that. I had never in the past felt the need to tap that resource. Now, not only was I in the midst of an operation that might require fire power, it was also one that could very well be considered beneficial to the U.S. Government.

One of the things that my years of negotiating for and with governments had taught me was, those that have been around for years, like ones in Europe and Asia, are motivated by tradition and institution. The teenage government of the United States, on the other hand, is different in that it is driven by personality. Both our politicians and our electorate get most enthusiastic when there's a bad guy to focus their attention on, i.e., Hitler, Stalin, Khomeini, Castro, Gaddafi, Saddam Hussein. It's hard to rally support against the impersonality of a foreign government's actions, even when those actions could be considered an affront. But when their leader can be depicted as a villain, taking compensatory action becomes a much more popular option.

That's where Roger Brisco came in. This villain was a thorn in the side of the United States Government and a living insult to the criminal justice system. The U.S. Attorney General had a standing order that Brisco was to be apprehended in Cuba using any means that didn't provoke an international incident. Unfortunately for the U.S. attorney, it was a meaningless mandate, because U.S. troops couldn't officially enter onto Cuban soil. So it had been a standoff – at least up to now.

I didn't have many friends on the base, but the ones I had could rattle a few cages. My political work with the Roca Group in Washington gave me a working knowledge of how to operate around the military. It took only one incident in my formative years as an operative for me to realize that most officers were frozen by both regulations and fear of being passed over for promotion. If you wanted some flexibility, find an NCO (non-commissioned officer). A few years earlier I had found a good one at Gitmo. If he was still there, I wouldn't have to look any further. He was a chief in the Marine Shore Patrol, the equivalent of the Military Police. If ever Roger Brisco was going to be apprehended in Cuba, the job would probably fall on him and his men. I knew I couldn't get Brisco to Guantanamo, but if I could get him nearby, maybe the Chief would stretch the boundaries of the base and make the grab.

The racial mix has changed in Cuba since the exodus of the million or so who felt they couldn't go along with Fidel Castro's program. Since many of those who opted to leave were well-educated, and many of the well-educated were advantaged whites, Cuba had been left with a greater proportion of dark-skinned citizens than before the revolution. Numerous times I had encouraged the Roca Group to make use of this demography by training African Americans as operatives for Cuba. As it happened, hidden amongst Wyndam Otnabe's numerous character flaws, there was also a strong discriminatory impulse.

I had no such predilection, and that made Chief Lou Grinnel and his black skin potential assets on this mission. His intelligence, boldness, and wit – the characteristics that had facilitated our friendship – would be indispensible if things got out of hand. If he could get some Puerto Rican marines to accompany him, they could all go unnoticed anywhere on the island – at least for the amount of time it would take to scoop up Roger Brisco once we knew where to find him.

As it turned out, Chief Grinnel was as flirtatious as ever and as good-looking as well. He would have jumped at the chance to grab Brisco anyway, but leaving the door open to future fraternization didn't hurt the arrangement either. It was all set. The Chief would brief his men and be ready whenever I called with the go-code. Our rendezvous point would be in Yateritas, only 30 minutes by car from the base, so his group's incursion onto Cuban soil would be limited.

The remote eastern end of the island that houses the U.S. Naval base is almost unknown to tourists – that is, the more recent ones, since the original tourist Christopher Columbus landed there. The only landmark I remembered in the area was an extensive artistic exhibit known as the Stone Zoo in Yateritas. Several years ago, a local sculptor named Angel Inigo completed carving 400 life-sized stone replicas of animals, and the government built a park around them. When I first met Lou, he had informally gone over the wall to show me around the place. So when it came to picking a location for my grand finale, it was the only one I could think of other than my first choice, which would have been the main gates at Guantanamo. A nice thought, but one that I knew was not going to happen.

Chapter 39

From a photo that Roger Brisco provided, the bartender at the Balneario del Sol identified the man he had spoken about. *No, he was not alone. Yes, he had been a guest of the hotel for several days, and yes, he was still registered in room 208 with a young red-haired lady.* Preferring a rendezvous on the beach rather than in a hotel room, Brisco arranged for his newly-acquired informant to hire on as a sentinel who would notify him when Eric Lynne was walking about. It didn't take too much checking to locate Lynne's rental car in the parking lot. So they were either in the room and not answering their phone, or out for a stroll up the beach or into town.

Covering the beach would be Brisco's first act of business. If they were lucky enough to encounter Lynne out there where there were no onlookers, then their work could be done without any more involvement at the hotel. Brisco gave Connert instructions to come get him if he spotted Lynne and not to let Lynne spot him. First stop on the way out to the surf would be at the beach bar where ten or twelve stools were occupied with backs facing the walkway.

While Connert was scoping out the beach, Brisco walked down to the end of the bar to get a look at the clientele before they got a look at him, and that's exactly what happened. Sitting on stools #5 and #6 were an attractive dark-haired woman talking to a stout, balding middle-aged man. It was Carmen Miranda and her assistant. Brisco had never met Manny, but he had dealt with Miranda years before when Roca Group helped shelter his money. Brisco was so uncharacteristically surprised, that he didn't back up in time so as not to be noticed. Miranda, who was facing Brisco's way, nudged Manny, and he turned around so that all parties involved were facing each other down the bar.

Within a few moments, the three had joined each other at one of the empty tables that skirted the sand.

"There's been a change of plans Mr. Brisco," Miranda said matter-of-factly.

"And what change would that be?" Brisco countered sharply.

"We now consider the implications of our previously planned action to be counter-indicated, so the arrangement you had with Mr. Otnabe has been terminated."

"Shouldn't I be hearing that from Mr. Otnabe?" Brisco retorted.

"Miss Miranda and I have been authorized to pay you for your services before we leave the island," Manny interjected. He hoped that he might be able to reach an understanding with Brisco by telling him that he would be paid the agreed-upon amount even though the contract had been canceled. Manny didn't know it, but he had just aroused Brisco's maximum suspicion, as his arrangement with Otnabe didn't involve any money.

"I'm afraid I'll need to confirm that with Wyndam. I'm sure you can understand my wanting to uphold conventional business procedures, especially when there is so much money involved," Brisco said, with a curious snigger and shake of the head. He had every intention of not only asking Otnabe about the questionable cancellation, but also informing him that he might want to check out the loyalties of his Roca Group compatriots.

"Certainly Mr. Brisco, we'll wait here," Miranda said, stalling for time. She was hoping that he would have difficulty finding a resource to make the prohibited call. Even if he found a nearby access to his Cuba / U.S. communications link, Otnabe might be unreachable for some reason or other.

"I can call from right here, Miss Miranda. You forget, communications electronics are what made me a wealthy man. That, and being a prudent borrower of course," Brisco added with a flourish. He pulled a cell phone out of his pocket and dialed a lengthy set of digits. He hung up, placed the phone down on the table, and proceeded to sip his drink.

In about thirty seconds the phone rang. Brisco announced who he was to whomever was on the other side of the line, and then involved himself in a series of *yeses, nos, and uh-huhs*. The call ended with Brisco describing his location as being at the Balneario del Sol on Playa Siboney near Santiago de Cuba.

While he was on the phone, Miranda subtly turned Manny around so that his back was to Brisco.

"Did you see that look?" Miranda whispered.

"What look?" Manny responded, craning his neck trying to see around Miranda, the confusion showing clearly at the furrow between his eyes.

"That little twist of his lips. Like saying, *you just gave it away* without saying it. I think we gave it away Manny,"

Miranda answered. "You don't steal two billion and walk around free without being clever as hell."

These were the moments when Miranda showed why she was near the top of the Roca pecking order. She was like a master poker player always reading her opponents, looking for tells. Most people are self-absorbed to the point that they are relatively oblivious as to what's going on around them. Miranda was the opposite, perpetually alert.

"It appears that Wyndam is on his way down to visit us. We can expect him here tomorrow morning," Brisco announced in a snide tone. "Of course we'll have to make sure that Mr. Lynne doesn't leave the hotel tonight, but other than that I think we can all relax until Wyndam arrives."

Chapter 40

Eric was safe, at least for now, and Chief Grinnel was on board and looking forward to some excitement. Next up was hoping I could talk to Miranda before Brisco got to her. I knew there was a good possibility that I would be late on that one. I rushed back to the Balneario Hotel from Guantanamo, knowing I could just as well run into Brisco as Miranda

The only way from Guantanamo to Siboney was through Santiago. Going through town was no fun, but after I got out it was very peaceful. Just past San Juan Hill up the Siboney highway is a huge rock balanced 3,000 feet above the road. I've heard that you can see Haiti and Jamaica from there on a clear day. It was a little too late in the day for that in more ways than one. It was nearly dark when I rounded the last curve and headed down the straight stretch of beach highway that led into Playa Siboney.

I had rehearsed my conversation with Miranda enough times to know that I probably wouldn't use a word of it. My plan was pretty simple. The only problem was that for it to work I needed Miranda in on it. That would be the only way I would be able to get Brisco to the reception that would be waiting for him at the Stone Zoo.

I got lucky. Miranda was registered under the second name I tried. Margaret Benetton was an alias I'd known her to use. Brisco was nowhere in sight. She answered her room phone and I was up in room 216 at the top of the stairs in less than a minute. Miranda told me that she and Manny had run into Brisco at the bar and she'd told him that the contract was cancelled. She went on to say that he insisted on verifying with Otnabe and called him right then. She was pretty sure that Brisco only got the office. They told him that Otnabe was on his way down to Cuba and would straighten things out when he got there.

Miranda sensed that Brisco was suspicious. She realized that he was probably being compensated with something other than money. Even with that, Eric was safe for now. Miranda guessed that Brisco had made a deal for either immunity from his past crimes, or some kind of asylum in a foreign country more to his liking than Cuba. The first seemed close to impossible, but the second? Miranda asked me how I wanted to handle the situation. Once Otnabe arrived she would be out of the picture. For now she was still a player.

As far as I was concerned, Miranda was only a player if she could neutralize Brisco. But since that hadn't happened, I really could only find one way that she could help, even if she wanted to do more. I needed to get Brisco to my party at the Stone Zoo and Miranda was the best person to leak that there was an important meeting where Lynne would be. I suggested that Miranda tell Brisco that he could talk to Eric there in person and maybe find a way to avoid violence. That would be sure to get him there, even though avoiding violence probably wasn't on his list.

There would be no reason for Brisco to be suspicious of the meeting, and all the time Eric would be 100 miles away. It was getting more and more attractive to jam up both Brisco and Otnabe, but I had some feelings for Fawn. Even though her dad wasn't her hero like mine had been for me, he was her dad. Having her lose him to prison would only be my choice if we couldn't call him off the hunt. I had dealt with so much duplicity and conniving over the years that my standard of good and evil was severely tweaked. Part of me even had thoughts like, *Well, he is a criminal, but aren't we all, and he's just doing his job . . . even if it is trying to kill the man I love – or should I say loved.* I had no such compassion for Wyndam, who I knew was on his way to get a surprise reception.

Chapter 41

Wyndam Otnabe was not about to risk the pedestrian inefficiency of the commercial airline system. That system would have had him transfer through two airports and onto three separate flights. Each one represented a possible threat to connection with the next, not to mention his distaste for sharing these inconveniences with what he disdainfully referred to as "the public." Instead, he called in a favor from a congressman who owed him one. It was not usual procedure to have a civilian transported in a military aircraft, but it did happen. In this case, Otnabe had the kind of influence that could make it happen.

Washington, D.C was just a couple of hours by train from New York, and the trains ran frequently. His plan to maximize his monetary reward could no longer depend on Manny and Miranda, as evidenced by their most recent interaction. He could still trust Brisco, not because of any mutual loyalty, a commodity that Otnabe found less than dependable, but because of the promise of retirement on the French Riviera that Brisco so coveted.

After a less than restful train ride, a short taxi to Andrews Air Force Base, and a 90-minute ride in the back of a C5A military transport, Wyndam Otnabe arrived at the small military flight hanger that was part of the Guantanamo

Naval Base. What he was not aware of was that his haste, his avarice, and his disdain for traveling as the commoners travel, were to deliver him to the one place on the planet that was likely to cost him not only his mega-payday, but very possibly his freedom as well.

A rain squall had blown through just before dawn, and the tarmac was shiny and appeared blacker than it actually was. Regulation procedure for all flight arrivals at Gitmo required a screening, though cursory, of all passengers, whether civilian or military. That screening was one of the responsibilities assigned to the U.S. Marine Shore Patrol. This morning the NCO on duty was Chief Lou Grinnel, who the night before had shared a glass of wine at the base PX with Callie Barton. It was an interesting story Callie had to tell, and a complex one. Had Chief Grinnel been any less sharp than he was, it would have been too confusing to follow. But the Chief was an old hand at intrigue as any longtime cop would have been. Whether Callie's inclusion of the name Wyndam Otnabe in her story was fortuitous or purposeful, its unique sound stuck in the Chief's memory. That memory only had to last till the next morning.

During the arrival screening process, which required giving name and purpose for travel, the Chief recognized the name Otnabe and excused himself to phone Callie at her hotel. After thinking that he was done with any scrutiny, Otnabe asked how to get to Playa Siboney near Santiago. Lou said it was close by. He added that as he was heading in that direction for an unofficial trip off the base, he would drop him off.

It was Monday and the zoo was closed to tourists. Not that there ever were many people who were interested enough to make the one-way trip to the Stone Zoo in Yateritas. An official call from Magelinos was enough to open the gates for the first group. Magelinos, two other officers from his unit, armed and in uniform for backup, and I were ushered in. The gatekeeper was instructed to allow entry to the additional players who were to arrive shortly thereafter. Even though in the movies these scenes are usually set in the dark of night, or at least as the sun is setting, this one was relegated to midday.

Magelinos and I knew that we had arrived first, so we walked around and looked at stone statues of animals. I noticed a Rhino whose right ear had been blown off. I hoped it was a white rhino as the black ones are on the endangered species list.

After a bit of satisfying our curiosity about stone animal sculptures, we found ourselves sitting on a bench in front of and almost under a life-sized sculpture of several lions attacking an antelope. At almost the same moment, we both turned around and took in the scene happening in stone behind us. Both of us spontaneously laughed at the trap we had set and what element of that sculpture we were hoping to clone. Our uniformed compatriots heard the laughing and hurried to our bench just in time to welcome the arrival of Roger Brisco and Barnes Connert – the man we assumed was tasked at being much more than Brisco's driver.

They were expecting to find their quarry, Eric Lynne, at the Stone Zoo. But it wasn't Eric Lynne they found. They found me, along with Enrique Magelinos and two other armed DSE officers. The officers wasted no time in ordering the two to drop their briefcase and put their hands in the air. Connert, clearly stunned by the sight of guns pointed at him, dropped the briefcase immediately. Brisco had a more delayed reaction of several seconds, but eventually obeyed the command. What followed was an awkward pause in which Roger Brisco, the consummate con man, found words to bridge the moment.

"So Callie," Brisco initiated, his hands in the air but his eyes on the ground where the briefcase lay. "I've clearly underestimated you. I think for the second time. In my business that is inexcusable and a definite program for disaster. Has my carelessness put me in line for a disaster, Callie?"

Enrique, being familiar with proper procedure in situations like this one, ordered Connert to kick the briefcase over to him. Brisco interrupted that Connert might break his toe if he kicked the bag.

His remark sounded so ridiculous that all I could think of was that there was a .45 in there like the one Manny had once handed me. A .45 is a side arm but it uses a larger caliber bullet than most rifles, and it's as heavy as some. It doesn't crack, it roars. It's not a discreet weapon, and the damage it does is closer to that of a shotgun than a pistol.

"Shut up and kick the damn gun over here!" I shouted impatiently.

"Gun, Callie? You didn't think there were weapons in the briefcase did you?" Brisco said, as though talking to a child. "Now you disappoint me Callie, and after all these years. Did you take me for a thug? There is nothing in that briefcase other than two three-and-half-pound gold bars."

"Gold! What the hell are you talking about?" I exclaimed as I walked over, grabbed the briefcase and looked in it.

As I was looking at the gold bars in disbelief, Brisco went on. "Your boss may have sought out my participation in such mayhem, but I couldn't face myself if the limits of my creativity stopped at murder. Callie, Callie, you've got a lot to learn."

"What the fuck are you doing showing up here with a briefcase full of gold bars?" I asked, frustrated but almost rhetorically, because while I was asking I was giving myself the answer.

"Can we put our hands down now?" Brisco asked while not waiting for an answer. "I may have misjudged your friend Lynne, but now we'll never know – will we? I have never met a man who wouldn't reconsider his position with a million dollars in gold dangling right in front of him . . . have you?"

We were on Cuban soil, so Enrique was in charge. The next move was up to him. He looked over at me while shaking his head in disbelief. "You know, the first thing I thought when I saw that kid Connert was that he didn't look like a hit man – more like an ivy league stock broker. But who knows, these days maybe he could do the deed with a computer," Enrique joked while looking at me, hoping that I knew where to take it from here.

Eric was out of danger and that allowed me space to gain some perspective about this intrigue. I knew I still had to deal with Wyndam, but Brisco was no longer in the enemy category. For some twisted ridiculous reason, any animosity I had felt toward this man, who at one time insisted I call him Roger, had disappeared.

"If you will help me disassemble Wyndam Otnabe," I responded, "I will do what I can for you. I promise. Not so much for the criminal I know you have been and still are, but for the father that I know Fawn would like you to become."

Roger Brisco, being a man who was eminently capable of assessing current conditions, and having learned from his stock market dealings when it's time to cut his losses, answered succinctly, "Deal." That's all he said.

Otnabe thought he was being driven to the Balneario Hotel, but never having been in Cuba, he continued to assume it. That is, until they parked at a place with a sign above reading Zoológico de Piedra (The Stone Zoo). Chief Grinnel played his part perfectly up to the sign, but there was no longer any reason to continue the ruse. Grinnel's imposing physical demeanor eliminated the chance for any bolting on the part of his charge. Anyway, that would not be Wyndam Otnabe's style. He knew some endgame was afoot, and even had a part of him that was curious what it was to be. Wyndam was, after all, a destined winner in his own view, and it was merely a matter of how that winning was to be played out.

He was wrong. He was looking at Callie Barton and Roger Brisco together with several Cubans, two armed and uniformed and none known to him. He was realizing that he had been the victim of a conspiracy that had whisked him away to this place by the United States Marines. That was enough to convince him that it would not be easy to gain control of this one.

Having realized that a member of the U.S. military was standing next to him on Cuban soil, Enrique Magelinos, as a Cuban law enforcement officer, was himself in curious waters. This was clearly a violation of basic Cuban sovereignty rights, and at one time a clear responsibility of his to defend. But times were changing, and honorable men like Raoul Castro and El Jugador were behind these changes. So Enrique glanced over at Grinnel, smiled at him, at his own men, and to himself, and continued to play his part.

"Wyndam Otnabe, you are guilty of conspiracy to commit murder – a crime demanding the death penalty in this country," Callie bluffed, having no such authority. "Roger Brisco has been given immunity for his testimony corroborating that fact. Not for the first time has your greed driven you to acts that are not only illegal but unconscionably immoral. Though I have never either condoned nor participated in your choice to use physical violence to attain your goals, I am certainly not one to judge, having participated in every other aspect of the Roca Group's activities.

"It would not further this aim of mine, nor would it help Cuba emerge from its past, to pursue a public demonizing of either the Roca Group or yourself, Wyndam. So if you will agree to the following you can go on your way."

Callie handed Otnabe a single sheet of paper on which were written four conditions, each beginning with the words, "I, Wyndam Otnabe, do solemnly swear to . . . " with a place for a signature and the witnessing of Enrique Magelinos of the Cuban Departamento de Seguridad del Estado and Master Chief Louis Grinnell of the United States Marine Corps.

Epilogue

The promise of a definite date for the removal of all U.S. restrictions on commerce with Cuba, including the lifting of the embargo, meant that modest economic changes could begin immediately. It would be years before Cuba's place in the community of democratic nations would be realized, but the beginning of the process was set in motion. Caroline Barton and Eric Lynne, acting as representatives of Cuba's newly-appointed finance minister Harris Barton, negotiated agreements with eleven multinational companies for investment in Cuba. Each agreement carefully stipulated that all new industry established on the island would be managed and staffed by Cubans, and that the majority of revenues from said industries would remain on the island to subsidize existing social programs.

Callie was successful in convincing the three major U.S. auto manufacturers, Ford, Chevy, and Chrysler, to form an investment consortium that would eventually build an auto production factory in Cuba, producing a brand that would be Cuba's own, the *Fidel*. The U.S. big three were awarded that contract over Japan's potential consortium of Nissan, Toyota, and Honda by agreeing to finance a program for replacement of antiquated vehicles. When the plan eventually went into effect, 150,000 low-income Cuban auto owners would receive subsidies in order to replace their ancient cars with new ones.

Callie made attempts to get the U.S. Department of Justice to drop its previous charges against Roger Brisco. The grounds she presented were his cooperation in revealing Wyndam Otnabe's part in various illegal manipulations involved with the Cuba deal. These attempts, although fruitless, were met with Fawn Brisco's deep appreciation and cemented what was to become a lifelong friendship.

The French government received an interesting offer that it subsequently accepted, granting it deferred rights to oil exploration off the coast of Cuba. The deal coincidently brought Brisco to the shores of the Riviera. He was welcomed with strict stipulations regarding his full retirement from illegal activities. Any departure from that retirement would result in Brisco's extradition to the U.S. Yes, he had been a criminal. But this last crime, the French rationalized, which was fortunately aborted in time, was motivated by a love for something French – the Riviera. Certainly this was reason enough for finding a compassionate resolve.

Wyndam Otnabe's future was to be much less secure. The board of directors of the Roca Group, which contained several highly-placed politicians, had to distance itself from Otnabe's revealed felonious actions, namely contracting murder. Even though he was not to be prosecuted, he could no longer be considered a viable director of the Roca Group, and so his resignation was requested and received. Carmen Miranda was rewarded for her years of service and prudent judgment by being given Otnabe's directorship, and this of course brought Manny into the executive circle as well.

Raoul Castro personally offered Enrique Magelinos the job of commander of a newly-formed National Police Force, with authority to establish standards and practices in line with his deeply held views of conscience. Enrique was encouraged by his friend Eric Lynne to accept. He eventually declined the offer in favor of passing that responsibility to a younger man with the same last name – one who had not been stigmatized by participation in unfortunate past events. Magelinos can be seen from time to time fishing in Cienfuegos Bay in sight of his family's home and the estate of his neighbor, El Jugador.

Both Callie Barton and Eric Lynne relocated, at least temporarily, to Cuba. The assignment of both liberating a country and its people from the economic restrictions of the past, and working to improve the living conditions of those people, brought the two together in new and uplifting ways. They were both committed to helping with the creation of a society that resisted cloning the lesser values of the capitalist world. One might say that the jury is still out on the subject of a permanent romance, but it does look promising.

It was an impressive but private ceremony – one that marked the end of an era in Cuba. Several carefully selected heads of state from around the world attended, and the keynote speech was given by William Jefferson Clinton, President of the United States. Fidel and he had been adversaries for all the years of his presidency, Clinton stated, but they had never been enemies. Other prime ministers and presidents spoke about the strength Fidel manifested and the love and respect that he won from his people. There was even a moment of lightness when his friend and ally, Hugo

Chavez, President of Venezuela, said that he would not let his speech last more than a few minutes, not wanting to challenge the record length speeches that Fidel had a reputation for giving. Everyone laughed when Chavez said that Fidel would forever keep his name in the record books.

At a meeting behind closed doors, Raoul Castro and Clinton confirmed that the process would begin slowly, and that the sweeping reforms agreed upon would not go into full effect for 20 years. It would take that time for the wounds to heal for the Cuban expatriate community living in South Florida. The U.S. Congress and Senate voted to remove the sanctions and travel restrictions that had existed only after the 20 year postponement was added to the agreement. Even with that, the vote was not unanimous.

Harris Barton, having permanently adopted the name El Jugador, opened his estate for a celebratory party. In the spirit of conciliation, he had Red-Jack use his skills to find, contact, and invite all of the participants in the drama that had led to that day. Over the past few weeks, Barton had managed to take time away from his duties to improve his sailing skills, with pointers from his houseguest and new-found friend. The Commander was a potential future relative as well, should their children see fit to continue on their current trajectory.

Roger Brisco was too enamored of his new living situation on the French Riviera to leave it so soon, but his daughter Fawn read aloud his congratulatory telegram. Two of the three Castro Brothers were present at the celebration. The third was in the midst of the latest of his miraculous recoveries. Manny attended, having been among the first

Americans to vacation legally along with his whole family on the beautiful beaches of Cuba. Miranda's new responsibilities as well as her aversion to leaving Manhattan kept her from attending. Both Enrique Magelinos and Arturo Gomez were there to represent the DSE and to announce their respective retirements.

Barnes Connert might not have shown up, but it was made part of his sentence that after 30 days in jail he would be required to make a public appearance at a gathering of El Jugador's choice. Connert's prison sentence was the idea of Eric Lynne. It took some creativity to come up with a law that Connert had broken. Enrique discovered a little-known statute that prohibited the ownership or transportation of gold bullion in any quantity. Connert having to spend time in jail was truly an inspired idea. He came away from the experience with a newfound respect for both his personal honesty and his freedom of movement. He even made a new friend at the party. It was a redhead on the prowl for a new flirtation.

If there were guests of honor, they were Caroline Barton and Eric Lynne. Raoul acknowledged both to have played an indispensable part in Cuba's recent metamorphosis. Between time needed for their new endeavor, and a shared desire to get reacquainted, the two had been in each other's company uninterruptedly for the past month. Perhaps they would continue to be for the years to come.

The End

The author sends his best wishes to Fidel on his 91st birthday.